For Cynthia

Standing your ground is hard when you can't trust what's underfoot. Sorting what's true and what's only wished is even harder in a place like Beaverdam, where stories sprout faster than grass on a new grave.

Beaverdam's children heard tell of the Witch Woman who lived in a ruined cabin, who would cuss you or worse if you dared knock on her door. They were warned of the Snakebit Girl, how the rattler's fangs struck her pudgy hand reaching into the nest for the hen's eggs. Rather than tell a soul of her plight, she swelled with poisoned pride, and for her silence she was buried in the sloping graveyard. They knew of the Failed Farmer who lost all in the last depression of the nineteenth century. He sold off his plow horse, but still found necessity for the useless halter: his body was found hanging from a rafter in his empty barn.

But the oldest story was of a curse that lay on the land itself. The first whites who crossed the gap encountered no Indians, but the occasional arrowhead could be unearthed in the black fields by the creek, once dammed by the creatures who lent the cove its name. Besides those napped flints, those first hunters had left behind a legend.

Royce Wilder learned about the Shadow Man when he turned seven, a good year to scare children, the age of accountability for a child's soul, as Baptists believed, when death and eternity become real and not just pretend.

It must have been summer, since the sun was prickly hot on his bare shoulders, and surely a Sunday, since his father and uncle wore starched, white shirts instead of their soft, blue denim, sitting in the Sabbath shade of the porch, doing no more work than allowed, whittling sticks into splinters with their Barlow blades. Royce was in the yard playing a game of his own invention called "Stomp Your Shadow." He pounced catlike in the grass, trying to land on the dark puddle of himself beneath the midday sun.

"Hey, boy. You sure that's your shadow and not someone else?"

Drawn by his uncle's strange question, Royce drifted to the porch. He sat on the steps and scratched his grass-green knee. "What you mean, somebody else's shadow?"

"Never can tell. That shadow might belong to you. Might be the Shadow Man on your trail."

Uncle Dallas proceeded to spin a strange tale about a creature that lived in the forest, preying on the shadows of Indian braves passing under the gloomy hemlock shade. After snatching their silhouettes, this being would follow their footprints to the village, and under cover of night, steal the dark profiles of their women and children, but especially those of little boys. When morning came, without their shadows to stake them to the ground, all the Indians blew away in the wind.

"See, the Shadow Man stashes all these stolen shadows into caves and closets and dark holes. Late at night—if you listen—you can hear them, all those lost voices, dying for a bit of daylight." Dallas closed his eyes and made a mournful sound. "Whooooo."

Sitting in the shade, Royce couldn't tell if he had his shadow or not. What if he stepped out into the yard and there was nothing to hold him to Earth? He was seven years old and believed anything his uncle said.

His father had been idly whittling through Dallas' tale. Now he sat there with his hand covering his mouth, trying not to laugh. "Quit pulling the boy's leg," he finally said. "He didn't sleep for a week after you told him about the witch woman up the road."

"That's not true!" Royce blurted.

His father's face darkened. He had just called his daddy a liar. He fled inside and upstairs, leaving only the slap of the screen door on his backside and not his father's hand.

He knew better than pray for protection from the Shadow Man. It was only a story, but he almost believed.

6

1

Rooted, down to earth, staking his ground was how Royce Wilder saw himself, a man who knew his place after having made his way in the world. As far as he'd come in life, building his own business, making a good home with a dear woman, rearing his boy, burying his father, becoming his own man—you couldn't ask that man to give up his history, surrender his soul, part with the past.

"Part with the past? You make it sound like a country song," Eva argued. "If you can consider selling the farm, for heaven's sake, you can do a yard sale." She raised the garage door on its rusted runners, and thin arms akimbo on her broad hips, studied the job ahead. "People shouldn't be allowed to own so much."

"Never knew I was married to a socialist."

"Don't get an attitude with me, Royce. Not today."

Royce and Eva Wilder, the deed holders midway through a thirty-year mortgage at 18 Chester Place in the township of Altamont, stood at odds in their cluttered garage on a crisp Saturday morning in late September 1992, hemmed in by the debris of two decades of marriage and more: dead microwaves, leaking coffeemakers, shot hi-fi speakers, the breakdowns and blowups of everyday life. Royce couldn't content himself with their private clutter; he had to collect the loose loot of other lives. Scrounging through woodsheds, corncribs, and barns across the countryside, he had salvaged artifacts of a pre-electric age—tack and harness from mule teams, a pile of weathered rail fencing that he aimed to erect in the backyard but never did, rusted watering cans, broken hoes and bent pitchforks, froes, adzes, scythes, awls, mauls, crosscut saws, and other forgotten tools, a treasure trove of the cast off, the discarded, the obsolete.

"How can you put a price on these things?" he asked.

"Easy." Eva peeled off adhesive stickers that she had labeled $1, $5, and $10 and slapped them willy-nilly. "Connie Mayhew from my book club said she made five hundred dollars in a two-family garage sale."

"You could put a sticker on me and Dean. Sell the kid, the husband, start over."

"Don't tempt me. Five hundred dollars. We can't afford to argue with that kind of money." She was right, that ever annoying habit of hers.

He kneaded the hollow of his neck; an unconscious gesture that threatened to turn into a tic, as if he were continually smoothing his raised hackles. "Look, I said I'd do lunch Monday with that Landrum fellow."

"He's still interested in buying in Beaverdam?"

"Who knows? Last time we talked, he complained about Beaverdam's radon levels."

"Radon, as in radioactivity?"

"It's pretty common. He's just trying to scare us into a lower price."

"Maybe we should take it. Tuition for St. Dunstan's is due."

The private school had been Eva's idea after their son had started coming home with Cs on the report card and bruises from the bullies. Get Dean away from the public schools to a more rarefied environment, boys in blazers and rep ties drinking tea and going to chapel. Royce only saw St. Dunstan's living up to its name, dunning poor parents like himself.

"Think our little prince will deign to come down and lend a hand?"

"I'm sure he will when he gets up."

"Right," Royce said.

The trouble had begun last night when Eva had asked Dean if he would please go post the yard sale signs for her. She'd drawn a dozen yellow posters in blue marker in her best finishing-school cursive and stacked them on the oak-block kitchen table, anchored on top by the staple gun. Once upon a time, Dean would have been there at the table, tongue poked out, crayon in his fist, eager to add his own designs. Nowadays, Dean stayed busy being bored, apparently spineless in how he could slump in the easy chair in the den, letting the TV wash over his pallid face.

8

"Do as your mother says," Royce said, wetting his thumb to turn the page of his *Time*. The cover said, "The economy: is there light at the end of the tunnel?" Not likely.

Dean muttered a word that Royce, of course, had heard before, but never from his son's mouth, something a boy is likely to pick up in the rough, wrong crowd, but not the kind of thing you ever dream of saying out loud, not face-to-face to your father.

"What?" Royce said. Though he had heard it perfectly—*oh, fuck off*—he still couldn't believe it. "What did you just say?"

Royce stood over his still-slumped son, raising the rolled magazine to smack the smart talk from the boy's mouth. But Dean ducked, bounded upstairs, and slammed his door, the punctuation to far too many family evenings as of late.

"What just happened?" Eva asked.

Royce had no answer but to grab the stack and rage out into the night, posting the signs with angry rounds from his staple gun. If he could only drive some sharp sense into his son's thickening skull...

"I'm through talking with him. Lip is one thing, but after what he said..." Royce trailed off, not sure where his ultimatum would take him.

"You know he didn't mean it. I'll talk to him." Eva changed the subject from the intractable problem of a son soon to turn fifteen to the more manageable chore at hand. "Everything without a sticker goes to the landfill."

"We never took anything to a landfill when I was a boy."

"No, they just dumped it in the closest creek."

Eva shook her head every time they drove to Beaverdam. The road wound by unpainted shacks, tireless cars propped on cinder blocks, and avalanches of rusted refrigerators down the ravines. As the executive director of Keep Altamont Beautiful, Eva never failed to be professionally disappointed by roadside litter or eyesore lawns, even outside her jurisdiction.

Digging toward the rear wall, they uncovered Dean's toys and souvenirs of vacations when their son was young and loveable: the sombrero from South of the Border on that trip to Myrtle Beach, a plastic tomahawk from the Cherokee reservation down in the Smokies.

"Remember this?" Royce notched an arrow with ragged vanes on a wooden bow.

"You've strung it backwards." This was from Eva's youth, a time when she'd won medals and taught archery as a camp counselor.

9

"So we're not getting rid of your stuff, only mine?"

"No." She ran her fingers down the grain of the longbow, then thumbed a sticker on the leather grip. "Everything goes."

Behind a cardboard box of busted Christmas ornaments and artificial wreaths, Royce found their first television, a twenty-seven-inch black-and-white Admiral, a model once made at the plant where Royce got his first real paycheck. He blew the dust from the pronged cord and plugged it in the outlet. A high-pitched hum gathered inside dusty vacuum tubes.

"Sounds like it might explode," Eva said.

"Wait. The picture's getting lighter."

But all they could see was their faces reflected in the screen, the humming light fading to a pinpoint.

"Bet Dallas could make it work."

"Like your uncle needs more junk. His barn's so full of stuff, we're going to have burn or bulldoze it someday. And your mother's, I hate to think of cleaning out that house when . . ."

"We'll worry about it when the day comes," Royce said.

"Like tomorrow. We're taking your mother to church, remember?"

Jesus, he hadn't remembered. Chores and church. This weekend reminded him too much of his childhood, hill-blocked and hidebound, that he couldn't wait to outgrow. Royce had spent an eternity of childhood Sundays burning up in Beaverdam Baptist. Let Eva and Dean troop off to the Episcopalian smells and bells at St. Mary's, his idea of keeping the Sabbath was a nice morning over coffee and the Sunday newspaper. But first the chores: Royce hugged the TV under his chin, hoisting it with gritted teeth and a disquieting pop in his spine. The weight tilted him backward. They once made things heavier, before microchips and plastic.

"Let me help." Eva danced in his way, stepping right as he went left, then left when he tried the right.

"Move!" He staggered to the end of the drive. He knew enough to squat rather than bend, but as he leaned over, the weight got away from him, smashing his fingers under the edge of the set, and a sharper pain jabbed his lower back.

"What's wrong?" Eva hollered from the garage.

"Nothing." He waved. But he was walking funny, listing to one side with muscle memory of an old trauma. Twenty years ago on a loading dock, he'd loused up his lumbar monkeying with these sets with the regular gorillas, football players working part-time. He'd woken the next morning, unable to get out of bed, let alone feel his toes. Slipped a disc, the doctor had said. Before he could see about any disability or worker's comp, the corporate bosses had handed out the pink slips and closed the plant.

"Don't you be giving this stuff away. That TV is worth at least fifty bucks," Royce huffed, stepping back into the garage.

"Where are you going now?"

"To get that boy up."

Royce limped upstairs. He didn't bother knocking at the door at the end of the hall. Although it was marked with a road sign, "Do Not Enter," he barged in.

In the darkness of Dean's bedroom, rock stars and comic-book heroes watched him sleep from the posters taped to the walls. Those two geeky guys from "Wayne's World" looked on from above his desk. Models of earlier enthusiasms dangled over his bed and dreams. Star Wars X-fighters leaking fat beads of airplane glue spun slowly overhead on filament lines strung from the ceiling. His stale breath wheezed through his retainer, trying to keep the orthodontist's work from spreading, but after four thousand dollars and two years, his front teeth still showed a persistent a gap—the inheritance of the Wilders.

The school blazer with the snazzy St. Dunstan's crest lay crumpled on the floor where it had slipped off the back of the chair, the striped rep tie still knotted in its noose caught on the armrest. Come Monday in his usual daze, Dean would roll it over his head and let it hang loose around his neck as he dashed out the door, Royce waiting in the car for his heir to emerge. "Why do I have to wear a tie and you don't? It's not fair," Dean would complain. "Life is unfair. Welcome to the real world," Royce would respond, rubbing his own neck.

"Dean, get up." He shook his son's shoulder.

"Wha—" his mouth opened, but his eyes seemed unable to follow.

"Get up."

"Okay." Dean rolled over.

"You have a choice. Get up and help your mother with the yard sale or go with me to the dump."

Dean had liked their last landfill outing ten years ago, impressed by the bulldozers and the flock of gulls from an ocean two hundred miles away scavenging piles of garbage. "Daddy, it stinks." Dean wrinkled his pug nose, inherited from his mother and continually running until the age of three. Royce unloaded the trash while Dean stood by mesmerized by the piles of rotting garbage, the discarded toilets the boy had just mastered himself. "Stay close, Dean," but the boy darted toward the mound of trash and grabbed a beheaded Barbie doll, which he wanted to take home. Royce tossed it aside, suspicious of his son's tastes, the makings of either a sissy or a serial killer. Now he had a lanky teenager with strange smells and a foul mouth.

"Dean?"

No answer. No drive, only drift. The boy dead to the world. He could sleep through Judgment Day, as his mother liked to say—another inherited trait.

Get up, he told himself. Royce slapped his palms loudly against his thighs, but he still sat there and did not move.

2

After all the taxes he paid, saving the city the trouble of picking it up at his curb, Royce had to shovel out ten bucks to throw away his garbage. He'd driven across the rutted road to Area 12 of the county sanitary landfill. Holding his breath, he'd emptied the trunk of his car while the roaring bulldozers buried the mounds of trash beneath the remote mountainside.

In his car, Royce could still smell garbage from the soles of his shoes. The empty trunk would reek for weeks, but at least the stench would be masked by the diesel clouds coughing out of his Mercedes—a sedan with 200,000 miles that he'd bought third- or fourth-hand. The traffic-cone orange paint job probably contributed to the criminally low sticker price, as Eva had pointed out, a garish shade that drowned out any hint of Old World class. He cranked down the window and slowly drove down the gravel road to the pavement, reluctant to return too soon to Eva's yard sale.

He fiddled with the radio dial, then snapped it off after getting only static, church music, or angry men bellowing about politics. Another season for patriotic pabulum and all-American bluster, though there was plenty to beef about—gas prices jumping to a wallet-busting $1.13 a gallon, unemployment at 6.8 percent, government spending money like there was no tomorrow to pay it all back . . . The politicians were promising paradise if voters only gave them the go-ahead.

13

Scattered amid the for-sale signs were the campaign placards stapled onto pine stakes, registered voters pledging their allegiance to the latest candidate. Perot catching on with his talk of deficit as the crazy aunt in the attic, but Buchanan's pitchfork peasantry posters surviving from the primary. Bush seemed out of touch, amazed that supermarkets had laser scanners at the checkout. When was the last time Mr. CIA had to buy a gallon of milk?

This part of town tended Republican with the rising property values, but Royce passed more blue Clinton-Gore signs dotting lawns and bumper stickers on Volvos parked in driveways. The candidate they were already calling Slick Willie was only a year older than Royce and the Tennessean Gore a year younger: it didn't feel right to Royce that a peer would be his president. The Oval Office belonged to older guys who could at least pretend to some wisdom.

In politics and population, Altamont had changed in the fifteen years since Royce and Eva had bought their house and watched their property taxes go up each winter. Where deer had once grazed in the backyards and raccoons rummaged through the midnight trash, Royce had seen the turnover of company transfers and Rust Belt transplants: more strangers and fewer neighbors. The small town had turned into more of an anonymous city. Condos and fake chalets, gleaming with walls of glass, dotted the northern slopes surrounding Altamont. Royce had appraised a few of those properties at a million or more, though he wouldn't pay to live that high on the hog. At those upper elevations, water pressure was as forceful as drool. Each morning a hillside of rich, wrinkled retirees squinted soapy eyes at recalcitrant showerheads.

At the corner of Edgewood Avenue, a new sign stuck in the brown lawn at a brick two-story: "Estate Sale Today." Royce parked and joined the curious swarm walking across the lawn, not even following the decorum of using the sidewalk. The grass needed mowing and two monstrously overgrown cedars guarded the entrance. He climbed the three uneven steps into the gloom.

Inside the open door a young man in sagging jeans stood on a stepladder in the foyer, wrestling with a clinking chandelier, cursing not so silently. Royce slid into the living room where two hulking boys in overalls manhandled leather sofas out into the backyard. Nail heads dotted the empty walls. Framed pictures were stacked on the floor leaning against the walls

14

where they'd once hung: amateur oils of autumn landscapes and Greek ruins, English hunting scenes—scenery for spinsters. Wives with their husbands in tow, their arms crossed under their breasts, carefully eyed the loot, looking for bargains in crystal and silver, estate jewelry.

"Bidding starts in fifteen minutes, folks. Fifteen minutes." A banty-rooster of a man flew through the crowd, clapping the stooped backs of bored husbands, patting the plump arms of eager wives. He sported a bowl-shaped red toupee that clung precariously to his crown. Red Penland, Royce would guess, the auctioneer as advertised on the truck parked in the drive. "Good stuff here, folks. Bargains abound. Hope y'all brought your checkbooks."

Royce roamed the rooms, taking note of the selling points: brick, hardwood floors, built-in bookcases, nice fireplace, brass fixtures. He estimated the house would list for one thirty-seven. With cramped closet space, dollhouse-sized rooms, cracked plaster and crumbling molding, a chill draft in the hall, it was only worth maybe $115,000 in this market. But you had to calculate in the intangibles. People buy a house for the sunbeam that creeps into a room like a lazy cat. They sign contracts for the aroma of apple pies in the kitchen (an easy trick to simmer water and cinnamon on the stove). The right light and smell closed more deals than mortgage points or assumable loans. Likewise, shadow and odor could kill a contract in a hurry. Buyers instinctively dislike dog hair and cat spray, mold and mildew. A house could sit for years on the market because of the sinister shape of water stains on a ceiling. Royce was glad to be an appraiser and not an agent. Better to deal with the hard, cold numbers than the whims of clients hunting for the perfect picket-fenced fancy.

He headed upstairs until a falling shadow halted him. He craned his neck up at a bulky man descending the stairs, a small head haloed by the light from the windows above. The man was so wide, there was no way to slip by until he had surrendered the stairwell. The shiny oxfords slowly descended, surprisingly small for the heft they supported, planting three-hundred-plus pounds of girth on a groaning riser, right foot first, a step at a time, the way a child uncertain of balance, afraid of falling, goes down stairs.

"Mr. Wilder? Fancy meeting you here."

Royce blinked in confusion, still unable to make out the man's obscured face.

15

"Lawrence Landrum? You don't remember?"

"Of course," Royce said. Who could ever forget anyone so fat? "I wasn't expecting to see you here on a Saturday." At an estate sale for that matter, wearing a pinstripe business suit.

"We're still on for lunch?" Landrum's voice was high and heavily winded, like it was an effort to force a sound through so many chins and folds of flesh.

"Sure." Royce didn't relish the idea of watching this man eat, but he had committed himself to a business lunch Monday to discuss his holdings in Beaverdam.

Landrum nodded and pulled a small device from his pants pocket. He began to sweep the wall and floor at their feet. The small box emitted a strange clicking frequency, like crickets singing in the floorboards.

"What you got there?"

"Oh, just a Geiger counter."

"Hobby of yours?"

"More business than pleasure." The fat man frowned at his readings. "Nothing out of the ordinary. Your typical background levels. Microwave, radon, even cat litter has a trace of radioactive decay. Though I have seen abnormally high readings in Beaverdam."

"You mentioned that. Still doesn't change my mind."

"I don't think you realize how high those levels are in Beaverdam. Rest assured, Mr. Wilder, radon is real. Second leading cause of cancer deaths in the U.S., after cigarettes."

"My Daddy died of cancer ten years ago, but he lived in Beaverdam all his life. Lucky Strikes, Mr. Landrum, not radon is what killed him."

"My condolences, but don't underestimate the danger," Landrum pocketed his device. "I believe the auction is starting. "Are you a collector, Mr. Wilder? Out for a bargain?"

"My wife would say so, but no. Just looking today."

With Landrum's bulk blocking his escape to the front door, Royce found himself forced into the yard by the one-man avalanche, where the crowd had assembled.

"Bidding starts at fifty for this silver set. Who will give me fifty?" Red Penland shouted. "Don't be bashful, folks. We need to start moving this stuff."

Royce couldn't believe what people were willing to pay for some things

16

and how other stuff went for a steal. Crystals, knickknacks, pots and pans, silverware, a pair of porcelain dogs, a peacock fan, chinoiserie, old lady stuff. The kitchen stove, an antique in its own right, sold for thirty bucks, a set of crystal goblets started at a dollar apiece. The auctioneer worked the crowd up to a dollar fifty. Penland paused to mop a red bandanna over his flushed face, like the dye was running off his bowl-shaped toupee.

"Here's an old-timey item, folks." Penland's assistant, a longhaired girl with buck teeth, paraded an ancient wooden radio overhead. "Let's start to the tune of ten dollars. Ten dollars? Who will give me ten dollars?"

Royce stood on tiptoe, craning his stiff neck, but when his heels came down to earth, he felt a lurch in his belly: his father's Silvertone set—that same radio when he was a boy. The house had been newly wired for electricity, and they plugged in the Sears and Roebuck radio with its varnished cherry wood, the brown Bakelite knobs, a glass porthole showing a red painted wooden pick that dialed to the various frequencies. From the mountain air came a whistling, static, then the faint sound of singing.

"Twenty-five," Royce croaked.

Red Penland pointed his way. "Twenty-five. Do I hear thirty?"

Out of the crowd came the answering figure. Someone was bidding against him, bidding to take his father's radio. Without thinking, Royce raised his arm and his bid.

"I'll take that as a yes. Do I have thirty-five?"

"Make it fifty!"

Royce scouted the crowd for this adversary. Who the hell was trying to tear his father away from him? Then he saw Lawrence Landrum waving his plump fingers.

"I've got fifty over here," Penland fingered Royce. "Do I hear sixty?"

"Sixty," he said.

"Seventy-five," countered the fat man.

"Yes, sir, I have seventy-five," Penland said. "Can we make it interesting now? Can we close it out? Could I hear an even hundred for this fine radio?"

Royce was running the numbers in his head, how far could he go for a probably useless radio? Did it even play? He licked his lips but he kept silent.

"Silvertone," Penland shouted. "One of a kind. Bet you can hear the Grand Ol' Opry if you listen close." The red toupee tilted on his head as he held the radio box to his ear. "Do I hear Dolly Parton? Do I hear Minnie Pearl? Do I hear a hundred?"

A lump kept working up his gullet. Royce was little again, lying on the wide pine boards by the woodstove, his head in his hands, his feet kicking the air: shoofly pie and apple pan dowdy, his father's boot tapping the time.

Royce blurted out: "One fifty!"

The fat man smiled, but wagged his chins.

"Sold to the gentleman for one hundred and fifty dollars."

Royce made his way through the crowd that parted for him, people smiling at his bold bid. "You got the radio, right?" said Penland's assistant, tossing her long brown hair over a thin shoulder like a sheaf of hay. "That'll be one fifty." She checked him off in the ledger. "Cash only."

Royce licked his thumb, counted out the last twenties from his wallet, then the fifty he always carried in the secret fold.

"Congratulations." Landrum stopped him in the driveway. "I have a soft spot for old technologies. The world is changing at such a rate, it's good to have reminders of those so-called good old days," the big man wheezed. "But you must have wanted it more."

"My father had one just like this. I was afraid you were going to outbid me."

"I could only go so far. Sentiment sometimes trumps good business sense." The fat man waved over his shoulder. "We'll talk more Monday. Have a good weekend, Mr. Wilder."

Driving home, Royce wasn't sure how to explain buying a useless radio for one hundred and fifty dollars, even if it did remind him of his father. Maybe it was the wood, the same grain of the collection plate he remembered handed down the pews of Beaverdam Baptist where his daddy had been the usher, the same slick varnish as his father's casket they had lowered into the slanted grave on the mountainside ten years back. Royce still flinched at the sickening thud of the rocks, the clots of clay dinging the wood as they heaped the ground over that yawning hole.

Royce rubbed the warm wood, imagined the dusty tubes stirring to life under his hand. Unmoored by middle age, he wanted nothing more than to resurrect a happier childhood for himself.

3

G lad to see you could finally get out of bed and join the world."
"What gives?" Dean yawned, grinding a fist into his sleep-encrusted
eye.

"Yard sale. Your school tuition." His mom sat on the stoop, fanning a
hand of dollar bills.

"You shouldn't sell my things without asking me." Dean flipped the hood
over his ball cap and shoved his hands deep into the sweatshirt's pockets.

"Are you cold?"

He shook his head. The black hood made him look like a strange bird
with the beak of his cap, thin legs poking out of baggy canvas shorts.

"I need to wash that someday. Maybe today?"

He shrugged one shoulder, a habit that Dean knew irked his mom. At
least she was talking to him after last night. All that aggravation over a
word, something you saw moving on the mouth of a football coach on the
sideline or a rapper in a music video. No big deal, but he'd let it out into
the open like rolling a hand grenade into the living room. Boom. In the
exploding silence, their mouths dropped, their eyes bugged. They about
died.

"We've cleaned out this garage. You are cleaning your room today. No
excuses."

"My room's not so bad. You should see Tucker's room at school. He's a
real slob."

19

"You haven't mentioned this Tucker. Friend of yours?"

Dean gave a noncommittal cock of his head, neither yes nor no, not a nod nor a shake. Friend might be going too far. Dean could only hope to be conferred that status—confidant to the coolest kid at St. Dunstan's, who lived in awesome squalor. Tucker was like the Gatsby guy they were reading about in English class, rich as hell and didn't give a damn. "Yeah," Dean allowed.

Her face brightened at this news, probably with the thought Dean was making friends at his new school, maybe even fitting in. "Mind the store for a moment." She patted his hooded and capped skull, as close as she could get inside his head these days. "I've got to go inside."

His mom would never say the word "bathroom" regarding her own personal needs, but her hurried motions and the empty thermos of coffee gave her away. Dean chewed the last of a stale bagel from his pocket and watched strangers scavenge through the spoils: his Dad's rusted, rustic junk, his mom's burned-out appliances, his own discarded childhood.

"This says $25 but I'll give you $15." A white-haired lady in a pink workout suit marched over with a glass lamp. She held the floral porcelain fixture to her drooping breasts like a long-lost relative. It was a pillar of Dean's world; the light that stood by his parents' bed, unremarkable, another daily detail of his life he never thought could be missed.

"Sure." He wadded the cash into his jacket's deep pocket about the time his mom returned.

"Anything happen?"

Dean looked around as if he had misplaced the right answer. He didn't regularly lie to his mom, but sometimes he didn't volunteer the truth. He hiked his thin shoulders in an exaggerated shrug, then let them drop inside his oversized sweatshirt. "Got to go." He hopped his bike with the soft tires and wheeled down the drive, nearly running down a couple of middle-aged ladies cooing over his mom's needlepoint.

"Dean, come back here. We have a yard sale," his mom called, but he was already around the corner, out of the cul-de-sac that was Chester Place.

Tires half-inflated, Dean rode the rims until he made the gas station and the free air pump. He monkeyed with the chain that slipped between the fifth and sixth gears and wiped the grease from his hands on his black sweatshirt.

"I feel STUPID and contagious, here we ARE now, entertain us," Dean sang along to the tape spinning in his Walkman, the grunge chords ringing in his ears.

Next stop was the hardware store, the automotive supplies, where the rack of spray paints had been waiting, beckoning in his dreams. Day-glo orange and a midnight black with cobalt for contrast. Two cans cost ten dollars and change from the fifteen he'd pocketed at the yard sale.

Back on the road he rode the shoulder while cars whipped by, nearly toppling him in their wakes. Finally free of the commercial strip, he coasted into a blighted neighborhood of broken-down cars and fenced-in yards advertising vicious dogs, down to the warehouse district. Dean had only caught a fleeting glimpse from the passenger seat of his morning car ride to school, passing high on the bridge over the brown river, a sudden splash of color amid the industrial gray. He wanted a closer look.

He coasted to the bottom of the hill and dismounted, letting the bike roll into the weeds by the cyclone fence. The gate was locked with a loose chain, but a skinny boy could slide right through. He clicked off Cobain on his Walkman and pulled the plugs from his buzzing ears. High overhead, on the steel spans of the overpass, he could hear the whining of tires, the wake of traffic. Below, there was only the sound of the river and his ragged breathing.

He rounded the corner of the abandoned building into the back lot, where the loading docks were deserted, the cement ramps cracked with weeds.

Oh God, they were real, colors exploded everywhere, like the aftermath of an acrylic nuclear event. It was like walking into a museum and seeing for yourself something famous, the Mona Lisa, maybe. Wait till he told Tucker.

He ran his hand reverently across the concrete canvas, retracing the motions of master taggers, working without templates, freehand, blowing up their signatures ten feet high, outlining echoes of rhythms, raps, and riffs from a boom box blasted onto the wall. Faces of beautiful women, hot bodies, fast cars, and fists raised in angry salute—an ocean of color, like the river ran red at night, overflowed its banks, and washed against the warehouse walls.

There was only a small empty patch, a place where he could make his mark. He shook the paint can, heard the ball rattling its percussive beat inside the contained cloud of hissing color, like a hailstone falling hard from a summer sky. He imagined himself darker and cooler, not just a pasty white boy, but a swaggering tag-meister in the Bronx, running with a midnight crew and bombing the side of a subway car, his hat turned backward and a heavy gold chain around his skinny neck. Yo, bro.

His hand hesitated in midair. The line wasn't as certain as he would have liked. He moved the can closer, and the line smudged, but he kept going, outlining the explosion. The orange blob became a sharp-pointed nova in a distant galaxy. Now the blue. He made the P fat, like an alphabet pumped on steroids, muscular rather than obese and soft. The O was even easy, but the W's last arm drooped a bit. Now the exclamation point.

"Pow!" He let his cheeks fill with breath then expelled the explosion out his rounded mouth.

"Hey you, kid!" A squat, uniformed man hustled his way.

Dean snatched his bag of paint cans and ran. He rolled under the fence where the raw clay had eroded. The sharp wire caught and ripped his sweatshirt but couldn't stop him. He plunged through the brambles, the cans rattling in his sack almost as loud as his heart hammered at his chest. He reached the edge of the briar patch only to find a bank and a creek. He flung himself over, still running in midair, and landed one foot in mud and the other foot in water. He scrambled up the bank, then ducked behind the trunk of a river birch.

When the sound of his own breathing and the blood pounding in his ears had quieted, he could hear the slow gurgle of the creek that fed the river. A flash in the air caught his eye. There were silver spoons and forks suspended by fishing wires from the surrounding branches, a charred fire pit, a tarp strung from the trees, a pile of bedding and clothing. It was out in the open, but it was like invading someone's living room. Any moment the owner was likely to come out of the woods, waving a knife or a broken bottle. He had heard of hobos along the rail tracks and had seen homeless people holding signs begging for food or work or mercy, red-eyed men who could burn holes staring right through you. Zombies and werewolves, crackheads and gangbangers, the monsters of modern life. Dean wouldn't have been surprised to see shrunken heads swinging from the branches, or the discarded shank bones of a cannibal feast. He lingered as long as his nerves could stand it, then he spied a faint trail through the woods and started running again.

He found a place to rock-hop the creek, still getting his shoes sopping wet and muddy, and picked his way through the briars to the front of the warehouse where he'd left his bike in the weeds, or thought he had. His bike was gone. Dean looked wildly up and down the road as if to catch the wino wheeling away his boyhood Schwinn. Hot tears came to his eyes. His hand was streaked with black paint where he'd accidentally sprayed himself. He felt a trickle on his lip; his finger was coated with red now.

A nosebleed.

He held his nose, walking uphill through the bad neighborhood. Drunks nursed hangovers and the first beers of the day watching him pass their porches with baleful eyes while babies were hollering inside over loud TVs and radios, but Dean was oblivious. He tilted his chin, breathing through his mouth as he pinched his nostrils, staunching the red tide thrumming through his sinuses. POW. POW. He could feel his life's blood pounding the hollows of his face.

4

She could always count on the men in her life to desert her, first Royce, then Dean. Eva was left to mind the yard sale and the strangers picking through the stuff spread on the drive and in the grass until they found their personal valuable, that something they never knew they needed so badly. Then they would want to know if she would take half of the sticker price.

Eva watched a hyperactive little boy snatch her bow and arrows and start to run up and down the driveway. "Look, Mama, look." The woman did and told him to put it back, an order she probably gave about a hundred times a day. "You got enough toys. Go sit in the car, Mama will be there shortly." The boy threw the bow down and stomped off to the car, while the woman paid him no mind.

At least Dean had been well behaved when he had been that boy's age, never an embarrassment to be with in public, Eva thought, and on second thought, she stashed the bow and arrows inside the front door.

That bow had brought her closer to the men in her life. Her father had encouraged her target shooting and driven her to meets. He'd set a bale of hay in the backyard of the rectory where she drew her bow, held her breath, aimed, and released—shot after shot into the gold center. Consistency was the key. "That's my girl," he'd beamed. They had driven down to Atlanta once for a Junior Olympics championship shoot. Maybe it had been a wisp of her blondish hair that lashed across the corner of her eye, or perhaps a bead of perspiration that broke in the divot of her upper lip in the humidity: something went awry and the arrow sailed an inch wide, striking neither gold, nor even red, but ranging out beyond the blue, even into the white. She was not perfect after all. He gave her his best daddy smile, but she could see it in his unblinking blue eyes, the light leaving them.

She'd nearly nailed Royce with a wayward arrow the first time they'd met. This was at Camp Hollyhock where she taught archery to anxiously proper Episcopalian girls only a few years younger than herself. She had gotten so good at her sport that, like Robin Hood, she could split arrows in the bull's-eye to the delight of the girls in her charge, but it had been the errant shot that had turned out so lucky. The yellow arrow ricocheted off the top of the target and sailed for the woods. Seconds later, a yelp came out of the dark woods, followed in a few minutes more by a young man trooping out of the tree line.

"Hold your fire," Eva ordered.

Her line of adolescent Amazons lowered their aim.

"This belongs to you, I reckon." He offered the wayward arrow politely, the tip pointed toward his heart, like a proper gentleman.

"You're on private property, you know. Didn't you see the ropes marking off the danger zone?" As the archery instructor she had run the perimeter herself, stringing the twine from tree to tree, warning the campers from the line of fire.

"I didn't mean to disturb your games."

"This isn't fun. I work here," Eva said, glaring at her giggling charges.

"Looks like fun to me, playing Indians. Guess that makes me the cowboy," he grinned a gap-toothed grin. And that country drawl. Still, Eva couldn't just tell him to run along nor did she want to.

"You're trespassing."

"I'm surveying the property line for the sale." He raised a scratched forearm to wipe his brow as the girls giggled. "If you see Mr. Pendleton, tell him I'm about through."

This was the first she'd heard about a survey or that the Pendleton family was selling Camp Hollyhock. Eva had camped and counseled here most of her life, like her mother before her. Generations of well-heeled girls had hiked the hills, paddled the lake, woven their baskets and lanyards, and shot their arrows, but now the land was worth more as private lots for retirees and people moving down from New York and D.C.

25

"Sorry." Royce caught her pained look, like he'd driven the arrow through her heart.

He was still apologizing days later when he phoned the camp office and left a message for her. He called for a week before he finally got her on the phone to ask her out on her next night off, their first date. When Eva returned to college in the fall, Royce pursued her there, and they were married the following summer, shortly before the camp was closed.

She hauled the bow and arrows and the shoebox into the kitchen. At her cubbyhole desk where she paid the power and water, the mortgage and insurance each month, she stacked and straightened the bills and sorted the loose change. Four hundred and eighteen dollars. Not as good as Connie Mayhew's haul, not bad, but not nearly enough. Maybe she should have sold the bow after all.

Royce would shoot her if he knew, but she hadn't told him yet to expect no raise with her executive director position with Keep Altamont Beautiful. Maybe even a cut after Christmas. With little public interest in litter control and less in donations, the nonprofit board was scaling back on payroll. They were fine for now with the monthly bills, but Dean's tuition was due, and after the first of the year, the numbers refused to add up no matter how many times she punched them into the calculator with the dying batteries and the fading digits.

A knock at the front door startled her. Probably a latecomer; the yard sale crowd had cleared about half an hour ago. The knocking grew louder. "Coming, I'm coming."

A man waited on her stoop, his back to the door. A braid of dirty blond hair fell from his hat and hung down his spine, straight as a plumb line. Cocked on his hips, his arms were wiry and sleeveless in a red shirt and a denim vest. A hunting knife was sheathed on a length of rope wound twice around his waist. His dungarees were tucked into the tops of his brogans, ugly dogs with black tongues that flapped over long laces wound twice around his shinbones. Between his legs, a burlap sack leaked a suspicious puddle across the brick.

The stranger turned to face her. A fierce, reddish blond beard blanketed his long jawbone and the high cheekbones. So weathered were his looks that his age could fall anywhere from thirty to fifty. But in the grime of his face, his eyes were set in a hard blue, flecked like granite. Glaring through the glass of the storm door, he didn't so much look at Eva as through her. A punch through the glass and he could reach for the latch.

"Can I help you?" The man mumbled, trying to hide his bad teeth. She cupped her ear toward the glass. "What did you say?"

This time she heard: "Thirsty...sorry...water."

"Water? There's a spigot around the side. Help yourself." She slammed the door and threw the bolt before the man could mutter: "Much obliged."

The pipes banged beneath the house and she could hear the splash of water. The back door was locked. She could check the windows, but she was afraid to meet those blue eyes again. She hoped a drink was all he wanted, not a bath, though he needed that as well. Eva had read about people like him in the paper, she'd seen their wild-eyed looks on the evening news, their slow shuffles along big-city sidewalks, but she'd never expected one to show up at her front door.

When Eva dared look again, the stranger was digging through the junk she had just hauled to the curb. She unlocked the door and stuck her head out. "Excuse me, what are you doing?"

"Just looking. You mind?"

Yes, she minded. But she didn't know what to say.

He fiddled with the knobs of the television. "This here TV, is it broke?"

"My husband is coming home any minute."

"I can wait." The man planted a boot atop the TV and retied the laces leisurely.

Stupid. She had just tipped this man off that she was alone in the house, a lone female. Eva scouted the sidewalk. Where was Royce? "You have no business here," she was shouting. "You don't even live here."

"Lady, do I look like I do?" The man rubbed his arm as if she had struck him with a rock.

She stood fixed in his baleful blue stare, not knowing how to respond, knowing he already had his answer. "Take it, whatever."

She slammed the storm door, then the interior door, and peeked through the curtains. He was gone, but she was furious at herself for being afraid, and at the men in her life who weren't around when she needed them. First Royce, then Dean, the male proved an unreliable species, starting with her own dad.

Long ago, she had watched her father, an Episcopal priest paid to be helpful, helpless in the face of a similar visitor. After her mother had died of breast cancer, it fell to Eva, only seventeen, to keep the illusion of a home going. He administered the sacraments, the bread and wine each Sunday. It was her job as the lady of the house to administer the dinner rolls and ice tea at the dinner table. They sat at opposite ends of the table in the rectory's cramped dining room. She watched her father fill his wine-glass, while she pushed her food about her mother's best Wedgwood, an overcooked chicken breast, some desperate vegetable, an effort at a home-cooked meal after all the parishioners' casseroles had finally given out. They were on their own now.

A knock at the door roused them both from the torpor of grief. Eva thought she saw in her father's face what was going through her head at that instant: "It's her." As if she had not wasted away in a hospital bed and then slowly turned on the bed and tried to pull the sheet over her own head, but passed only when they had both left the room late at night. No, she was at the front door, as if she had forgotten her key. But that hope seemed silly and the pit in Eva's stomach swallowed that bright thought.

"Wonder who that could be?" Her father daubed his lips with the linen napkin before he rose from the table.

She could feel the draft coming from the front door, a cold wind that snatched away the voices of her father and whoever was calling at this hour. Someone, a man, was begging her father for help. "I didn't know where to turn. You've got to help me, mister." She could imagine a man with bruises and a three-day beard, the bleary blast of whiskey breath. She could see her father, leaning against the lintel, listening, nodding with his practiced pastoral nod, his slight frown, not unfriendly, but as if pon-dering the terrible problem put to him, until you realized he had been merely biding his time, readying his excuse. "In God's good time. We can't know the mind of God. It's a mystery . . ."

The platitudes her father could spout. How he could hold these on his tongue without choking, Eva couldn't imagine, but that was his job.

"Where else can I go?" And her father: "I'm sorry. What do you want me to do?"

He reentered the dining room and shook his head curtly at her, not now. He grabbed his plate of half-eaten food and carried it to the foyer. Eva could hear the door close on the conversation, then he returned to the table and sat with a heavy satisfied sigh. "Poor devil. He looked hungry. Giving him money, he would have just gone for the nearest drink." Her father filled his wineglass again.

At seventeen and even now, Eva could not forgive him for that mindless charity. Her mother's china. Ever after, there would always be one odd setting.

5

Kyle McRae staggered with his new TV on his shoulder, its pronged tail dangling down his back. Fishhooks and metal buttons pinned in his hat clicked against the blank screen of the television. Brogans slapped the sidewalk, the burlap sack banged against his hip. Coming and going, Kyle made such a commotion he could hardly hear himself think.

A decent haul today. He'd bagged a broken radio-alarm clock-telephone, a burned but intact coffee carafe, a dozen aluminum cans, three refundable glass bottles, a pair of women's bedroom slippers, and one black-and-white television. Like the button he'd found the other day said: "God Don't Make No Trash." Kyle smiled at that thought now pinned in his hat. Not everybody could stomach this line of work, but you got used to the smell—even in the summer when garbage got so ripe that oily rainbows danced atop the trash.

Eyes closed, Kyle could tell the neighborhood and its potential by aroma alone. Lift a lid in Altamont and out wafted the smell of Scotch bottles, yogurt gone bad, espresso grounds, the perfumed strips in women's finer magazines. Try the trash in the projects and the fumes turned funky with malt liquor cans, greasy cornbread, baby diapers. Nose knows, but a body's got to dirty the hands.

But a body got tired lugging a TV. Kyle unshouldered the set and rested. Hiking his trouser leg, he checked the bankroll wrapped with a rubber band and stuffed in his brogan: five crumpled twenties. He bet the TV might bring twenty more at the Dreamland flea market.

A police cruiser slowed, showed red brake lights at the corner. Kyle knew how that conversation would go: "Nice TV you got there. Donation, you say? Got a receipt? Live around here?"

Shouldering the TV, Kyle crossed the street, cutting up a driveway and through a backyard. But a block over, the cop car came creeping down the street. At the corner, an off-duty domestic waited with her battered shopping bags. The city bus was in sight, but the cruiser was gaining on him.

The bus whooshed to a halt. Kyle made the bottom step, jostling the broad beam of the black lady. "Watch it, mister! Don't you be pushing on me!"

The black lady slowly managed the steps, support hose drooping around elephantine ankles. He shoveled the correct change into the meter beside the stoic driver. The bus took off, throwing Kyle and his TV into the nearest seat. He scooted to the window and waved as the police cruiser passed. Kyle watched the fancy houses slide by, neat lawns dotted with his progress, scraps of paper, bits of trash.

The woman turned in her seat, sniffing. Her eyes lit on the burlap bag in the aisle. "What stink so bad?"

Kyle smacked his lips. "Dinner."

At the last stop, Kyle tumbled down the steps with his television. The Dreamland gates were open under the marquee promoting a double feature at dusk: "Deaths-head Revisited" and "Prom Night at Hell High." Behind a row of white pine and a chainlink fence, the huge screen loomed over five acres of gravel and crabgrass. Tonight the screen would flicker to life with bloody images. Tinny screams from speakers propped in car windows would mingle with moans in back seats as teenagers licked salty popcorn from each other's lips. By day, the Dreamland doubled as a flea market. Trucks and vans parked beside the speaker posts, hawking antiques, country and western cassette tapes, NASCAR caps, heavy metal T-shirts, Elvis collectibles, fresh produce, stenciled leather belts, cotton candy and helium balloons, jars of homemade relish and pickles, painted whirligigs.

Kyle toted his TV toward the back rows, where a rough table had been erected from warped sheets of plywood propped on sawhorses. A man in a straw cowboy hat and horn-rimmed glasses was clearing his wares from the table and loading the open trunk of a Plymouth Rambler.

"I said move, dammit!" Underfoot, a child squatted, busy pounding the dirt with a rock. He wore cowboy boots like the man's, elastic play shorts, and a tank top stained with grape juice.

The man piled the junk into the trunk with a clatter, but relieved of their load, his shoulders didn't straighten. The crook in his spine gave Hump Humphries his nickname. Kyle dumped the television on the sagging plywood table. He rubbed his own stiff shoulder. Lugging this old set all day, Kyle felt like he could share Hump's name.

"This for sale?" Hump wet his finger and tapped the TV, hissing between his teeth. "Feels hot to me."

"Charitable donation," said Kyle. He knew for a fact that Hump Humphries had never worried about the propriety of any property he dealt with at Dreamland. Half the stereos he sold were covered with glass from break-ins.

Hump pretended disinterest. "What makes you think this thing works?"

"Listen." Kyle rested his good ear on the console. "You can still hear some electricity. Plug it in and see."

"No outlets out here."

"It works, believe me." Kyle pounded the top of the console as if to resuscitate it.

"I'll give you five bucks."

Kyle shook his head. "Twenty."

"Ten would be stretching it for something you know don't work."

"It works. Twenty."

"All right, fifteen. I'm a fool, but I'll give you fifteen."

"Twenty." Kyle stuck out his palm.

"Twenty it is, you old sumbitch." Hump shook his open hand. "How you been, Kyle McRae? Last I heard you were pulling time up in the jail."

A man who rarely let people close enough to touch him, Kyle never knew exactly how to act when shaking hands. He let his fingers go limp until Hump was through. Kyle didn't trust a handshake; he only trusted the cash he could close his fist around.

Kyle felt a gentle tugging underfoot. Beneath the table, he saw small fingers pulling at his bootlaces. "Dammit boy, I told you to leave folk's feet alone." Hump yanked the boy by the arm and half spanked, half wiped his shorts, raising a faint cloud of dust. As soon as Hump unhanded him, the boy slid beneath the table. He didn't cry, but with arms squeezing

31

his scraped knees, he rocked to and fro on the heels of his cowboy boots. "The old lady usually has him. This weekend, she decides I ought to spend some quality time with the little booger. He poured dirt down my boot this morning."

Kyle tapped the top of the television. "So twenty, that's the deal, right?"

"We shook, didn't we? But I ain't seen you in ages. Where you been keeping yourself? They had the Windsor boarded up. Heard tell they're going to pull it down for a parking deck."

"Ain't been back to the Windsor. Rent's free if you don't need a roof. Food is too if you know where to look." Kyle lifted a dead rabbit by its hind legs from his sack.

"You going around picking things off the road?"

The boy under the table barked out a laugh, then covered his mouth with his dirty fingers. Kyle swung the carcass close so the child could touch the cold fur.

"Your mama don't want you touching dead things," Hump scolded him.

Kyle stuffed supper in the sack. Hump still hadn't reached for his wallet, but fiddled with the knobs on the TV. "So where did you lift the tube?"

"Like I said, found it."

"Likely inside somebody's living room."

"No. Out on the street. I got a truckload of stuff like it back at the camp."

"You got more?"

"TVs, toasters, all kind of things. So how about the twenty?"

Hump was hard at thought, pulling his hat brim low over his eyes. "Tell you what. I'll pay you twenty, maybe more, after we go camping."

"Camping?"

"You, me, and the boy. Try some of the rabbit. Hey, Randall." Hump leaned under the plywood table. "How would you like to go camping with your old man?" The boy shook his head side to side so hard it seemed like he could get whiplash. "What if you could watch Uncle Kyle skin that bunny rabbit?"

"Whoa, now," Kyle protested, but the kid was already bobbing his head yes.

"Rabbit!" Randall squealed.

"Rabbit, that's right. Let's eat us a bunny rabbit."

"Hold on now. Only got one rabbit."

But the boy kept shrieking: "Rabbit! Rabbit!"

"Go get in the car, Randall." Hump lifted his son and swatted his behind, steering him in the direction of the Rambler. "That's it, hop. Hop like that bunny rabbit."

"Look, this ain't just for the kid," Hump confided. "I can help you out. The Windsor might be gone, but you can't stay out in the woods all winter. There's probably some stuff at your camp I might pay top dollar for."

"You said twenty. We shook on it."

As dusk fell, Kyle led the way into the woods, carrying the TV, which caught stray branches and whipped them over the boy's head, smack into Hump's face.

"Damn. Watch it. Don't know why the hell you wanted to lug that TV all the way in here. We could have just locked it in the trunk."

Hump wasn't trustworthy. Kyle wanted to be sure the set stayed in his eyesight until he got his money.

"How much further?"

"We're here." Kyle plunged into a thicket of rhododendron, fighting through green leaves and tough boughs to a clearing beside the stream. A branch snagged Hump's grocery bag, ripping the bottom. Out fell hot dogs, frozen potato slices, and two big wine bottles. One bottle landed in the leaf mold, the other cracked against a rock.

"Damn, after all that way!" Hump said. "We'll have to go back for more."

Kyle set his TV down, rubbing his tired shoulder. "Think you can find your way?"

Hump stared into the darkening woods. "Well, this one bottle might last the night, but no sharing. Yours was the one that got busted."

Kyle walked to the creek bank to relieve himself. Randall followed, pulling down the front of his shorts, too. "Watch what you're doing," Kyle said. "You'll get your hands all wet."

Twin yellow streams arched over the water. The creek was foul anyway: bits of trash and beer bottles glinted under the slow-moving water. Upstream, a discarded refrigerator stored dead leaves and broken twigs. Kyle zipped up and winked at the kid who did likewise.

Kyle emptied his burlap bag, sorting through the day's haul. Randall squatted, poking at the dead rabbit. Kyle slapped his hand. Curiosity must run in the family. Hands clasped behind his crooked back, Hump strolled about the camp, eyeing Kyle's collection. Besides the latest TV, there were several remote controls, a telephone without a receiver, a video cassette recorder, an eight-track player, a dusty turntable, various speakers, burned toasters, mixers, stacks of dog-eared paperbacks, crates of glass bottles, crushed aluminum cans, miscellaneous flatware.

Hump unscrewed his bottle and took a swig. "I don't see why you drug us out here to look at this crap."

"Weren't my idea." Kyle unsheathed his knife and lifted the rabbit by the hind legs. A weird laughter filtered through the trees. Hump stared into the woods, the bottle frozen before his lips. "Highland Hospital is just over the rise. You hear 'em hollering late at night."

"You would live right next door to the loony bin." Hump quivered then took a long pull at his wine and stepped backwards, bumping the TV.

"Careful, that's my twenty dollars."

"Damn thing don't work."

Kyle dropped the knife and went over to a rotted stump where he pulled on an orange extension cord, covered with leaves. Actually, a series of cords, connected one after the other, snaking through the woods and over the hospital grounds until it reached an unlocked work shed and an unused electrical outlet. Kyle switched on the set. From the woods flowed the surreptitious current, bringing a babble of voices to the box, like nightmares drained from the psychiatric patients. The picture tube faintly glowed.

"I'll be damned."

"Courtesy of the crazies," Kyle said. "Hey!" He retrieved his knife from Randall who was stabbing the ground with the blade. "Don't be playing with this." Kyle wiped the blade on his pants and tested the edge with his calloused thumb. "Why don't you go watch the TV?"

But Randall wagged his head, bangs flying from his low forehead.

"Hey, Randall, wrasslin's on." Hump crouched on his heels, the TV screen glowing in his face as he swigged from the bottle.

"Look," said Kyle. "I'll tell you a story when it gets good and dark."

"Promise?" the boy whispered.

"Sure, but right now, I'm gonna skin this rabbit. Best go watch the wrestling." But Randall wouldn't budge. He rocked in a tight ball, blowing his lips against a scraped knee. He stared at the furry body on the ground. "Suit yourself, but don't say I didn't warn you."

The knife blade flashed in the television's blue glow.

34

6

Of all the things Ruth Wilder prided herself on in her largely blessed life, family was of course high on her list, ranking only a little below her perfect Sunday school attendance for the past forty-four years.

So on the rare Sundays when they visited Beaverdam Baptist, Royce and Eva set the alarm to rise at dawn, rousting Dean out of bed, bolting down breakfast, and dashing in and out of the shower, everybody dressed and into the car, driving the forty-five miles from Altamont to Zebulon County, off the main highway and threading the hairpin twists over the gap, then descending the ten miles of curves down into the bottomlands of Beaverdam where Ruth sat, waiting on the front porch in her best dress, clutching her black clasp purse on her lap, rocking impatiently for the past hour.

"I knew you would be late. You have always been since the day you were born." Ruth never failed to remind her son that he had been born on a Saturday in a fierce labor that wouldn't let her get out of bed the next day for church.

"We got plenty of time, Mama." Royce kissed the tightly permed top of her aging head as he helped her into the back seat of the Mercedes, then drove the quarter mile to the church.

They took their places in Ruth's usual pew, ushered past the watchful eyes of the regulars already seated, trailed by the whispers of women hissing into the jug ears of their deaf husbands: "Them's Ruth's kin. Jake's boy and his family from over in Altamont."

35

This morning, for this special occasion, Ruth wore a pretty lavender-colored polyester dress, dug out of the closet from last Easter. As soon as she took her seat, she started digging around in her purse for her tithe and her tissues. Ruth was bound to weep when her perfect Sunday school attendance was again rightly recognized.

Eva reached out to squeeze Dean's restless leg to keep him from kicking the pew ahead of them. Good, Royce thought. If he had to suffer through church, so could his delinquent son, flushed and steaming in his blue hopsack blazer, off in his own world.

When Dean was little, Eva had let him take crayons and paper to services at St. Mary's. While the Episcopalians rose and knelt according to traditional forms, Dean squatted on the plush velvet kneeler and used the polished seat of the pew for his desk, copying his versions of the stained-glass windows overhead. Growing older, he had to sit up like the rest, but he'd drawn his secret comic books on the order of service held inside the worn cover of the Book of Common Prayer. But even Episcopalians could indulge their youth only so long. Now officially in high school, Dean was expected to act like an adult, pay attention like a regular grownup, and be bored out of his expanding skull.

"Don't be so jumpy," Eva whispered, trapping his scribbling fingers, interlacing them with hers. He had been practicing his painting, memorizing his moves, angles, and arabesques, quick cuts and curlicues, against the nap of his worsted trousers.

At the ringing of a tinny bell, Ruth leaned around Eva and tapped his knee. "That means it's Sunday school," she whispered. "Go on with the young'uns."

"Just like catechism class," Eva reassured him. "Just behave."

The young people filed from the sanctuary into a classroom behind the pulpit, leaving a handful of widows and aged farmers for the adult class. Eva always steeled herself for these Sunday visits to an alien denomination. "Mama's almost got used to you being Episcopalian," Royce had teased her on the drive over this morning, "though she still thinks you all pray to the Queen of England."

"Funny," she said at his familiar joke, screwing tighter the smile that she wore around her mother-in-law.

Eva had grown up in Sunday schools and church services, living in a succession of ever smaller rectories as her father kept finding himself

36

shepherd of increasingly thinner flocks. These Baptists made those chapels look like the Vatican. No stained glass, no organ, let alone the embroidered kneelers she was used to at St. Mary's. They sang a few rusty hymns, made long-winded prayers, and stumbled through a reading of Judges, an object lesson from the crude customs of an ancient tribe given to stoning its wayward women and disrespectful sons. Royce kept squirming on the pew burnished by decades of Baptist backsides. "Be still." She elbowed his ribs. "You're worse than Dean."

Nothing had changed in the church in the twenty years since Royce had left home and the stifling services here. He saw the handwriting on the wall. A painting behind the pulpit depicted a disembodied hand writing across an unfurled scroll: "Where will you spend eternity?"

Royce had no ready answer to the terrible question, sucking his lip bloodless between his gapped front teeth. The other painting on the back wall was no better: a portrait of the Savior, with his heavenward gaze under thick eyelashes. Shave off the beard and his brunet locks bore a resemblance to Lucy Greene's.

Royce couldn't help himself. Every time he went to church, he thought of sex. He used to sit beside Lucy Greene, daring damnation in the eyes of the Lord, their thighs touching, her fingers tiptoeing up and down the corduroy of his trousers. The Wilders and Greenes countenanced this, since it was commonly known they were courting and likely would be married before any baby or wrongdoing could show. The pew was just another station, like the swing on Lucy's front porch where they sat most Saturday evenings and talked about their life after high school, how they would always be happy in the world they knew in Beaverdam.

Royce couldn't imagine bearing his life if he had stayed in Beaverdam, sitting in this stifling sanctuary Sunday after Sunday. He would have hanged himself like that farmer whose story of failure haunted them all.

When the offering plate passed down their pew, Royce set the bowl in his lap and raised one haunch while he fumbled for his wallet. The only thing worse than suffering through church was having to pay for the pain. Handing the plate over, Royce was surprised to see that the man who took his money wasn't his father. Each Sunday, Jake Wilder had passed around the offering plate he'd cut from a walnut bough and turned on a lathe. He patrolled the center aisle, counting in his head what went in the collection, who had tithed and who had not. "Let every day provide for itself and God

37

send Sunday," he used to say. Now the old man would never see Royce slipping in a guilty five bucks instead of the five cents he used to grudgingly give as a kid.

The preacher took the pulpit to call the names of those with unsullied Sunday school attendance in the past year, starting with the youngest children and on up through the adults, saving the best for last. "And of course, Mrs. Ruth Wilder has her 40th anniversary of perfect attendance," the preacher said. "Miss Ruth, we got you a special fruit basket."

Ruth waved to the applause she'd been waiting for all year, but her moment was short-lived. The piano sounded an off-key chord. The congregation staggered to their feet, reaching for the hymnals in the racks behind the pews. They sang halfheartedly in the heat, a choir of apathetic angels, then took their seats, feeling their mortal bottoms numbed through the duration of the sermon.

"Jesus is coming," the preacher wailed. "Sinner, are you ready?"

But if Jesus was really coming any minute now as the preacher said, why did they keep the doors closed? Imagine a knock. How many would believe it was Christ's own knuckle softly rapping?

Royce had quit listening to this stuff years ago and used the time to tally columns of mental figures in his head. Paying off all his debt, his bills, amortizing mortgage rates, divvying up dividends from stocks he could buy when he was well-to-do. He wanted to climb to Royce's Rock, the cliff where the ravens roosted that his father had willed to him. All the good land and the tobacco allotment of course had gone with the bulk of the farm to his mother, but Royce was grateful his sire had remembered him in his will.

Landrum could ask all he wanted for the land, but no one could build there. It was more of a view, something you would buy for a development on the Buckeye on the other side of Beaverdam Road, but that all belonged to his uncle Dallas, who had no more interest in turning loose of his holdings than in voting for a Republican copperhead, as the old Yellow Dog Democrat called those partisans in the bitter inbred politics of Zebulon County.

The altar call came and faltered. Nobody came forward to be saved, no backslider slipped forward into good graces. Thank God, Royce thought.

Dean was ready to bolt until his mother caught his elbow. "Please, wait for the rest of us."

"Quarter past twelve." Royce eyed his watch. "Mama, you ready?"

But Ruth sat down again to dig through her purse. "Thought I had some money in here somewhere. Need to make my tithe."

"Mama, the offering already came around. We'll give it on the way out." Royce helped her up. His mother seemed so frail that too rough a touch might snap some bone in her loose skin.

"Why, Royce Wilder. You didn't think you could run off without saying hi?" Lucy Greene Gudger must have run halfway down the aisle to hug him.

"Where's Junior?" Royce searched the sanctuary for the good old boy Lucy had snagged after Royce had shed her and fled Beaverdam.

"Sleeping in today. Worked a late shift last night. Royce, you're a sight for sore eyes."

Eva prodded his ribs before Lucy and her cheap scent of soap released him.

"Hey, Lucy," Eva showed her forced smile. Royce could tell she was trying her best not to stare at Lucy's disfigurement, but she couldn't help but mark every wen, sty, goiter, and glass eye, each birthmark and amputation evident among the backwards populace of Beaverdam, marred from birth or maimed in the barnyard. In Lucy's case, it was the missing tip of the middle finger of her left hand, the sawed-off stump ringed with her wedding band.

"You must not know what to think of our little old church." Lucy laid on the drawl a little thick, Royce noticed.

"Oh, not at all, I rather enjoy the singing," Eva said.

"You ought to come more often."

"I usually go to church in Altamont. St. Mary's. I try to take Royce, but he won't go."

"Episcopal. Too fancy for me," Royce said.

"Dean didn't give you any trouble in Sunday school, did he?" Eva patted her son's slumped shoulder.

"'Course not. This is one sharp son you've reared here. Though we did have a bit of a discussion about Genesis."

"Dinosaurs didn't ride on the ark with Noah," Dean hissed, continuing the argument he had waged in class.

"I know in a fancy school they teach all sorts of things—evolution and all—we don't get way back here. But no, we straightened him out. You come and see us soon, honey. We'll talk more."

To Dean's evident horror, she patted his sleeve with the disfigured hand, that missing knucklebone.

"We've got to be going now, Lucy. Good to see you. Say hi to Junior for us." Royce prodded his mother forward.

The aisle filled with the faithful and the smell of talcum powder and strong soap, cigarette smoke, sweat, manure, aromas of the barnyards and woodstoves. Royce could see daylight over the threshold, freedom ahead, but not until he passed another reminder of his past, those dents in the double doors, the shadowy indentations his uncle had once pressed his little fingers into.

"There, feel that? We're talking pure meanness." Dallas showed him where the hatefully flung rocks had scarred the wood. "Sure as you and me are standing here, she stood yonder and stoned the house of the Lord, if you can believe it. Dog-cussed us all on a Sunday morning."

She was Wanda McRae, the witch woman who lived over the ridge from the Wilders at the end of a long dirt road Royce had been up only once in his life—a secret he'd never shared with Dallas or his daddy or anyone.

Ruth balked at the door. "I forgot my fruit basket."

They had come this far and Royce didn't want to have to wade into the crowd and face Lucy again. "You've got a whole bushel of apples at the house. Why not let someone have it that's truly needy?"

"I am needy. I'm a widow woman and I need a fruit basket. Dean, go fetch it for me."

Royce escorted his mother to the car, her pumps shuffling through the loose gravel, her weight leaning on his arm. He suspected she walked slower on Sundays to keep up appearances as a church elder. At home, she shed the fake feebleness and rushed from room to room, chore to chore. She was turning eighty-two next March, but she only acted her age when she had an appreciative audience.

Ruth lowered herself into the back of the Mercedes while Royce held the door. "Seat's hot! I told you to park in the shade!"

"It was all shade when we got here, Mama. I'll turn on the air conditioning."

"Never mind. I'll just crack the window." Ruth always complained about the smell of air conditioning, saying she just as soon have wind with no conditions on her face.

"Boy, what's your hurry? You act like a Methodist scared of getting

40

dunked by a bunch of Baptists." A rough, familiar hand grabbed the back of Royce's neck.

"Hey, Dallas. How you doing?"

"I'm just an old mailman with a message. You better come to church more often."

"I'm here, aren't I?" Royce said.

"Morning, Ruth. I see you got this pagan in a pew today." Dallas Rominger tipped his jaunty fedora to his older sister. The green hat matched the plaid of his jacket, which must have hung in Dallas' wardrobe since the Eisenhower administration.

The old bachelor draped his arm around Eva's shoulder, smooching her temple. "Um, you sure smell good today. Royce, come smell her hair."

"Who poked you in the eye?" Eva tilted Dallas' chin. "Royce, did you see this?"

Royce crouched to look beneath his uncle's hat brim where a sty glowered like a coal in his left eye.

"Pretty, ain't it? If it don't go away soon, I'll have to do something to keep from scaring the ladies. Maybe a black pirate patch?"

"You'll need a peg leg," Ruth called from the back seat. "Show 'em what else you done."

Dallas hiked his trousers, showing a scabbed shinbone and a purple bruise.

"What in the world?" Eva asked.

"Fell through the loft of that old barn is what he done," Ruth said. "He'd still be there if nobody'd heard his heifer bawling at the hay bin."

"It wasn't near as bad as she makes it sound. Boy, you ever scrape your knee this pretty?" Dallas pirouetted on his good leg and showed his wounds to Dean who had returned swinging the cellophane fruit basket, about to send the Granny Smiths into orbit.

"Gross." Dean wrinkled his face in disgusted admiration.

"Dean, be careful." Eva rescued the swinging fruit basket from his grip.

"What's this I hear about you making monkeyshines, arguing evolution in Sunday school with Lucy Gudger?" Dallas thumped his fat, soft Bible on Dean's hard head.

"What did you say?" Royce dreaded his wayward son had let off another f-bomb in the church like he had at the house.

"Nothing." Dean rubbed his head. "She was saying God created the

Earth about four thousand years ago if you counted all the begats in the Bible. I told her my biology teacher said the Earth was more like four billion years old."

"Old! What you know about old, boy? Talk to me about old." Dallas pinched the boy's shoulder playfully. "Can't see, can't hear, can't hardly walk. We're getting so old we ain't hardly fit to kill. Ain't that right, Ruth?"

"Don't talk like that," Royce said. "You're not dead yet."

"Oh, I don't plan on dying," Dallas wasn't joking now. "World's going to go before me. Any day now, that trumpet's going to sound. The heavens shall pass away with a great noise, the elements shall melt with fervent heat, the Earth also, and the works that are in it shall be burned up."

"Burned up?" Dean asked. The usual curiosity of teenage boys for death and destruction, Royce thought.

"Doomsday. That's another Baptist thing like the Creation," he explained. He always felt nervous when Dallas started quoting scripture.

"No, that comes after the Rapture," Dallas corrected him. "Born-again believers won't have to see the Tribulation that follows. The trumpet will sound and you'll be looking into that graveyard yonder and all them holes will open."

"Cool," said Dean.

"You'll see them rising into heaven, even your granddaddy, I'll bet."

Royce squinted at the cemetery on the hill behind the church. He had been raised to believe that all the good Baptists buried there would walk out alive in the end, but the thought of his father shooting out of his grave like a stalk of bone unnerved him.

"You don't believe that, do you?" Dallas pinched the funny bone in Royce's elbow. "You think you're too smart for all that now. Let me tell you, the Secretary of the Interior wanted to sell off the federal forest because the Lord was due any day."

Royce worked free of his uncle's clutches. "Say what you will on a Sunday, Dallas, come Monday morning, you wouldn't sell your land to Satan or St. Peter."

"Don't be so sure. Half million is what one jasper was offering me just last Monday."

"Who in their right mind offered that?"

"This Japanese feller," Dallas said. "Fight a war against them fifty years ago, now they're over here buying up the land."

"You're not seriously thinking—"

Dallas doffed his green fedora from his broad shining pate, then clapped it down like a tight lid. "Boy, I'm always thinking."

"Dallas, why don't you come eat with us?" said Eva. "We bought fried chicken."

"Store-bought?" Dallas looked disappointed. "That Colonel cooks the scrawniest chicken. No, I'm headed to the house, wait and see if the end comes today."

His uncle waved goodbye as Royce backed his car out of the lot. In the mirror, he saw Dallas gaze at the sky then check his wristwatch.

7

"hat woman, how did she lose her finger?" Dean asked what he was dying to know.

"Poor Lucy," Ruth said. "She's done her best after the accident."

Dean rested his chin on the bench seat, pestering his father. "What accident?"

"She was cutting wood. She never did pay attention," Ruth said.

"She cut it off? Oh man!"

"Story is the chickens ran off with it after her little brother brought the axe down," Royce glanced in the mirror.

Poor Lucy, trying to hide her mutilated hand. A slip of the axe blade. She lost the first knuckle of her middle finger, but no matter, she had that next finger to slip on Junior Gudger's cheap wedding band, dropping out of high school, married in the nick of time, eight months before they would cut the cord on her first, stillborn. No real funeral, just one day a new smaller patch of red clay in the Beaverdam Baptist graveyard, like a trap-door into the hereafter. Bad luck. Bad judgment. Bad things happened all the time in Beaverdam.

"Check the mailbox," Ruth ordered just as Royce was turning onto the wooden bridge.

"It's Sunday. Mail doesn't run today."

"I don't recall if I went to the mailbox yesterday. It was better when Dallas was delivering the mail. He'd leave all my letters right on my kitchen table."

44

Dallas had been retired from his Rural Free Delivery route for the past twenty years, but she still pined for her personal service. Royce shifted into reverse, backed up the car, cranked down the glass, and reached inside the rusted mailbox for a stack of shopping circulars, magazines solicitations, a sweepstakes entry.

"Here you go. Says you might have won a million dollars."

Seeing her name and the dollar amount on the front, Ruth ripped into the manila envelope as if expecting greenbacks inside.

"He's teasing you, Ruth. There's no money," Eva said.

She sniffed. "Never hurts to check."

"What's this?" Royce reached again into the mailbox where a slender envelope was wedged in the side seam. No telling how long it had been stuck there. He tore off the perforated edge to find a computerized form. "Mama, you do remember paying your tax bill?"

"Oh, Dallas handles all that, has since Jake passed."

"Says here you owe eight thousand, and if you don't pay these back taxes, the county will start foreclosure proceedings."

"Probably a computer error," Eva said. "Isn't it, Royce?"

"I'll ask Dallas." He folded the tax bill and put in his blazer pocket.

"God, are we going to sit in the middle of the road all day?" Dean banged his head against the glass as he mimicked hanging himself with his school tie.

Royce shifted into gear and drove across the bridge. The two-story farmhouse with its peeling whitewash and rusting tin roof had been built decades ago for far less than the eight thousand dollars the taxman wanted. But with the ninety-eight acres of land that sloped down Frozenhead Mountain, along with the barn, outbuildings, and a tobacco allotment, this was a valuable piece of real estate. Skip a few years of payment, and the tax bill could quickly mount.

Ruth dried her eyes then replaced her spectacles on her red nose before she climbed out of the car. "Jake never liked to be in debt to anyone. He always paid what we owed. You tell that taxman we always settle our accounts." She slammed the door and hobbled across the yard to the porch.

A sharp wet snap came from the back seat. Eva and Royce turned to see their son biting into the apple he'd snitched from Ruth's basket. "Whaa?" he said with his mouth full of white, fruity flesh. "I'm hungry."

"Take that basket inside to your grandmother," Eva said. "We're going to eat in just a moment."

In the trunk, the cardboard container had overturned in one of the mountain curves, spilling chicken parts and gravy. Eva was furious, throwing wings, thighs, drumsticks, and breasts back in the bucket, while Royce tried to wipe up the spill with old newspapers. "What's this doing in here?" Eva spied the wood radio jammed in the trunk and mistook it for detritus from their garage. "Wasn't it supposed to go to the dump?"

"Shush, this is a surprise for Mama." Royce cradled the radio under one arm and carried it into the house. In the parlor, he set his prize find beside the worn leather chair where his father had once held his dour court. "Brings back memories doesn't it, Mama?"

"What's that?" Ruth asked.

"A radio just like Daddy used to have."

"I don't remember no radio. Besides, I've got one in the kitchen. I can pull in Bristol and Johnson City and the farm reports and weather."

She meant the cheap plastic transistor radio Eva and Royce had given her for Christmas years ago.

"Not like this radio. This is real old, just like the one Daddy had. I paid good money for it at an estate sale."

Eva's ears perked up as she walked into the parlor. "How much money?"

"Some. Not much. Never mind."

"Does it work?" Dean poked at the frayed cord.

"No, it's broken." Royce waved him away.

"Broken?" Ruth had no use for the past, for junk. "Why you bringing me an old, busted radio? Son, sometimes I don't know about you." She stomped into the kitchen with her fruit basket of perfect attendance.

For all their churchgoing, and Ruth's perfect Sunday school attendance, the Wilders no longer said grace at mealtimes—a family embarrassed with too much piety since Jake Wilder's passing. They kept silent, almost in his surly honor, the quiet broken only by the sounds of forks scraping chipped china, the clink of the ice melting in tea glasses, the loud tick of the mantel clock from the next room, the gurgle of water in the springhouse adjacent to the kitchen, the smacking of their lips on greasy chicken, until Eva could hardly stand it.

"What was Dallas talking about—somebody wanting to buy his land?" Eva asked.

"Oh, he means this Jap fellow who came by," Ruth said. "When was it—Tuesday? I forget."

"You talked to him, too?" Royce asked. "What did he want?"

"Wanted to know who owned back of the Frozenhead and across the Buckeye. Government, I said, then Dallas, and us, of course. He seemed real interested in the house here. Wanted to look inside, but I wouldn't let him. You just can't tell with strangers nowadays. I thought at first this feller might be with one of them cults, Mormons or Jehovah's Witnesses, the way he kept saying the world as we know it is ending."

Again with the world ending, Royce thought. Something as big as the Earth, four point five billion years old, should be immune to change. The land should outlast them all.

"Royce is meeting with a man tomorrow who wants to make an offer, too. Beaverdam must be booming in real estate," Eva said.

"Market's in a slump." Royce shook his head. "He's just looking for a bargain."

"This Jap feller said this was prime property now."

"Japanese," Eva corrected her, shaking her head for Dean's sake so he wouldn't repeat any ethnic slurs.

"He said what with folks retiring here from Florida, they are going to be knocking at my door wanting to buy. He said I could get half a million."

"Only if they don't know any better," Royce said.

"I ain't going to become a millionaire, but half that would be fine with me. With that kind of cash, I could fix this place up, put siding on the outside, a new stove in the parlor."

"Mama, if you took the half million, you'd have to move. I'd think the house would be part of the deal, not just the land."

"Move?" Ruth frowned at this bit of logic that had escaped her. "But I've always lived here."

"And you'll live here lots longer, I'm sure," Eva tried to calm her.

"But I'll have to move someday, won't I? I've lived way too long, way past my time."

"Quit saying that," Royce said. "Look, you still live here and no one's making you move. I'm going to go check on that spring like you've been talking about. I'll clean it out if you just stop all this talk about living too long."

Ruth wiped her nose with her napkin. "Never mind me. I'm just a silly old woman at times." She carried the platter of chicken bones into the kitchen.

Royce pushed his chair free of the table. "Want to head up the mountain, take a look at the spring?" he asked Dean.

"Nah."

"Oh, go on, why don't you two spend some time together," Eva said. Dean shrugged.

"Dean don't need to go into the woods," Ruth said as she returned for more dirty dishes. "There's ticks and snakes, poison ivy. You don't want to go, do you?"

A second sulky shrug.

"It's all right, I don't need the company." Royce stalked from the room.

❖

"I hope you're happy," Eva hissed as she cleared Dean's plate.

He sat there, smirking, that habit that drove her crazy. He scraped his chair back, then shuffled from the table. His shoulders rounded in the blue blazer like he was carrying the weight of the world. He resembled his grandfather, Jake Wilder, a man he probably barely recalled. Eva remembered her father-in-law as a small, shutdown man, coughing into a calloused fist a dry smoker's cough that turned darker toward the end when the cancer finally caught up with him. No hospital, no doctor for him. Ruth had ministered to him with corn whiskey that Dallas had procured from somewhere, Ruth didn't ask.

"Eva!" Ruth called from the kitchen. "You bringing the rest of them dishes?"

"Coming," Eva sighed. She brought in the stack of dishes and set them by the sink.

"My ring," Ruth called too late, as the two women watched the gold band, the widow's last reminder, suddenly slide down the metal sideboard into the frothy suds. Ruth plunged her plump hand into the water, full of dirty knives and plates and forks, then as quickly snatched it back. "Look what you done now." Ruth sucked at the crimson bubble of blood and soap on her sliced fingertip.

Bad luck always happened in Beaverdam.

8

Royce carried his antique radio from the parlor to the car. No one appreciated his memories, all his efforts. He leaned against the trunk, slipping off his leather loafers to change into his brogans, lacing them tight for a hike up the mountain.

He swung by the woodshed to pick out a tobacco stave for a walking stick. The stick served to stir the brambles ahead for any snakes, but Royce found the staff a welcome support. The slope seemed to have grown steeper over the years, straining his hamstrings. Good thing that Dean hadn't come. He tended to thrash his stick at the brambles and briars. Last time he'd swung wild and caught Royce in the mouth. For once, Dean hadn't been the one doing all the bleeding.

Royce gained the fence to the upper pastures, then stopped to catch his breath and look back over the house and farm. Smoke purled from the chimney, which had lost a few bricks on the rusted tin roof. All of the outbuildings—barn, shed, chicken house— leaned precariously closer each year toward total collapse. What was it worth? For a man who made money off the land, who could calculate square footage by the dollar, it was hard for Royce to put a price on the place where he'd been reared.

He pivoted on his stick and started again uphill, passing into the shade of the woods. Clouds were massing over the Frozenhead, and Royce wondered if a storm might brew up. It had been raining down the road in Altamont when they woke up this morning, but here in Beaverdam, it was dry as bone. You could have a foot of snow up here, and only an inch over in Altamont. Even the weather couldn't make up its mind in these mountains.

It was only two in the afternoon, but too late to climb to the granite cliff that his parents called Royce's Rock, where he would perch, swinging his legs in midair, surveying the church steeple and the lightning rods on the roofs sheltering all the folks he knew, his boyhood haunt where he dreamed of the day when he could fly away from here. At least his father had left him his dreaming spot if no money in the will. He could no more sell Landrum that barren rock than he could turn loose of that useless radio.

Royce had always known his old man was awful with money. Turning all those decisions over to Dallas as executor in his last will and testament only confirmed his cowardice with hard cash. How many times had Royce tried to talk his daddy into making the land work for him, instead of him working the land so hard? "Tobacco's turning into nickel-and-dime stuff with what RJR and Philip Morris pay at auction. Why not try Christmas trees? You sell 'em direct. That hill would be perfect for Frasier firs." When the new highways brought tourists, Royce suggested rentals. "You could put Swiss chalets or log cabins on top of the Frozenhead. With that pretty view, people would pay to stay in 'em. You'd never have to break your back again."

And to each of Royce's get-rich schemes, Jake Wilder would say, "Hunhh," not even bothering to pause his Barlow knife whittling whatever stick he would have in hand, just "Hunhh," his standard response, the same serviceable monosyllable that conveyed skepticism, disdain, or simply the end of any disagreeable discussion.

"Hunhh!" Royce heard his father's voice deep in his throat.

He couldn't find the path to the spring, following what he took to be a trail until he hit a dead end beneath a rock overhang. He doubled back, crisscrossing the slope, his rubber-soled shoes slipping in loam. Water seeped from all over the mountainside, but he couldn't locate the iron pipe that fed the springhouse below. Flailing through the laurel, Royce had to fight a growing claustrophobia and the unsettling sense that he was not alone. Stopping, he heard nothing but his own belabored breathing where before he could have sworn there were footsteps. At last he located the pipe, tripping over it snaking through the leaf mold. The line ran farther to the left than he remembered, following a dry streambed a hundred yards uphill through laurel and galax before disappearing under a stone slab.

Royce raised the mossy rock and saw his reflection in the water. A salamander shot across the bottom where the spring bubbled from the Frozenhead. Why his mother ever worried about this spring running dry, he didn't know; it was like not trusting the sun to rise each day over the Buckeye. He cupped his hands and drank. This was the way water should taste—so cold it tingled the fillings in his back teeth. What did Dallas always say? "If once you take a drink of lonesome waters, you'll come back someday." Royce scooped out the leaves that clogged the pipe, then replaced the stone lid, leaving the salamander to its sleep.

He stood and dried his hands on his pants. A shadow fell over the woods as a cloud drifted across the sun. Trees creaked overhead with a sound like a closing door. Royce sensed again that he was not alone. He grabbed the stick and headed downhill. He tried slowing his descent by grabbing at branches but the hill was too steep. He stumbled, half running across an overgrown logging trail. The tobacco stave caught his foot, tripping him headlong into the low branches of a hemlock.

When the tree branches stopped spinning like the spokes of a wheel, Royce came to, lying on a bed of soft, brown needles. He had knocked himself silly against the trunk of the tree. He sat up, surrounded by a curtain of green.

"Thought you could hide!"

Royce flattened his tingling spine against the tree trunk, searching in all directions. Through the screen of branches, he saw a cow trotting down the logging trail, chased by a woman with a long switch. "Git now! Git on home!"

The screaming woman wore a man's hunting coat and a felt hat clamped over her gray hair. She stopped. "I know you're there!"

Royce froze. He could see her profile through the boughs as she kept watching the logging trail behind her.

"You can't hide from me!" Her voice quavered. She seemed to sniff the breeze stirring the branches of Royce's cover. What if she could smell his cold sweat?

"Damn you!" She flicked her switch in the cold air. "Damn you all!" She lashed the rump of the grazing cow. The poor beast bellowed and bolted down the trail, chased once more by the cussing woman.

51

When he could no longer hear the harridan nor the heifer, Royce crept out from beneath the hemlock. He had not seen Wanda McRae this close in years, not since he was a boy foolhardy enough to hurl a rock at her house.

Royce had been no more than eight when he walked what felt like forever up that red dirt road forbidden to him by his father, a dry knot in his windpipe and a rock sticky with sweat in his fist. Lucy Greene, squatting in her pinafores, had selected the proper heft of mica-flecked granite and placed it in his hand, double daring him. After all, hadn't the witch woman thrown rocks at their church?

At the top, the ramshackle cabin teetered on piers of river rock, threatening to tumble down the dirt road. Various coats of paint had been tried on the clapboards but had dulled to shades of rust and ditch water. As he crept closer, the peeling paint turned out to be long snake hides hung by the lintel: diamondbacks, canebrake, and timber rattlers, their fangs fixed into the rafters, the pearly buttons of their rattles touching the floor. A rusted Ford Fairlane was parked out front—no telling how long since it had run any blacktop. A scrawny brood of chickens clucked and scratched about the flattened tires. Besides the noisy fowl, Royce heard another, peculiar babble. He crept along the side and raised his head over the hood.

Squatting in the dirt was a small child in a man's torn undershirt, blue-eyed, mouth stained red by the clay he was gnawing. A frayed rope was tied to the child's thin ankle, trailing up the porch steps and inside the door. So it was true. Dallas, who told so many tales that it was hard to believe anything he said—how she kept rattlers for pets, brewed liquor for drunkards, hexed cattle and folks with her spells—he was telling the truth about this: Wanda was a witch who favored stewed young'uns for her supper.

Rock in hand, Royce stepped out from behind the car. The boy was maybe his own age, or a little younger, hard to tell as small and scrawny as he was. The bound boy stared at him—marble blue eyes that never blinked. Royce wanted to say "hey," but he was afraid.

"Hey, you!" A woman yelled from the porch. It was Wanda, as close as he'd come to this woman he'd been warned to keep clear of. Her hair was wild, the wind licking wisps around her sharp face. She wore a dress and a man's boots, an apron stained with what might have been blood. She waved a broom as if to sweep him from her private property. "What you doing here?"

Royce flung the rock in her direction. He couldn't believe it would come unglued from his hands. He didn't see where it landed, but he heard the kid begin to bawl.

"Damn you, boy! Come back here!"

Royce raced down the road. He stumbled and ripped the knee of his dungarees, then jumped up and kept going, terrified to look back lest he see Wanda flying on that broom.

9

I'm scared to go up that mountain lest I run into that crazy Wanda McRae," Ruth confessed. They were at the kitchen table, hearing Royce describe his adventure on the Frozenhead. Ruth had spread out a newspaper and was peeling an apple from her church basket.

"Did you say anything to her?" Eva asked.

"I don't think she saw me. I was sort of hiding under a tree."

"You can't say a word to Wanda." Ruth jabbed the paring knife to make her point. The bandage Eva had applied to her hurt finger was already dirty and loose. "Folks have tried and failed. Your daddy used to post no trespassing signs and she'd just tear 'em down."

"That's not very nice," Eva observed.

"Nice ain't her problem, she's just mean. You know she once threw rocks at the church and dog-cussed the congregation on a Sunday morning?"

"Dallas showed me the holes in the door when I was little," Royce said. "He used to say she'd come get me if I did something bad. It used to give me nightmares."

"Dallas was always bad to tease you," Ruth halved her apple with the dull knife. "But they do say she can hex people."

"Oh, now, that's just make-believe," Eva said.

"It's no make-believe when a healthy heifer births a two-headed calf or when the Cantrell girl gets bit by the rattler coiled in the hen nest," said

Ruth. "You wind up on the cross side of Wanda McRae, you best watch out. Look what happened to Dallas, how he got stuck in that barn."

"Clumsiness, if you ask me," Eva insisted. "I'll bet this Wanda's nothing but a little old lady."

Royce thought of worse, of a boy tied to a porch post, of Wanda waving a broom, but he kept quiet.

"Hunhh, I'm the one who's old," Ruth sighed. "Too old to worry like I do. Times are troublesome. I tell you some days I'd like to be free of it all. Go ahead and put me in that rest home like you want."

"Mama, now you know we're not going to put you in a rest home, not while we've got a spare bedroom."

Ruth didn't answer, but spit the apple from her mouth. Spittle hung from her lip and bits of fruit flecked her chin, and for a horrifying instance, the dementia that Royce feared seemed to have finally overtaken her. "Apple's no better than mush. Look how they treat old folks." The old woman wadded the bad apple in the newspaper and took the trash into the next room to toss into the woodstove.

"She's been driving me crazy," Eva whispered. "It's not fair having to watch her all the time."

"What do you want me to do?"

They ceased their whispering when Ruth returned. "I wrapped the rest of this banana pudding for Dean and you can take the rest of this fruit basket. I don't believe all the apples are bad."

Royce glanced at his watch. "About time to head back to Altamont."

"Where is Dean?" Eva asked.

"Last I saw, he was headed to the barn," Ruth said.

"I'll fetch him."

Royce walked out of the house. He heard a strange rattle and hissing in the air from behind the barn. He turned the corner and saw a bloody mist spraying from his son's hand. "Damn it all to hell, Dean! What have you done?"

10

The barn had beckoned with its gray, weathered planks, just begging for a tag. He'd come armed with the paint cans in his rucksack, stuffed under the homework he'd promised to do on the ride home. After crucifying his morning in the backwards Baptist Sunday school, hearing that freak-fingered woman babbling about creation happening the day before yesterday, he'd show them. Dean was ready, by God, to rewrite Genesis. Just watch.

He'd shaken the can of red in one hand, the can of black in his left, the ball bearings rattling inside, small planets swirling through the pressurized plasma of paint, the universe he was about to unleash. A forefinger atop each valve, he let creation come hissing into being. He swirled his wrists tight in mirror writing, and red and black streamed together in midair and speckled the grained wood. He conducted the symphony of design, great sweeps that echoed each other, the mysterious glyph that was his true name written on the wall like a doorway he could step into. Oh man, oh man.

From one end of the barn to the other, the red and black line danced, swirling around a gigantic POW painted in the center. The closer he looked, the more the chaotic swirls and lines seemed to shift and take new shapes. He thought he saw faces in the clouds, apelike creatures surfing ocean waves, giant hands and midnight eyes staring out of crimson jungles.

"Damn it all to hell, Dean! What have you done?"

His father was suddenly screaming in his face, flecks of spit flying from his lips. POW! was right. For the second time this weekend, Dean was afraid his old man was about to slug him.

Royce grabbed a fistful of his sweatshirt, but Dean was more shaken by the language he'd never heard before from his buttoned-down dad. "God damn it, haven't I taught you to respect what belongs to other people? You're going to clean up this shit. You're going to learn your lesson."

Dean ducked his small chin, dropped his eyes, but stood his ground, responsible enough not to run off.

"Dean, are you all right?" Eva was hurrying from the house, Ruth following behind her. "Royce, what's wrong?"

"Just you wait, mister, until your mother sees this." Royce released Dean's sweatshirt from his shaking fist.

"Dean, what in the world?" Eva halted.

"It's called tagging," Dean said. "It's art."

"You always were a scribbly kind of boy, handy that way." Ruth frowned as she tilted her head, trying to get a focus through her bifocals, a proper perspective on the damage done her barn. "But I like that red, if you could even it out a bit."

"Even it out?" Royce said.

"I always told Jake I wanted the barn painted. Now seems like the time I can get it done and in a color of red that I like. When you reckon you can do the job?"

57

11

Deep in the woods, the light from the television flickered against Hump Humphries' half-lidded sightless eyes. The dead wine bottle lay in the crook of his arm. He'd passed out before the station returned to the air with dawn's religious programming.

Randall curled against his drunken daddy. The boy had had a big time too, running about the camp and generally getting in the way. He helped haul firewood and watched as the spitted rabbit dripped what little fat it had over the flames. After supper the boy threw rocks in the creek until his clothes were soaked, then he fell into a fitful sleep, dirty hands pawing the air like a dreaming dog.

Kyle squatted by the fire and watched the sparks spitting into the dark. The iron smell of rain hung in the air and a prickling of his neck hairs warned of an approaching storm. Nothing to do but watch the weather change; not that he minded. Wind, sun, sleet, rain, snow, hail—Kyle had seen all manner of meteorology come down on his head and roll off his back. Over the years he'd learned to make his own weather, a necessary talent in any season. Stretched out on the humid riverbank in July, he could make his toes turn blue with cold. Curled under a frigid overpass in January, he could work up a sweat by just dreaming of hell in the trunk of an old car.

When he was little, no more than Randall's age, his mother had locked him in the trunk of a Ford Fairlane outside a feed store. She couldn't trust him to go inside with her lest he wander off or start talking with strangers or eating the seed like candy. "Git in," she'd said with a look that warned against any sass or lip. He climbed in to keep the spare tire company. The lid slammed once, twice, until the latch caught and everything was dark. Sweat trickled down his face as the invisible sun beat down, but he fought the urge to beat on the underside of the metal. He waited like the good little boy his mama always threatened to trade him for. He thought of blowing snow and sharp icicles until he couldn't feel his fingers or toes. He shivered simply imagining winter.

Kyle opened his eyes. The kid stood before him, scratching his belly. "Hey," Kyle said.

Randall took this as an invitation to crawl into his crossed legs, surprising Kyle with a lapful of little boy.

"Better, huh?"

Randall nodded. "Story?"

"I don't know any, and I ain't your mama." Kyle tried to push the kid off his knee, but the boy slumped like deadweight.

"Story!" he said stubbornly.

"Your mama, she tell you bedtime stories?"

The boy nodded again.

"Your mama, she ever lock you in the trunk of a car?"

Randall giggled.

"She ever smack you silly with a frying pan?"

He snorted.

"She ever tie you up and make you sleep on the porch at night?"

Randall laughed in his lap.

"Guess not."

Thunder rumbled in the far hills and the sky glowed on the horizon. Randall squirmed as if trying to burrow behind Kyle's ribs for protection.

"Don't worry, rain won't reach us for a few hours." And as soon as he said it, Kyle knew the story he would tell. "'Course you ain't seen real rain," he cleared his throat. "Let me tell you about real rain."

The voice was not his own. It sounded more like a hoarse woman's, his mother's. She'd told and retold the tale so many times, dredging it up from her past or pure fancy, over and over, until it was like knowledge he'd suckled from her breast.

"Listen, this happened not too far from here and not so long ago."

She would start the story anytime a bad storm blew across the cove with the power out, the single light bulb dangled from the rafters dark as the new moon. Rain fell down the flue and hissed on the grate. Evenings like these, she didn't make him sleep out on the porch. Small mercy. He lay on the floor by the fire, by the creak of her rocker, and listened.

"All summer you could see the lightning in the sky, storm clouds dragging dark bellies over the ridge. You could hear noise, big booms that made your ears ring. They were building a dam downstream—making power for city folks—but all a body heard was the dynamite."

Lightning flared at the windows. The night cracked open overhead. His heart fluttered, but her rocker kept its steady creak.

"Independence Day, the clouds let loose and it commenced to rain. You think you seen it rain? You ain't seen nothing. This was the sky turned to water. Your lungs felt soggy after a while, like there wasn't air enough to breathe in between the raindrops. It was a hard rain. Hold a dipper out from beneath the eave and the rain dinged the bowl and bent the handle. Stick your tongue out on a dare? Why, the rain would raise blisters on the tip of it."

Randall stuck out his tongue just as Kyle once had, trying to imagine such a hurtful downpour. The boy darted the wet muscle behind the safety of his baby teeth.

"Now, here's the scary part: the creek kept coming. The more it rained, the higher the waters rose. One morning the creek jumped the bank, rolled across the yard, climbed the steps, and lapped into the house. At first, it was only at your ankles and you had to be careful not to step on tadpoles and crawdads. But by the time you sat down to lunch, water was up over your knees. By supper we had to open the windows to let the creek out, but otters and minks came diving over the sills. Daddy was in the back asleep. I dog-paddled into the bedroom to roust him, but when I lifted the blanket, he'd turned into this big, whiskered catfish. Last I seen of my daddy, his tail splashed water in my face as he swum off."

The voice gave out, surrendered to the silence. Kyle cleared his throat, but that was all he remembered.

Randall tugged at Kyle's beard. "Was your daddy a fish?"

"I believe that was my granddad."

"My daddy drinks fish," Randall solemnly repeated what he had always thought he heard.

As if the words had pierced his stupor, Hump stirred, burbling his lips. His chest rose slowly under the empty bottle.

"Don't speak ill of your old man. Least you got one."

Randall yawned. "Fish smell funny."

Kyle watched the fire. The flames guttered in the rising wind. When he looked, the child in his arms was asleep.

❖

It was raining. Hump eyed the purple dregs and tipped the bottle, trying for the last drop. "What time is it?" he asked.

Kyle craned his head out from under the tarp, looking for a sign of the sun in the overcast sky. "Say about ten."

"Damn store won't sell wine till one." Hump licked his lips. "You ain't got nothing to drink here?"

"Plenty of water coming down," Kyle observed.

"Funny." Hump turned on the TV, in need of some intoxicant for his brain.

"Cartoons," Randall piped up.

"No, no cartoons," Hump snapped. He kept switching the channel. "Shit, it's Sunday. Nothing but preachers and politicians. Well, lookee here. Wish I was in Florida with them." A commercial came on with sunny beaches, women in bikinis, the famous mouse bestriding a globe in the fantasyland built in the swamp. "Yep, me and Mickey Mouse," Hump said.

"Rains in Florida, too."

"How do you know? You ever been?"

"I seen windshield wipers on all them Cadillacs that come up here every summer."

"Least it's warm down there," Hump argued. "About the time it snows on your ass, you'll wish you were in Florida."

Digging through his gear, Kyle produced a plastic baggie of dried buds. "Want some?"

"Shit always gives me headaches."

"And that cheap wine don't?"

He rolled a joint and lit it off a glowing twig from the fire. Hump relented and took the joint in a deep drag. "You grow this shit in the woods?"

61

"Nah. Bought it downtown from a migrant. Snakeweed, grown hereabouts."

Another commercial flashed on the screen, models in swimwear cavorting in the surf, then shots of beer foaming in a mug. Hump bent closer, blowing smoke. "Ho boy, that looks good."

"The beer or the bikinis?"

"Both." Hump leered. "Bet them's May's work clothes now since she took her business down to Florida."

"It wasn't business, her going to Florida. Last I seen her, May was real sick." May would have looked silly in that string bikini, built as she was. Her hipbones spread like brittle bones from the place she called her only selling point. She grew thin and sharp as the needle she jabbed between her toes and fingers, into the yellow crook of her arm, searching for a vein that wouldn't give. "It wasn't business," he repeated. Hell, that was a lie: May always meant business.

"You think your mama abused you? Mine named me Maybelline, after a goddamn mascara." Before she became a junkie and one of the regulars walking Asheland Avenue, Maybelline Carter was raised a farm girl amid half a dozen squalling siblings, a flock of chickens, and no indoor plumbing. When she was fourteen, she walked out of junior high and hitched a ride to the city, still carrying her algebra book. She never threw away that book but clung to it as a keepsake, its margins doodled with hearts and initials of boys and secret crushes. Did she keep anything of him, Kyle wondered. When was May coming back?

A kung-fu movie was on the TV with its terrible dubbing, the unnatural sound effects of pummeling fists, whirling numchucks, bone-breaking blows. The mayhem switched to a commercial for a national sweepstakes. Ordinary people in obscure places swooned before the camera, laughing and weeping when they were anointed instant millionaires.

"Wish I could win me a million bucks," Hump said.

"Not likely." Kyle scratched at his shin. His bankroll was safely tucked away in the top of his brogan, five crumpled twenties, not a million, but enough for a new start when May came back.

"If I had me a million, I'd go to Florida," Hump said.

"Not there again."

"Least a body can be warm in Florida."

Kyle tapped a finger to the side of his head. "Weather's all up here."

"Oh, go to hell."

"It's warm there, too."

The kung-fu movie resumed and Hump shut up about Florida. Kyle hated how the mention of the Sunshine State kept bringing May to mind. She used to talk about this mermaid show in Wikkiwachee where the girls put on golden fins and swam underwater in this big tank for the tourists. "You could wrestle 'gators for a living," she teased Kyle, "and I could be a mermaid."

Kyle stared into the space between the raindrops. He saw May with long hair, bare breasts, and a fishy tail.

"Damn TV." Hump tried to adjust the antenna. He snapped his hand back like he'd been snakebit. "Shitfire." He leaped and upset the tarp, spilling a collected puddle of water on them all. "Damn thing about electrocuted me!" Hump hopped around the clearing, shaking his hand. Kyle couldn't help but laugh. Randall joined him, giggling.

"It ain't funny," the hunchback whined.

Kyle and the boy roared.

"I said it ain't funny!" Hump kicked the TV.

"Hey, that's my twenty dollars!"

Hump grabbed a crate of soft drink bottles and hurled them into the creek with an angry grunt. The barrage of glass exploded on the creek rocks. Then he grabbed a carton of silverware. Forks flew into the water. Kyle came in, swinging a right haymaker, but Hump moved and caught the blow on the neck. Hump stumbled forward, butting his head into Kyle's chest. The two men fell to the wet ground. Kyle locked his legs around his opponent in a scissors hold. Hump raked his nails down Kyle's cheek, trying to gouge his eye.

"Daddy!"

Kyle's head jerked back, pulled by the ponytail. Randall had a hold of his hair and was kicking his kidneys. Kyle let go of Hump's neck and backhanded the boy. Randall fell on his butt. He began to scream. The two men froze. Kyle let go and rolled across the wet leaves. Hump sputtered, holding his throat. Randall sat on the ground, head tilted to the rain, bawling for all he was worth.

"He ain't hurt, is he?"

"Nah, you just scared him." Hump touched his mouth. "Damn, am I bleeding?"

"A little."

"Mama!" Randall screamed. His cries came in pants and spurts, unable to catch his breath so as to bawl properly.

"Sure he's okay?" Kyle squatted beside the caterwauling kid. He couldn't see too well, pressing the heel of his palm against his burning eye.

"Get up, you ain't hurt." Hump tried to hoist the boy, but Randall refused to budge. "Mamaaaa!" he wailed.

Kyle covered his good ear, trying to muffle the boy's screams. Hump turned his face to the woods. "Mama's boy," he muttered. "What time you reckon it is?"

"Not likely noon yet."

"Damn. Another hour before the store opens." Hump flicked his tongue over his bloodied lip. Randall was merely whimpering now, his crying jag about spent. "How the hell do we get out of here?"

Kyle couldn't focus his raw right eye. He pointed blindly west toward the psychiatric hospital and the road where Hump had parked his car last night.

"Move it, crybaby." Hump jerked the boy to his feet and pushed him in that direction.

"You still owe me twenty for the TV."

"You know what you can do with that TV."

Kyle let them go, father and son, hung over and hurt. Long after he'd lost sight of them in the trees, he could hear their feet shuffling through the wet leaves.

He hadn't meant to scare the boy. Hell, Randall had scared him with that racket. And calling for his mama? Kyle couldn't figure. Last person on the planet he'd holler for would be his mama. He'd learned early on that crying was asking for trouble. She'd be on him in a heartbeat. "Stop it, stop that right now. You'll sleep outside, you keep carrying on like that."

But maybe Randall actually loved his mother. Maybe she didn't lock him in a car trunk, slap the side of his head, or tie him up like a dog at night. Kyle didn't know what he had done wrong as a kid. Had he spilled the bucket of ash shoveled from the woodstove? Or a glass of milk at the supper table? But when it was time for bed, she took him out the door onto the bare porch and tied his leg with a rope. "I've got hold of this other end," she warned him, "so I'll know if you try to wander off. Untie this knot and the Shadow Man might snatch you off this porch."

64

Tied to the porch with his mother's magic knot, the boy he once was had been unable to sleep. He'd gone to the window shiny with moonlight, and in its reflection made funny faces: upturned pig nose, wide-mouthed frog, squinty snake eyes. Then on the other side of the glass, deep in the darkness, he thought he saw something move. He blinkered his eyes with his hands, pressing his face to the window. As he watched, the diffused darkness in the corner stirred and seemed to take shape. The Shadow Man emerged, and then, in the moonlight that lay on the floor, his black hide fell away and puddled about his feet. He was naked, white as bone, creeping toward the bed where she lay. Don't watch, turn your head, close your eyes, you never want to see this. Look.

The flicker of orange caught Kyle's good eye, yanking him out of the past. At first he froze, thinking it was a hallucination of the snakeweed. Then he jumped, thinking, Snake!

The extension cord slid over his boot, sliding into the wet leaves. The TV jerked on its side, then the cord pulled loose. He lunged for it, but the slick plastic cord slipped through his hands. "Sonofabitch!" On his hands and knees, he crawled as fast as he could after the retreating cord. He knew Hump was out there in the woods reeling in his power supply hand over hand. He made a last dive. The pronged cord bounced and skipped across the ground, whipped around a tree trunk and disappeared. He sat up, spitting bits of bitter leaf from his mouth. Then he remembered something else.

His hand went to his boot, and he dug his finger under his sock. The bankroll was gone. On his hands and knees, he scoured the camp, wiping away the leaves, trying to find the green bills in the clearing where he had pinned Hump. It was gone. The five carefully folded twenties must have fallen out of his shoe during the fight. Hump could have pocketed them easily when the crying kid distracted Kyle. He could cry himself at the damage done to his camp. The TV he had hauled all day yesterday across Grovemont was busted. His beautiful bottles were broken and the silverware glittered in the bottom of the creek. The tarp was torn and his gear was all soaked. The fire sputtered in the still falling rain.

He fell backward in the wet leaves. Rain struck his face, stinging his scratched eye. He felt so tired he could lie here forever. Tired to the bone. Dead tired. But if he lay here long enough, he would be just that. Flesh would flay from his bones and slide into the black earth. Rest here and soon enough the falling leaves would catch against the exposed ribs. Stray dogs would find him, chew his shanks, scatter his limbs. Insects would march into the marrow, rooting out the last dried clots of him. He'd be gone to earth before winter was done. Come spring, vines would crown his bleached temples as empty eye sockets stared at the blue sky.

Kyle made himself sit up. He wasn't dead yet, even if he felt nothing. He envied the boy, bawling as if the world had ended. But he dared try her name aloud. "May. May."

He must be alive for it to hurt so.

12

"Come on, let's go. We don't have all day," Eva muttered into her stainless steel travel cup, blowing on her coffee before sipping its bitterness. Monday morning—7:16 by her sports watch that always ran fast—she was already behind schedule. Her leather-bound daily organizer showed both a star and three exclamation marks for this morning's meeting with her board of directors. Top of the agenda were the cuts in next year's budget. She was most likely losing a part-time position, unless a miracle came through in the latest salvo of grant applications, or a new donor materialized at the country club tea. If she spent as much time picking up cigarette butts and burger bags as she spent chasing dollar bills, one by one, her world would be impeccable if not perfect.

Dean sauntered out the front door. At her angry horn, he broke into a halfhearted trot, slowed by the book bag slung over one shoulder.

"About time. You've got everything?"

"Yeah." He slammed the door and slumped against the window.

She shifted the second-hand SUV into reverse and backed onto Chester Place. She could relax a little now that they were on their way. "You have English class?" Eva tried a little quality time with her teenager, as all her magazines for working moms suggested. Dean was turning into a long-term project now, more than a check mark on a daily to-do list: hug your child, say something nice to your spouse.

"Yeah."

"So what are you reading?"

"Great Gatsby."

"Oh, I love that book, don't you? You know F. Scott Fitzgerald visited Altamont, wrote in the big inn while Zelda was in the hospital?"

"I know," Dean hesitated. "You don't think that will be on the test, do you?"

"Don't worry. Just read the book. You'll do fine on the test. You're very smart when you apply yourself. You've got gym today? It's about time you brought those clothes for me to wash. They must be getting ripe now, those socks and the athletic supporter." She rubbed the fabric of his knapsack, his one souvenir from his short-lived career in scouting. Was it her imagination or had that old bag gotten worse looking, new drips of paint? Where had those come from? "We should get you a new book bag. That looks about like what that homeless man had the other day."

"Mom!"

She slammed on the brakes, pitching them headlong into dashboard and windshield, until the seat belts caught them at their collarbones, and bounced them both, their hearts in their throats, deep into their plush seats.

A gobble came from the grille. Eva saw the turkey peer around the headlight, its wattles aquiver, then a clawed foot planted itself on the pavement. The old tom she'd nearly plowed over bobbed its small head and smaller brain, unaware of how close it had come to being flattened like a tetrazzini noodle. Gobble, gobble. She gripped the steering wheel, waiting for the neighborhood flock of tame turkeys to cross the road.

"Those birds are going to get killed if they aren't careful."

"Dumb birds." Dean pulled a toaster pastry from the knapsack and peeled away the foil. He chewed the crumbling sweet crust, the unnaturally red filling.

She pressed the accelerator and sent the trailing bird flapping into the air with a squawk. She checked her watch again. The morning might yet be salvaged. By the time she swung by St. Dunstan's, then back downtown and parked, she would only be fifteen minutes behind in her day, twenty tops.

Dean swallowed the last of his pastry, and without thinking, cracked the window and pushed the wadded foil out into the air stream.

"Dean!" Eva slammed on the brakes. "What are you doing?" She flung her arm over his headrest, and he flinched as if she were about to hit him, but she was twisting in her seat, maneuvering the Subaru into reverse down the graveled shoulder. "How could you throw litter out of the car? You know better."

"Jeez."

"Don't you 'Jesus' me! Don't you blaspheme like that!" Eva heard herself shouting. "Get out and find that wrapper."

"But I'll be late for school."

"I don't care. Be late, but this is a lesson you need to learn."

He almost fell out of the car, stumbling into the ditch and weeds. Eva swore she would not cry, but she was so angry. First, the swearing at his father, then vandalizing his grandmother's property, now this trashing of what she did for a living, part of the paycheck that helped feed and house and clothe and school him, and this was how her only offspring repaid her. She remembered the first time he'd whined as a toddler, "I hate you."

Of course Dean hadn't meant it, but it staggered her how much it hurt, still hurt a dozen years later. To think she had tried to defend him last night in bed, Royce and her pulling the covers between them, pulling at each other, their usual argument lately.

"I'm no more happy about Dean than you are, but we have to believe in him and that this is just a phase."

"This isn't a phase. It's him. It's his personality. He's always had this streak in him."

Like son, like father, she wanted to say, but bit the underside of her lip, very gently, restraining herself.

She watched the rearview mirror, worried that some careless commuter might clip her prodigal son. Don't blaspheme. Quite the outburst, but she couldn't comprehend that after educating the public about the eyesores of roadside litter for years, her own child could sit there and shrug and not even say he was sorry that he could toss a wrapper from sugared junk food. Obligated as both a Keep America Beautiful official and an American mother, she felt guilty that she didn't make Dean eat a proper breakfast.

"Don't be such a drama queen," her own mother used to chide her. Her mother had raced their big Buick, maneuvering around curves as she deftly applied brilliant lipstick to her pouting mouth in the rearview mirror. Eva had been a little girl, trying to show her mother the picture she had drawn in class, a portrait of their rectory next to the church, with her with a pair of ponytails and a sunny yellow smile and a skinny Daddy with his white collar and black shirt and the midsized Mom with her bright red mouth and white apron, the Trinity of their happy family beneath the steepled cross. Barely paying her any mind, her careless mother had cracked the window, and the wind had snatched the drawing from Eva's chubby little fingers. The drawing flapped like a bird in her mother's powdered face, before it flew out the window.

"My picture," Eva wailed, all of six years old and four feet tall, standing up in the seat to see her portrait of home waving goodbye down the receding road.

"Tough toenails. Sit down now. You're a big girl." Her mother drove on, her gloved hands on the wheel.

What have I done? Eva watched in the rearview mirror as Dean slowly searched the shoulder, blown in the wake of passing traffic, growing smaller and smaller, looking for an insignificant bit of litter to appease his mother.

13

The numbers flashed upwards in the elevator, ascending the floors of the high-rise hotel toward the Criterion, downtown's priciest restaurant. Royce pried a finger beneath his too tight, too stiff shirt collar, buttoned down over the unusual tie. Two days in a row of having to wear the uniform of a good banker or bad lawyer, but this was the real deal, a business lunch, and Eva had insisted the tie was necessary for the Criterion. The oak-paneled compartment shuddered to a quiet halt; the doors parted with a soft chime. Royce blinked in the sudden sunlight glinting from crystal and silverware. Then he spied the dark bulk of Lawrence Landrum waving from a tiny table by the wall-length window.

"Good of you to come." Landrum offered the tips of his plump fingers for Royce's handshake. But Royce needed that small support as he neared the wall of glass, a vertigo-inducing vista of graveled rooftops and chimneys, car parks, and dirty sidewalks. Royce lunged into the nearest chair.

"My associate will be joining us," Landrum nodded at the empty third chair. "He just made a visit to the facilities. I've heard the food here is wonderful. You've been here before?"

"No." Royce nervously fingered the several forks aligned to the left of his plate and moved the wine goblet and the water glass. "Once. My wife. For our anniversary."

"Let's get you a drink. I hear their martinis have quite the reputation." Landrum raised his half-empty glass, beckoning the waiter.

71

"Sweet ice tea," Royce ordered.

"How Southern." Landrum sized him up, sipping the last of his drink.

Royce didn't like business lunches and certainly not drinking lunches. He wanted his wits about him and the numbers straight before him. But Landrum wasn't from Altamont where most businessmen were Baptists with reputations to uphold, willing to do their whiskey drinking after work rather than risk being seen sipping big-city martinis and manhattans at noon.

"Ah, there you are. Mr. Wilder, meet my associate, Mr. Matsui."

Royce turned awkwardly in his chair. Bowing before him was a small-boned Asian man with large, golden-rimmed glasses shielding a delicate face—very serious, very sad. Matsui took the chair with his back to the immense view, produced a small leather portfolio and placed it beside his napkin, then laid a silver pen on top. "Have we started?"

"Still on the drinks," Landrum said. "Anyone getting hungry?"

The menu described twenty-dollar entrees with French names Royce wouldn't try to pronounce. When the waiter came around, he was still debating.

"Soup, please," Matsui snapped his menu shut. "And salad, thank you."

"Matsui here is a vegetarian. He eats like a bird. Go ahead, Mr. Wilder."

"Um, porterhouse, well done. Baked potato."

"Ah, a meat-and-potatoes man, I should have known. Fruit plate for me, I'm afraid," Landrum surrendered his menu to the waiter. "Diets are hell, but the doctor keeps insisting."

To Royce's eyes, here was a man who hadn't passed on a meal in his life.

"I trust you're enjoying that radio? The Silvertone?"

"Yes, well, no. It doesn't play or anything. It brought back memories for me," Royce hesitated. "Probably paid too much for it."

"Never apologize for investing in what you value. That's the basic definition of a treasure, is it not?"

As if on a secret signal, Matsui opened his notebook and clicked his silver pen. Landrum set down his martini glass. "So let's talk about what we treasure, shall we?"

Royce crossed his arms. "Not a lot to say. That property of mine isn't buildable. It's just that rock face and about an acre. It really doesn't make sense to sell that landmark unless you get the rest of the farm, which belongs to my mother."

"Rest assured, we do our research. Mr. Matsui?"

"We have a good grasp of the current prices, and what the future market might—" Matsui stopped with a panicked look like he'd forgotten what he was saying. His head shook, then he let loose a terrific sneeze, muffled by the soft napkin he buried his face in. "Excuse me. Something in the air, I'm allergic." Mr. Matsui wiped his nose.

"You're wasting your time, I'm afraid," Royce said. "I know my uncle, and he's not going to turn loose of any of that land any time short of Judgment Day." He could hear the thickening drawl in his tight throat. He was laying on the cornpone kind of thick, an instinctive defense against these flat-landers making not-so-subtle jabs against his choice of drink and dinner.

Landrum and Matsui exchanged querulous looks.

"Have you spoken to your uncle recently?"

"Just yesterday. Saw him at church in Beaverdam." But this answer didn't seem to erase their uneasy smiles.

"I see you're not in the loop. Your uncle has already sold us one tract of ten acres on the south side of Buckeye Mountain. We're in negotiations for more."

Royce's mouth fell open.

"Ah, here's our food. That was fast."

Landrum picked up the napkin folded to suggest a swan. The illusion of a bird flew apart with a flick of his wrist. The fat man poked at the mounded cottage cheese, the slices of seasonal fruit. He gazed helplessly at Royce's plate. "How's the steak?"

Matsui frowned his vegetarian displeasure, sipping the broth from his spoon.

Royce sawed into the slab of meat. "This isn't exactly well done."

"Send it back."

"It's fine. I'll just eat around the red."

"You should get what you ordered," Landrum insisted.

"That's okay," Royce chewed stubbornly. He couldn't swallow the idea that Dallas would sell off anything, let alone the land. "So did you give my uncle half a million like you offered my mama?"

Matsui sipped his water and licked his thin lips. "We never quoted an exact figure."

"Mr. Matsui did not mean to mislead anyone." Landrum forked a peach slice dripping with syrup. His chins waggled as he vigorously chewed the soft fruit. "Besides, that doesn't take into account the $8,871.79 in taxes owed from the last five years on land deeded to Jake Wilder and wife in Beaverdam, along with a two percent penalty. Your uncle has an even bigger bill to settle with the good folks of Zebulon. What was that figure again, Mr. Matsui?"

Matsui flipped through his pages and readjusted his spectacles neatly on his nose. "Ah, roughly $35,000 with a two percent penalty."

"We pay what we owe." Royce felt his face flush.

"I'm not judging you, Mr. Wilder, far from it. Just stating the financial facts. As an appraiser, you can appreciate that. You also realize the market may be weaker than you anticipated in Beaverdam."

"How so?"

Landrum wiped his wet lips and placed the white napkin in his lap. He slipped a pudgy hand inside his pinstripe suit, pulled out the Geiger counter, and laid it on the table. "You recall our conversation about radioactivity the other day? While Mr. Matsui was in Beaverdam, he took some readings inside the church, your mother's barn, and inside your uncle's house. The numbers were rather alarming. Ten times the normal background levels."

Royce laid his knife and fork on his plate. He felt his face burning, but he spoke slowly, deliberately slipping into his best drawl. "Mr. Matsui, when you were in Beaverdam, did you happen to look at all the lightning rods? Roofs just covered with them. Slick salesmen used to go door-to-door, scaring good Baptists and poor widows half to death lest they get struck by lightning." He took his fork and speared a piece of steak to make his point. "Why do I get the feeling you're trying to sucker my kinfolk into buying a lightning rod with your radon story?" He popped the bite into his mouth.

"Cut that hillbilly crap."

Royce gagged, then gasped for air that would pass the lump in his windpipe. Black spots swam around the corners of his vision. The clatter of silverware and conversation around the restaurant faded away in the commotion he was creating himself.

"Mr. Wilder, are you okay?" Landrum scooted his chair back. "I know the Heimlich maneuver."

Terrified that the fat man might hug him, Royce retched. A piece of gristle flew against his teeth.

"Got stuck." Royce carefully spit the meat into his napkin.

The waiter approached warily. "Everything all right?"

"If one is able to speak, one is not choking," Landrum said. "Water, please."

The waiter returned with a glass of water that Royce sipped with embarrassment. Everyone in the restaurant was looking at him.

"Very frightening, I know. I once choked on an artichoke at the Four Seasons. Maitre d' pounding on my back, my life flashing before my eyes. Now I shudder whenever I hear coughing in a restaurant," Landrum said.

"As I was saying," Matsui tapped his pen against his notebook after Royce's rude interruption, "we've researched the area's mortality rates, and Beaverdam does show a big blip in the curve for cancer deaths. But where some might only see the downside of excessive radioactivity, others might see the advantages. Remote valley, limited access, small watershed. Perfect for certain industrial facilities."

"You're talking about a power plant in Beaverdam?" Royce still felt lightheaded, fighting to keep from pitching face first into the gristle and bone on his plate.

"Keep in mind much of what we're telling you falls under national security or our company's proprietary information." Landrum sloshed the olive in his glass, then plucked out the garnish with his thick fingers. "The government has been going about its business, hush-hush, the whole Cold War over in Oak Ridge. Nuclear warheads. The first step is clearing the cove of the current inhabitants for their own safety and well-being."

"You're talking about families who have lived there for generations, my family—"

"Please, I've read my history of the region, the Cherokee Trail of Tears, Horace Kephart's 'Southern Highlanders.' History is always sad. All those mountaineers forced off the family farms when the TVA needed to build its dams, when Roosevelt decided we needed a national park down in the Smokies. America has always been about people losing the land. We move on."

Landrum wagged his several chins. "Take Mr. Matsui here, he was herded off to a California detention camp. His parents are running a dry goods shop in Sausalito, then, bam, the Japanese come out of nowhere and hit Pearl Harbor. Matsui, a native-born American citizen like you and me, spent his childhood behind barbed wire in the middle of nowhere.

His family lost everything. His father even committed suicide. Then of course we dropped the bomb on Nagasaki, where Matsui's family originally immigrated from. Ironic, I suppose. Certainly, sad, wouldn't you agree?"

"Could I interest you in dessert?" The waiter had returned. "We have a cake called 'Death by Chocolate.'"

"I'm allergic, unfortunately," Landrum said. "The facilities are that way?"

Royce was left at the table with the dour Matsui. "What he said about your family? All that really happened?"

Matsui's eyes flashed behind the wire-rimmed glasses. He bowed his head only slightly to his history. "Yes. Very sad, but true."

"Sorry to hear that."

Landrum returned to his seat, huffing. "Did the waiter bring the check?"

Matsui shook his head.

Landrum's hand slipped inside the breast pocket of his coat. He produced a slip of paper and slid it across the table. "Enough talk. This should speak louder than words." A check made out to Royce Wilder for five thousand dollars. The voucher was drawn on the account of Current Inc., but there was no signature. "What you have in your hand is what I'm willing to pay per acre for whatever land I can get around Frozenhead Mountain. Call it a finder's fee. Just say the word and I'll sign."

14

What was with his mom this morning, Dean had no idea. She just went apeshit on him about the pastry wrapper. Okay, so he felt bad about roadside litter, but he hadn't meant to desecrate the landscape or freak her out. She was on edge lately while his father kept giving him dark looks. He just wished they could lighten up, cut him some slack. Every day they deposited him on the green swards and ivy'd halls of St. Dunstan's. He was one of only a handful of day students; skinny guys all sporting the same blazer dropped off by pushy parents, they dashed up the stone steps as the bell rang for first period. The resident student body sauntered out of the dorms—rich kids from all over who weren't quite bright or connected enough to make the serious prep schools up north.

Monday mornings were interminable. First homeroom, then English and the dreaded pop quiz. Then Latin: *amo, amas, amat, fuck, fuckum, fuckorem.* Followed by algebra: what is the square root of a complete and total fuckup? But he had made it thus far and was now headed for the lunchroom where he would forego the Episcopalian mystery meat, only marginally better than public-school gruel, and have his home-packed daily bread with the sorry slice of bologna, hoping that no one noticed him, but secretly wishing that someone might deign to speak to him.

Crossing the parking lot toward the cafeteria, Dean was nearly clipped by a red Camaro. "Watch where you're going, asshole!" Came the raucous laughter from the open window.

But then the car hesitated and backed again over the yellow speed bump. "Hey, Wilder, isn't it?" Tucker rested a tanned forearm out the open window of the coupe. "Need a ride?"

"I was going to lunch."

"Get in."

Dean piled into the back seat with his book bag. An empty beer can rolled across his sneakers.

"You know Fairy, I mean, Perry?" Tucker introduced his roommate slouched in the front seat.

"Oh, very funny, Fucker, I mean, Tucker." Perry sighed an insolent cloud of cigarette smoke. "We gonna eat or what?"

Dean stuffed the poor, brown paper bag that was his bologna sandwich into his rucksack and scraped enough coins from the lint in his pocket to order a burger at the fast-food joint.

"Anything happen this weekend?" As a day student at a boarding school, Dean always felt like he was starting over every Monday. The guys had lived whole lives over the weekend, made new friends, had fallings-out, fights, a whole forty-eight hours that was old news. Who was gay and who wasn't in the dorms? Who had the best dope, the hottest porn?

"Nah, watched Fairy here jerk off under the sheets."

"Who's the fairy for watching, fucker?"

Tucker and Perry didn't like each other much, but they were roommates and both of them rich as hell. It was no big deal. Tucker bragged how he was doomed to be a corporate lawyer like his dad. "I'll have no soul. I'll be filthy rich, but I won't be able to buy my way out of hell."

Perry's father was a lawyer as well, and like Tucker père, an old-money alum of St. Dunstan's.

"What does your father do, exactly?" Perry asked Dean point-blank.

"Appraiser, land or something."

In the awkward silence that followed, Dean found himself trying to explain. "It's like he figures out the prices of houses and property that's about to be sold. He runs his own agency. It's just a little office in a little old house. Realty Ranch. All this lame cowboy stuff, but that was there when he started work."

Perry and Tucker stared at him as if Dean were explicating the daily life of a primitive stone-age tribe of hunters and gatherers.

Dean kept digging the hole deeper. "My mother, she runs this nonprofit charity, Keep Altamont Beautiful."

"I think my ex-stepmother probably writes checks to them when she's not shopping."

Dean tried to steer the conversation away from his hopeless parents. "I saw this really cool warehouse down by the river. You wouldn't believe the tags and pieces going on down there," Dean prattled on, but Tucker didn't seem taken. He slurped the last of his milkshake through his straw and then Perry joined him in a duet.

It was going on one o'clock when they got in the car. Tucker handed out cigarettes from a pack stuck in the sun visor.

"This would be better if this were Jamaican, mon," Perry attempted an island accent.

Dean bent over the flame from the plastic lighter Tucker offered over the seat. Dean could still catch a little buzz from nicotine—he was that new to smoking. "So where was that warehouse?" Tucker's eye trained on him in the rearview mirror.

Dean thought better about mentioning his 1:30 class. "Take a right here. It goes down to the river."

They drove fast, the smoke streaming from the open windows, Axl Rose at full scream on the tape deck. Dean showed him the dirt drive to the warehouse. Tucker pulled the sedan off to the shoulder.

"We have to be careful. There was a guard here on Saturday." Dean led them under the gate and around to the back of the warehouse. Tucker and Dean walked down the wall, looking over the work.

"Amateur stuff. Strictly amateur," Tucker said, a connoisseur of the cool. "Gang wannabes. Wait, here's a guy maybe knows his stuff."

Tucker reached into his pocket and pulled out a roll-on deodorant bottle. He'd emptied the deodorant and refilled the container with black paint, his own DIY crayon. He painted his tag over the work.

"Is that cool?" Dean asked. Wasn't there an etiquette or an honor system of sorts for street artists, he wondered.

"Welcome to the jungle, man." Tucker laughed.

Way to look like a wimp. Dean instantly worried. Desperate now, he brought up his adventures on Saturday. "Over there's a secret camp I found."

"What kind of camp?"

"It was deserted. I guess bums live there, hobos." He pointed like the faithful Boy Scout he never was.

"Let's go, then."

They leapt the creek and negotiated the bank with its gnarled roots of trees and long vines that hung from branches, picking their way across a deserted bridge and the shattered glass of a thousand wino midnights, following a dirt path across the floodplain.

"Wait." He hesitated until Tucker bumped into him. Could he have missed the opening in the brush where he'd first found the hideout?

"You know where you're going or not?"

"Here," Dean said with some relief. He ducked under a thick rhododendron.

The camp seemed different from Saturday, like a great storm had rolled through. Everything was busted and scattered, the bottles broken, the tarp torn down. A television lay in the creek; soggy clothes burrowed into the mud. They tiptoed gingerly through the muck. Tucker found the wooden crate of empty soft drink bottles. "Bombs away."

He tossed a Coke bottle into the creek, smashing both bottle and picture tube. They hurled the bottles, shattering bright, loud glass on the rocks in the muddy creek. So this was vandalism. It was fun. His mom would be mortified, Dean thought casually as he smashed glass against the rocks. He could live like this. Down and out in the woods. No school, no parents. Freedom.

Tucker sprayed his initials on a tree, then spewed more paint across the tarp. They threw the chairs in the creek, then the piles of blankets and the sleeping bag. A little boy's jacket spread its small arms over the water and wrapped itself against a rock downstream before it sank.

"Hey, look." Tucker squatted and dug up a muddy roll of money. "Man, there's a hundred bucks here."

Trashing the leftover junk was one thing. Stuff like this you could throw away without a thought, but money was a different matter and Dean knew it.

"Shouldn't you..." Dean started to say.

"Shouldn't I what?"

Dean hesitated, then turned away. "I don't know. Keep it, whatever."

There was nothing left to destroy. They stood shocked and more than a little awed at what they had done amid the sparkle of busted glass. They walked silently through the trees to the car.

Shit, his nose was bleeding, a warm trickle in the channel of his upper lip. He flicked his tongue over the sticky flow.

"Gross," said Perry.

"Must have cut myself with all that glass," he lied.

Tucker eyed him coldly in the rearview mirror. "You better not bleed in my car. That shit doesn't come out."

Shit. *Why does this always happen to me?* Dean pinched his nose, and swallowed that terrible warm taste.

15

Eva slipped into the nave, taking her seat in a strange pew, guilty that she was somehow cheating on St. Mary's. But she'd heard that St. Thomas' had a new rector, a younger man from Atlanta whom the bishop liked, but women loved. A few of her friends had already ventured downtown to the crumbling brick sanctuary, braving the winos who slept on the sidewalks, the reek of urine from alleys that glittered with broken glass, all for a glimpse of this Father Michael "to die for," according to Connie Mayhew.

Eva had never been in St. Thomas', but she had nowhere to go, not after her meeting this morning. It had felt like a funeral. The board members wouldn't look her in the eye, but had stared down at their feet, their fine oxfords and pumps, ready to walk away.

"The donations just aren't there, Eva. No reflection on you. Litter looks to be of little philanthropic interest these days. The board appreciates your hard work all these years. Purposes are served. People move on. It's time."

"Time?" It was the only thing she said as they broke the news. The one word she wished she could take back now.

"To move on. January specifically."

Her head bowed, her feet had taken her this far, a staggering zombie walk across downtown to St. Thomas'.

My baby. They're taking away my baby. She had felt the same exact hollowness after her miscarriage, of all things. That was what she couldn't believe. It was only a miscarriage, the doctor had told her. It's only a job, the board had said.

She secretly knew but had never fully admitted it: her childhood faith had died along with her first child. Jesus loves all the children of the world, why hadn't he loved that first baby, never quite forgotten? She had been happy, a mother-to-be, even sewing something although she was not that patient with crafts, when she had pricked her thumb with the needle and stuck it in her mouth, the same as the girl inside her, she suddenly saw, and then the pain like a giant needle had gone through her.

So it was all a beautiful myth. God, who had once gripped her so securely, had turned on his heel, crushing her hopes, insignificant as an insect. Yes, he watched the swallows fall from the sky, but did he ever bother to intervene in the daily deaths of so many small things? In time, Dean had come along without trouble, but she had no real faith, only an abiding fear that he too would be taken from her some day. God was watching, waiting for when she least expected it, like this morning.

The candles flickered on the altar while traffic sounded through the thin stained-glass windows. It was a thin congregation, a scattering of women, mostly white-haired widows and a few middle-aged gals with their sunglasses perched like plastic tiaras against their honey-colored hair, gathered here for a gander at the hunky rector.

The door opened on the side and a man came floating out in a white surplice, like a spirit that made her catch her breath. She scrambled to her feet like the other women.

"The Lord be with you." A baritone as warm as the polished wood of the pews, the altar where the flames bowed their little heads.

"And also with you," the women said in unison.

She knew it all by rote, but the words were empty.

"The Gospel reading says the poor you always have with you. The Old Testament reading tells us, 'Happy are those who consider the poor and needy. The Lord will deliver them in the time of trouble.'" Then he began to talk and she was surprised. Father Michael was more than a pretty man. "So how do we translate those scriptures? What's our brother Jesus trying to tell us?"

He seemed to be looking right at Eva with those watery, warm eyes.

"Are you happy? Maybe you're asking yourself that. Are you happy? You have the car, you have the house, you have this nice food with nice cooking pots you learned to use in cooking class. You have the latest cook-books, and you're buying the freshest, fanciest food, and yet you're not full. You have closets full of nice clothes. You have finely furnished rooms, yet you look around you and see only piles of junk and things turning to dust before your eyes. Consider the poor and the needy. Are you happy?"

He strolled the aisle, looking over their heads toward the door as if expecting someone to walk in. "Each week we open the doors of our church and make a soup kitchen to feed the homeless. I'll tell you these people do not smell good. They often don't bathe. Some have mental troubles and can't look you in the face. They talk to themselves. These are God's children. I invite you to consider them. Consider how you might help them, how that may indeed be the way to the happiness you so desperately seeks, which only the Lord bestows."

AMEN.

She felt the catch in her throat. Eva closed her mouth, which had been agape in wonder with this man's preaching. She pressed a finger to her tearing eye, careful not to smudge her slight makeup.

"Anyone desiring the laying on of hands can come forward at this time."

Eva stepped forward, stood in the chancel in her sensible shoes, and felt Michael draw a cool cross on her forehead with his thumb dipped in the oil. She kept her eyes downcast. He was wearing sandals. Like Jesus, he was wearing sandals, and his feet were so strong and masculine. What pretty toes, straight and not crooked or humped like Royce's calloused dogs. She closed her eyes.

"Name?"

"I'm sorry?"

"What is your name, my dear?" he whispered.

"Eva."

"Any special requests for prayer, Eva?"

"I just lost my job." She let out a short laugh, then a sob.

"I'm so sorry, Eva." And he gently put his warm hands on her head, wiping the tears from her check, cradling the ache in her skull.

16

They lay in bed, exhausted but still wired at the end of a crazy day. The mattress was worn and lumpy, and in the past year, neither of them had slept well on the sagging springs, but they secretly attributed their tired bones, their sore sides to time itself, even old age. A car passed on the hilly curve, throwing high beams into their second-story bedroom, panels of light that loomed against the walls and then slid down into the shadows.

"So you didn't take the check?"

"Didn't feel right."

"So you're not ever going to sell that land?"

"When the time is right. Someday. I don't know."

Royce hadn't mentioned all the talk about radon. He was sure the land was worth more than the five thousand Landrum was offering. The talk of radon was just a bluff, or so Royce wanted to believe. He squirmed.

Eva sighed, a pensive exhalation that seemed to fill the darkness. "Royce, don't be mad. I've got to tell you something."

He pushed her hand away. His arm was losing circulation under the weight of her head. "What?"

"What would you think if I quit? Work, I mean," Eva said.

"What?" He didn't like the sound of this. "I thought you loved your work."

"I had a talk with the new board today. Litter and beautification don't seem to be high on the agenda. Maybe I should find something else to do."

"Now's not the time to be quitting. Economy's still in a recession. My appraisals are running behind last year. Dean's in that new school, and God knows, that's pricey."

"Oh, and you don't waste any money?"

"Like what?"

"Don't play dumb. The radio, Royce. How much?" She sat up in the bed and pounded her pillow furiously, but her voice was even harder. "We clean out the garage and first thing you bring home is a piece of junk radio that doesn't even work. You're just going to stick it in the closet or in the garage, and I'll have to throw it out. So how much did you pay for this new treasure?"

"I won't lie," he said at last. "One fifty."

"Royce!"

"Hear me out. So it doesn't work, but it's not junk."

The silence from her side of the bed was glacial, and that was even worse than the heat of her tirade. Royce kept talking, trying to chip through the ice in the air. "You have to understand, somehow it was like my father's radio. It just brought back memories. Okay. I got carried away, you're right, we can't afford one fifty now, but business will pick up."

"You don't get it, do you?"

Royce sighed toward the ceiling. He hated when they fought at night. They wouldn't speak. They wouldn't sleep. Morning would come with a bitter taste like a hangover. "Eva?"

Silence.

"You can't be this mad about a stupid radio."

"Would it be just an imposition if you just held me once in a while? Maybe made love to me? Selfish."

Royce rolled over again. He felt the small of his back cramp in the too soft, too old mattress. He rubbed his fist to his bare skin, but the pain was like a mouse burrowing to the bone. He could feel them all in the dark, Eva curled up and cold on her side of the bed, and down the hall in his room, Dean with his headphones, the Walkman under the pillow, feeding his brain with the noise of his generation, Cobain, Axl Rose, Van Halen—dirty, tattooed, and longhaired. His beloved wife, his only son, neither had a good word for him as husband or father. They were as cold and distant as the planets burning in the night sky.

And none of them could sleep this dark night. They were all exhausted but awake, waiting for sleep, for relief, for unconsciousness that wouldn't come. Like that disembodied handwriting on the scroll: "Where will you spend eternity?"

17

In leaf season, traffic started early. The first thousand cars crossed the Woodfin Street Bridge. Tires whined the length of the girders, then thumped a final tattoo over the concrete ledge where Kyle was curled, dreaming of Florida. He was not on cold concrete, but warm sand. Tropical sun pried at his fluttering eyelids. Surf broke, foamed at his bare feet. May lay beside him. He heard her whisper, her warm breath brushing his cheek. Her hand—or maybe only the wind—ruffled the sparse hair in the hollow of his chest.

"Where are you going?" she whispered, although he hadn't moved.

"I never seen the ocean."

"Here, silly."

A wave broke over their naked bodies and he tumbled on top of her. Her ankles locked around him. They rode the waves, crest and trough, rise and fall, gasping for air, drowning.

He awoke with a shudder. He was curled on his side, hands clenched between his thighs, neck cramped on the burlap sack. His blanket covered only from his shoulders to his knees. His toes were numb inside the boots he'd unlaced but kept on last night.

Knees popping, joints cracking, he rose and stiffly shuffled down the slope to where he could stand erect under the bridgehead. Balanced precariously, he unzipped and peed in painful spurts. A yellow stain steamed down the concrete. Kyle spat. His tongue was coated with the taste of the marijuana from last night. His head still buzzed like a nest of rattlers in the sun. Snakeweed had itself a bite.

Boots laced, blanket rolled, bag shouldered, stick in hand, Kyle emerged from under the bridge. He toted a scrap of cardboard he'd saved for a sign. He walked along the chainlink fence that divided town from bypass, private from public property, until he reached the exit. The sun peered over the mountaintop. The first weak rays lent a little warmth. Soon he stood on the shoulder of the eastbound lane. Kyle raised his cardboard plea: "FLA."

Drivers squinted into the sun as they sped by. Many hid behind sunglasses and visors, and he could not catch their eyes. "Florida!" he hollered in case they could not make out his crude print. But no one stopped.

Kyle kept an eye out for cop cars. They had caught him once before trying to thumb a ride after he had robbed the convenience store. Waving that two-by-four at the clerk's head had bought him nearly as stiff a sentence as if he'd had a gun. Hauling ass from the store, pockets stuffed with bills, plank in one hand, a bottle of wine in the other, Kyle had been caught only half a mile down the road.

In and out for twenty years all told, with time tacked on for once walking out of a work farm for a two-week spree, and then after assaulting a guard who as a real wiseass only had it coming, Kyle finally walked out of the North Carolina Department of Corrections system a free man. Then he met May and not much later, he was back on the thirteenth floor of the courthouse where the windows showed prison bars.

At least that high-rise jail had heat. In the woods and under the bridge, winter came early. To keep his blood moving, Kyle stomped his brogans and clapped his hands wound with old rags, walking backwards with his sign in his teeth. "Florida," he muttered every time a car passed. "Florida," like an incantation to make someone stop. He'd run down the road and land in a heated front seat for the long haul to the Sunshine State.

He recalled his dream, the good part with May in the sand and water before it turned into a nasty nightmare with his mother's appearance that he blamed on the snakeweed. Having never seen the ocean except in pictures and on TV, Kyle had to guess what it felt like to lie on a beach. But he knew May; he'd been with her. He knew her skin, the grain of goose flesh on her thighs, the down on her forearms, the bruises and scabs at the hollows of her elbows.

A van approached, gleaming in the morning sun. Through the windshield, Kyle could see the driver, a man drinking coffee from an oversized plastic mug.

"Floridafloridaflorida..."

Kyle imagined the plush interior: shag carpet, curtains on the porthole windows, sweet stereo, soft seats with holes in the armrests to park your drinks. The van barreled along the right lane and pushed him back with a wake of exhaust. He saw the green peninsula of faraway Florida receding on the license plate.

After an hour, Kyle had walked backwards over the cut and down to the next exit. He followed the grassy shoulder to an intersection where a restaurant sat on each corner: a pair of steakhouses, a burger stand, and a fish camp, each venting their specialty in grease from metal steam pipes. His stomach knotted. Since leaving his camp, food had been hard to come by. No berries left on the briars by the highways. His rabbit snares had all been empty save one, but dogs had gotten there first and eaten his catch, saving him only bones and bits of fur. The river was no good either. He'd walked the banks and seen the foamy scum, a few fish floating belly up. He'd be a fool and perhaps a dead man to eat from those tainted waters.

Kyle fished a half-burned joint from his pocket. He popped it in his mouth and swallowed—anything to ease the hunger pangs.

Day before, he'd seen a cheese giveaway from a tractor-trailer at the Social Services. He fell in line behind black women bent over canes and walkers, but when he reached the head of the line, the social worker said he needed welfare papers to get his cheese. Kyle didn't even have a social security card or a valid driver's license. Since when did a body need a number to eat?

The traffic signal at the intersection blinked red, yellow, green, and back to red. People waited in their cars for the light to change in their favor, some munching on burgers or sipping soft drinks.

Kyle found a piece of cinder by the asphalt and scrawled a new message on the flip side of his Florida sign. "Will Work For Food."

When did you ever work?

"Shut up."

It was just his belly speaking with a mind of its own, but the voice reminded him of his mother's. *You always were so lazy.*

"I said shut up!"

89

He could work. He could chop wood, cut grass, clear brush, tote things—so long as no one got on his back. Once he'd signed on as a carpenter's apprentice, but that had only lasted about a day of busted thumbs before he chucked a claw hammer at the foreman's thick head.

Kyle raised his new sign at the traffic waiting at the light. Drivers turned their heads, hid behind sun visors. Women reached over to lock their passenger doors.

Can't blame 'em none. You always were a sight that made eyes sore.

"Who asked you!"

The light changed. The cars accelerated away, drivers going about their own lives. Kyle held his sign until the sun reached its zenith and he was about to pass out on his feet. The day half spent and he was no closer to the Sunshine State. He started walking.

In the parking lot of the fish camp he passed Cadillacs with Florida tags. Why not sneak into the back seat of one and lay in wait for the blue-haired and bald couple to come out picking their teeth? Up he'd pop, surprise, surprise. Wouldn't hurt them none, just a ride, if you please. But all of the cars were locked.

Kyle scouted the trash behind the restaurant. The stench was bad but he dug until he hit pay dirt—an overripe tomato. Juice gushed down his beard as he chewed the pulp. He licked his fingers of broken eggshells and coffee grounds for a taste of breakfast. A cold piece of fish that some finicky eater had pushed aside on the plate he swallowed whole to silence his stomach. Farther down in the debris he found a few stale bread heels and a damp box of sugar packets, handy bursts of energy he could pour on his tongue. At the bottom, he scraped a slab of yellow cake soaked with strawberry juice so sweet the blood boiled in the top of his head.

"Hey, buddy, move along. This ain't no cafeteria!"

A woman materialized behind him, a cop in a blue uniform, her hand resting on a leather belt with revolver and baton. Her eyes were earnest and blue behind the glasses set on her wide face.

Sooey, sooey. Like calling a hog to the trough.

Kyle swayed on his feet, leaned against his stick. It was hard to make out what the woman was saying over the voice grunting in his gut.

"You been drinking, bud?"

Kyle shook his head. He could feel his brain sloshing softly inside his skull. It was the snakeweed curled around the brainstem.

"Did you deface this dumpster?"

"What?"

"Did you paint this shit on the side here?"

A grinning skull had been painted in white aerosol on the green metal, fancy scribbles that swam before his eyes.

"First the owner complains he's got vandals, now he's calling in bums snacking in his parking lot. Restaurant don't appreciate you poking around in the trash. Scares off the paying customers."

His belly let out a loud rumble.

"Look, if you're hungry, there's a soup kitchen under the Episcopal church downtown, St. Thomas'. You can eat there tonight and maybe bed down if you ain't been drinking."

Oink, oink. Like a pig in slop.

"I ain't no pig." Kyle talked back to the voice.

"What did you call me?" the lady cop asked.

Like a sow wallowing in shit.

"I said, shut up!" Kyle raised his stick and struck the bag of garbage by his boots. The plastic seams split and spewed food across the parking lot. "Shut up, you!" He kept flailing his stick. It felt good to hit something.

"That's enough! Drop it now!"

He swung his stick against the side of the metal bin, sending a jolt along his arms.

"I said hold it, mister!"

Breathing hard, his hands tingling, Kyle only now saw the gun aimed at his head.

"Pick up that shit! Now!"

Kyle squatted, keeping his eye on the gun as his hands felt for the greasy paper, the spilled food.

"All of it!" the cop screamed. "Hear me!"

"Yes'm."

And he heard faint echoes of the other voice that had crept away during his outburst. *Oink, oink, oink.* His hands were filthy. The air busy with flies. His stomach heaved like he might lose what little food he'd managed to get down.

The cop holstered her gun. "Get moving and I better not catch you poking in anybody's trash today. You understand?"

"Yes'm."

He took the cracked staff and slipped the rope of his bedroll over his shoulder. He walked along the two-lane road into the tunnel that drilled through the mountain. The passage smelled of dampness and diesel and earth. Cars flicked on headlights and blared their horns in deafening echoes inside the belly of the mountain. Kyle trudged on until he reached the daylight on the other side.

18

So are you sure you want to volunteer? This is not very glamorous work, I'm afraid."

"And picking up trash is?"

Father Michael smiled. Eva shifted in her chair and smoothed her skirt across her thighs. She had dressed professionally for this visit, but now she worried that her skirt might be a tad short, too provocative for the occasion. Which was? A pastoral visit, a blessing, spiritual consolation? After all it was his homily that had wormed its way into her conscience. But if she were honest, she'd have to say she wanted to be in the company of this handsome man of the cloth, not necessarily feeding the hungry and clothing the needy.

"I'm losing my job. I thought I should be doing something meaningful with my time."

He frowned now. "Are you sure you're up to this? They're our brothers and sisters, perhaps, but they may not be exactly the kind of people you may be used to."

"You sound like my husband, now."

"Really?"

"Royce likes to quote scripture when it suits his purposes. You know, Jesus saying, 'The poor ye shall always have with ye. The homeless aren't going away. What can we do?' I think that's crap—excuse my language."

Michael laughed. "You're right. That's no excuse. I think Jesus is on your side. What can we do? We can start by giving them a bite to eat, a place to stay out of the cold, warm clothes to wear. Christ said that too, you know."

The priest leaned back in his leather chair, clasping his hands behind his curly head. "Your husband, he's not a churchgoer?"

"Oh, no. Royce says he's not much of anything, but he was raised Baptist. Dunked and everything when he was all of eight."

"Some of our Baptist brethren they don't hold under the water long enough in their baptism, if you ask me. Sorry, old seminary joke. Your husband and you disagree?"

"No more than any married couple. Our son—"

"Royce Jr.? Just a guess."

"Dean. Named after my father," Eva said. "He's turning fifteen, acting out. Just a phase. I hope. We hope."

"Sounds like you have your hands full with the family. You're sure you want to take on the homeless?"

It was like he was trying to talk her out of doing this. Maybe it was a test of her mettle, a pop quiz on her persistence. Did she have the right answer?

"I don't know. A man came to my door the other day. I gave him an old TV—or he took it. I didn't know what to do; I just know someone ought to do something about these people. I mean, you make donations, write out checks to charity, give away your old clothes, but it seems like so little."

"We can do no great things, but we can do small things with great love." The priest shrugged, offering only this stale leftover from a past homily. He casually crossed his legs and scratched his bare ankle. He was muscular, this Michael, she had felt that under his robes when they traded the peace; the discreet hug the priest gave all the women in his congregation at the Wednesday eucharist.

"Come by to talk any time," he had offered. It was the first time she had seen him out of uniform. Stripped of his robes, he seemed collegiate in a sweater and slacks, Birkenstocks. How old was he?

Eva bowed her eyes as if praying. "My husband says I shouldn't worry about these things. That man—he was so rough—I can't get him out of my mind. He wanted to ask a question."

"What? What did he want to know?" The priest leaned forward, suddenly interested, elbows on his knees, his fingertips steepled under his chin from the habit of genuflecting.

94

"He asked where people like him could go."

Michael turned serious, or put on a face that made him look serious, something they taught young seminarians to look more mature, though he would need more years and wrinkles and gray around the temples to carry off the gravitas. He looked like an Adonis hemming and hawing whether to ask a girl to wear his letter jacket. Eva felt her neck flush down to her collarbone.

"Home," Michael said at last. "Isn't that what he wants? What we all want? Just to go home, to be at home somewhere? To not to be alone."

Eva felt a flutter behind her breastbone. *If you only knew how alone, how lonely I am.*

"Of course, volunteers only go so far. Paid staff actually does better work, and with how fast our soup kitchen and outreach is growing, I'm thinking we will want to add some staffers here shortly. I know you're busy, but maybe you would know someone who might be interested."

"I might be interested myself, Father—"

"Stop being so formal. Call me Michael. I mean, we're going to be spending the night together."

19

Wanda McRae whetted the blade of her bush ax with a rusty rat-tail file, squinting one eye as she ran her calloused thumb along the bright edge. She'd been honing it for the last half hour, the protest of the metal grit against the steel, the shaft leveraged against her thin thigh, the butt wedged in her unlaced boot. She'd let things get too dull when she needed to be sharp.

She kept an eye on the skinny cow tearing tufts of grass from the bank, edging slowly down the road. Another stupid beast not even thinking to make its escape from the ax she was sharpening for the slaughter.

Occasionally, she jerked her head as if to catch a sound from the woods waving their slow green leaves at her, the crack of a twig in the under- brush, or a shadow flying overhead, crow or cloud. The world full of whis- pering. Her eyes had never been that good, even as a girl. She probably could have done with spectacles but that would have ruined her looks and maybe made her look twice at the too ugly men she found herself with, but her hearing had always been unworldly sharp. She could hear mice breathing in the rafters of the drafty cabin or rattlers sliding their thick bellies in the den back of the Buckeye.

The mountain had gotten windier in the years she'd lived here on its northern side, where the sun rarely shone more than just a few hours a day, long shadows lay in the summer, and the last snows lingered in slowly melting banks. Rain and thaw scored rivulets into the clay where the road had been cut years before and never healed, like a red welt zigzagging up the Buckeye's belly. She could hear the crunch of gravel, any car coming her way, from a quarter mile down below, giving even her old bones time to duck into the weeds around her cabin.

Social workers used to come to the door guarded by the snake hides and peep through the warped glass panes. "Miss McRae, Miss McRae, you home?" they called and called. She had to stuff her toothless mouth with her knuckles to keep from laughing out loud, squatting on her thin haunches in the kudzu. They wouldn't catch her so easily.

She had lost a step in the woods. Her foot was not certain of purchase on a slope, climbing the ridgelines up through the laurel hells, along felled rail fences, rusted barbed wire, the property markers she never minded. Who could keep her off the land? She'd tell them where to go.

She could hear a shadow slide across the planks of the cabin, even before the wood complained of the weight. She held her breath, waiting in the dark for the Shadow Man to come lie with her.

"Watch it." The cow paid her no mind, having several more stomachs than brains in its heavy skull. She would fatten it up. It had no idea what was coming. She ran her thumb down the blade until it sliced her thick skin.

She shouldered her ax and walked down the dirt road to the mailbox that stood by the pavement. Property of the U.S. Postal Service, the lid of the box said, like that mattered. She poked through mailboxes across the cove, opened mail that looked interesting, thumbed through catalogs and magazines. He'd told her it was illegal, of course. Worse than the revenue men if you cross the postal inspectors. Worth hard time down at the women's unit in Black Mountain. Stay out of them boxes. You'll get us both in bad trouble. She'd paid him no mind. Never had, or at least pretended that to his ugly face.

She felt blindly for her messages, arm swallowed in the recesses of the metal box that didn't even carry her last name. No family, so she expected no postcards, the likes she found in other folks' boxes. Nor bills or magazines nor coupons or newspapers. Her mail was much more practical. Packages of food, tins of evaporated milk and tomato soup, peanut butter, pouches of dried beans. Uncle Sam or the Shadow Man did provide. Used to be a regular envelope of loose bills first of every month, but then the money dried up. She still had plenty of money. Jars of it, stuffed with bankrolls like leaves of pickled cabbage. Jars of quarters and nickels and pennies and dimes. Loot aplenty lining her pantry shelf. Years of payback.

But the food, that was different. She didn't drive no more to town for provisions. Her box had been empty too long. Damn him. She slammed the lid shut, stepped back and swung the back of her bush ax, striking the empty box until it shook on its post with a pleasing clamor that echoed across the cove. Damn them all.

She listened intently with something like a smile twisted on her small face as she swung her hooked bush ax in wide swathes, listening for the soft slicing sound it made, beheading the last of the dandelion's fuzzy manes in the ditch.

20

So you like to paint? Here's your chance, pal." Royce unlocked the trunk of the Mercedes and handed the buckets of paint to his son. The boy about buckled under the weight of the ten-gallon cans, but didn't say a word.

"Hang on." Royce gathered the brushes and the screwdriver that had rolled about the trunk all the way over the gap. He hadn't replaced the spare tire, and the gravy stains from last weekend had clotted into the interior carpet. There was the paper bag from their stop at the hardware store, an extra purchase he'd slipped into the cart while Dean was getting the paint brushes, but that chore could wait until he had Dean doing penance painting the barn on a Friday, a teacher workday, when he should have been at home goofing off, wasting his time on music videos. Royce slammed the trunk. "Let's go."

Dean's chin trembled as the wire handles bit into the soft flesh of his hands. Still, he didn't say a word. Good, Royce thought. He marched his young vandal through the barn lot to the scene of the crime. "So this is your idea of art, huh?" Royce crossed his arms, squinting at the giant red squiggle on the side of the barn. "Was it supposed to be something?"

"I dunno."

"I dunno," Royce mocked his son's lame excuse. His duty as a parent today was giving his offspring no breaks. "Think you can get that lid off while I get the ladder?"

99

Royce rummaged around in the musty barn, filled with all sorts of squeaks and groans. The building was on its last legs, slowly twisting askew from the square of its post and beams, dangerously leaning and likely to fall into the creek come the next hard wind. The barn had been part of the dowry that Ruth Rominger had brought to her marriage to Jake Wilder, built by her side of the family to store a poor dirt farmer's implements, shelter plow horses, mules, and the occasional cow, store their provender and cure tobacco in the loft, but in all its years, it had never seen a lick of paint or the swipe of a brush until Royce's own flesh decided to deface it with a spray can.

Royce dragged the wooden ladder into the barnyard, kicking aside dried cow pies, hard as the stones that littered the ground. "Give me a hand," he grunted, feeling the muscle pull again in his lower back.

Father and son wrestled the ladder upright, leaning it against the side of the barn. Royce tried the bottom rung, then thought better of it. "Up you go. You work on the top and I'll do down here."

"Whatever," Dean said.

"Whatever?" Royce repeated. "What did I tell you about attitude when you're working?"

"Yes, sir." Dean raised his eyes up the rickety ladder. His spirit visibly sank with his shoulders.

Good, Royce thought. Life's tough and it's about time you learned to take your licks. He had lectured Dean on the drive about how nothing was ever done without hard work and the right attitude, both sorely lacking in his son. Dean stared out the window. If the kid would just say, "I get it, I give up, I get the point," they could get in the car and go home.

"Whoa, now." Dallas hobbled into the barnyard. "Ruth said you two were out here having a painting party and you didn't even invite me."

"Anytime you want to grab a brush, go right ahead," Royce said.

"Oh, no, I rather play Tom Sawyer and let you boys have all the fun. You having fun, boy?" He pinched Dean's shoulder and the nerve there, trying to make the usually ticklish young'un giggle, but Dean twisted from the old man's grip. His chin thrust out defiantly, his fists dug deep into his fleece pockets, Dean didn't plan on having any fun today.

"Listen, we need to talk," Royce pulled his uncle aside, lowering his voice. "I called the Zebulon County tax office. They say you haven't been paying your taxes. They're talking a lot of taxes on a lot of land. Foreclosure."

"Don't you believe a word they say. That's my business, not yours."

"You were supposed to pay Mama's taxes. That makes it my business, family business."

Dallas waved his hand as if swatting a pesky gnat. "Not to worry. Took care of the bill just the other day."

"Landrum and Matsui, right? They said you sold off a little property."

"I said I took care of it. Now, let's see what Dean's done here." The old man squinted at the graffiti, just as Royce had done earlier. "Yeah, I can make it out now," Dallas nodded sagely. "Believe it says 'mene mene upharisen.'"

"What? Where?" Royce bent for a second look.

"Boy, you forgotten just about everything you learned in Beaverdam Baptist? Mene mene upharisan. What God wrote on the wall when Nebuchadnezzar was having his big old party. Invitation to destruction."

Dean burst out laughing, clapping his hand to his mouth. Royce glared.

"Dallas, you coming or not?" Ruth called at the gate. She had her purse and was ready. Fridays, first of the month, were the days that Dallas ran Ruth into town for groceries.

"Coming, sister!" Dallas squeezed Royce's arm. "We'll talk later."

"That red's looking good," Ruth said.

"I hope so," Royce swiped some paint on the wood. "Y'all take your time in town. And you..." he motioned at Dean to start climbing and painting.

Dean perched on the penultimate rung with the dripping brush and flicked his wrist, flinging a spray toward Royce's thinning crown. Royce craned his neck, like he felt rain out of the blue. "Do that again, bud, and I'm coming up there after you, I mean it."

Dead silence passed between the two of them, nothing but the scrapping of the bristles against the barn, like the rough lick of a dog's tongue. Atop the ladder, Dean dabbed the brush onto the bare boards, which drank the red deep into the grain. Down below, Royce was angrily slopping over his son's handiwork, broad brushstrokes that took out Dean's mess.

"Yeah, looking pretty good," Royce stepped away from the barn, then set the brush on the rim of the paint bucket. "You're getting the hang of it. I told your grandma I'd check the furnace while I'm here. Promise not to fall off the ladder?"

"Promise."

❖

101

Dean waited until his dad walked through the gate and out of view behind the huge boulder that stood between the house and the barn. Now he could play with the paint, what he'd been waiting for all morning. He practiced the skull that Tucker had whipped on the side of the dumpster the other afternoon in broad daylight behind the fish camp.

On their way from lunch, they had pulled into the rear of the restaurant. Tucker was out of the car, shaking the can of paint with its ball bearing rattling inside. A few quick swipes through the air, then a man yelling out the screen door of the kitchen. But Tucker was already behind the wheel, chucking the empty aerosol can out the window. He floored it and the car fishtailed with the squall of tires and the smell of burning rubber. From the back seat, Dean stole a last glance at Tucker's handiwork, a great grinning skull that covered the green side of the metal container, with Tucker's little tag like a scar on the skeletal face. Awesome.

He tried the same move in miniature, but the brush was too big. Dean's attempt looked like a lame smiley face rather than a cool skull. The balls of his feet were aching against the rung and his arms were starting to shake, so he climbed down for a break. He lit a loose, bent cigarette that he'd stashed in his pocket, waiting for this chance to blow smoke at his fate and his father's lesson. He was still learning to smoke and like it. More than just a few puffs still made him lightheaded, a little head buzz, but not like the rush of snakeweed that first time in Tucker's dorm room.

"Shotgun," Tucker had said. He'd placed the burning joint inside his puckered lips and brought his face close to Dean's, blowing a steady stream of smoke into Dean's mouth. Dean had opened his eyes to see Tucker's delicate, fluttering lashes. He was a fraction of an inch away from kissing Tucker full on the lips, when he coughed out a cloud of cannabis.

You dumb ass, Dean still flagellated himself over that awkward moment. Smoke trailing out of his mouth, he watched the woods behind the barn where the green leaves waved hypnotically, though there was no wind. The grove stood dark and deep, a green gloom. He shuddered and ground the cigarette underfoot.

Dean studied his work of the last hour spent slopping on the red oil, but he could still make out the message, the krypton curlicue he'd whisked through the air, an afterimage that kept bleeding through. POW! How many coats would it take to cover that mistake?

21

Royce found the front door locked for a change. Ruth had been spooked by a recent rash of break-ins and had taken to locking her door at nights and whenever she was away. She had even moved the spare key from beneath the welcome mat to the doorframe's ledge, but Royce found it just the same.

Inside he held his breath, listening to the empty house: the clock ticking on the mantel, the water running in the springhouse, the rattle of a loose window sash upstairs. The stairs creaked under his feet; his clammy palm clung to the banister. At the top of the landing, a curtain billowed over a half-open window. Down the hall, Royce unlatched the door to a bedroom used for storage. A cedar wardrobe leaned in the corner. Cured hams hung from the ceiling.

He slumped on the sofa in the corner and emptied the contents of the paper sack: a homeowner's guide to radon and three testing kits. The radon detectors were brown cardboard folded into small pyramids. On one side, a red arrow pointed at a scale going from a black zero to a red two. You activated the test by pulling a small hook at the apex. The instructions said to leave the detector in an enclosed space for seven days. If during the week the arrow rose into the red danger zone of 0.08 picocuries or more, immediate inspection by a licensed professional was strongly suggested. Royce tugged at the hook. He almost expected it to start ticking like a bomb, but to his relief, the arrow did not perceptibly budge.

On his hands and knees, he shone his flashlight under the sofa. The beam played on another intruder—a dead mouse caught beneath the bar of a sprung trap. Rodent teeth grimaced at the orange cheese that had lured it to death. With his flashlight, Royce batted the victim and trap out from under the sofa. He dropped the remains into the paper sack and wiped his hands on his trousers. He'd have to ambush the radon elsewhere, some place undisturbed by mice or his mother.

He opened the wardrobe. A warped rod held a row of his father's old suits, sheathed in plastic. Through a rent in one filmy shroud, he fingered the dark fabric. He lifted the plastic and slipped the coat from the wire hanger. His arms slid down the cold tunnels of the sleeves. He sniffed the lapel for some scent of astringent sweat or pipe smoke, a reminder of his father, but there was nothing but the masking odor of mothballs. The coat bunched across his shoulder blades and his wrists dangled from the sleeves. He sucked in his belly to button the jacket; his father had been much thinner. Royce offered a profile to the mirror. He patted the inside pocket and discovered what was breaking the drape, a torn photograph.

He recognized his father on the left as a young man squinting into the camera and future from fifty years ago, his head with wavy black hair pointing to a widow's peak. He was dressed in khaki, though to Royce's knowledge he had never served in the war. There was a woman next to Jake Wilder, or half a woman in the torn photograph, but it wasn't his mother. There was at least a third person in the missing part of the snapshot, a man's hairy arm draped across his daddy's shoulders. He turned the photo over. There was part of a handwritten message beneath the impression of a lipstick kiss.

Remem—

Al—

The rest of the message had ben lost with the other half of the photo, but the kiss remained unfaded, bright red. Who was the woman with his father? Who was Al? Sweating in his father's snug suit, Royce scratched his neck where the wool collar fretted. He should put it back, but instead, he slipped the photo into his shirt pocket, the same motion his own father had made once before, then forgotten in the breast pocket. Royce shed the coat and hung it again in the wardrobe. He hooked the radon test inside the breast pocket, then lowered the sheath of plastic, and closed the door.

Downstairs, he opened the closet beside the wood stove. Inside hung an outdated 1977 calendar, charred potholders, and the blackened poker his mother used to tend her fire. The oil furnace took up most of the long closet. Royce squeezed by the furnace to the rear wall, where he squatted and pried open the trap door with the poker. Cobwebs clung to the underside and a chill draft rose into his face. He shone his light into the hole and softly cursed. His daddy had to have built a house with a crawlspace instead of a cellar and Dallas had to have invented that story about the Shadow Man.

He slid his legs into the darkness where a coolness crept up his pants, tingling the hairs on his calves. He lowered himself through the opening until his feet touched solid ground. Holding his breath like a man going underwater, he ducked under the floor. He swung the beam of light around the crawlspace, blinded by all the glittering reflections, like a dungeon full of jewels. His eyes adjusted and he saw the bare dirt was strewn with broken glass. When he turned on his haunches, he knocked over a circle of intact Mason jars tied with lengths of string. Most of the jars were dry as bone, filled only with decades of dust. But a few still had their lids and liquid sediment inside.

He held a jar before the light, then unscrewed its rusted top and took a whiff. After all these years, the cheap corn whiskey still scorched his nostrils. Old hypocrite passing the plate down the pews every Sunday, signing the temperance oath in the family Bible, and all the while pulling up stringed jars from a private liquor cabinet beneath his family's feet to toss back at his leisure. Carrying kissed pictures of girlfriends in his Sunday suit. Damn that old man. He'd buried him ten years ago and he still kept coming back to haunt him with that derisive "hunh!"

Forty-five years old, Royce felt like such a fool. Pursing his lips, he poured the last of the liquid out into a dribble on the dust under his light. He slung the emptied jar against the brick foundation, listening to the pleasing sound of shattered glass. Nothing moved but the slow dance of dust motes raining down on him. He switched off the flashlight and sat in the dark, waiting for his anger to subside.

Overhead he thought he heard the front door slam shut. They couldn't be home this early. Then, just as he thought it had only been his imagination, the floor creaked overhead, showing a faint sliver of light where a body's weight bowed the jointed board. "Dean," he nearly called out, but he didn't want to scare his son with a voice from the underworld, then have to explain what he was doing down here with drained whiskey jars and a bag of tests for radioactive gas.

Another creak of the floor under a furtive step. Someone was there, but he knew it wasn't Dean. Royce eased his head through the trap door, peering through the crack in the door. The telephone rang. He ducked. The phone kept ringing, that black Ma Bell rotary under the window, resting atop the thin Beaverdam directory. His mother would never let it ring like that. She would have come running from wherever she was in the house to answer. Even Dean, a sulky teenager, couldn't resist talking on the telephone and had been trained to take a message.

He hoisted himself through the square opening and crouched inside the closet. His fingers closed around the plastic flashlight, but it wasn't much of a weapon. He found the poker on the floor. The closet door swung open on creaking hinges. He bobbed his head out then back, like he'd seen actors do on television cop shows. The room blurred in his brief take: brown sofa, black iron stove, white wall. The room was empty. The phone quit ringing.

A sudden draft from the kitchen raised goose bumps on his arms, then he jumped at the slam of the back door. He ran through the kitchen into the springhouse. The door his mother always kept locked was wide open. He raced out of the house, hoping to catch the intruder. He heard a car door slam, once, twice. They were stealing his Mercedes. He tore around the corner of the house, poker raised in his fist.

"Royce, what on earth?" Ruth and Dallas froze on either side of the truck, grocery sacks in their arms.

"You aiming to hit us with that?" Dallas asked.

He dropped the poker. Then he saw his car: the left front tire was a puddle of rubber on the grass. Royce poked a finger into the cuts in the vulcanized rubber. One gash went deeper than the rest, biting into the steel belt. The hubcap was dented, the wheel rim scored by some sharp heavy instrument like an ax.

"Looks like you got yourself a flat," Dallas observed. "You hit a hole coming over the gap?"

"Someone slashed my tire."

"Let's put away these groceries, then y'all can worry about that tire." Ruth climbed the porch steps with her purchases.

106

"Wait," Royce bounded up the steps and blocked her from going inside. "Something funny's going on here."

"I don't think this is a bit funny."

"Hush, Mama. You stay right here."

Royce double-checked the parlor, then the kitchen for any signs of the intruder, but the house was still empty. The storm door hung crooked on its hinges, broken when it had been blown open. He tried to shut it, but the aluminum frame was bent and he was afraid the glass might break if he forced it.

"Okay" he hollered. "Come on in. Door's broke, but I think it can be fixed."

Ruth and Dallas came into the kitchen, set their bags of groceries on the table, and sat down in their coats. They were still looking for an explanation for all his foolish behavior.

"First you jump out and scare us. Then you won't let me come in my own house. Next you tell me the door's broke. What's got into you?"

"It wasn't me. I heard someone in the house."

"What were you doing in the house? You were out painting the barn when we left," Dallas said suspiciously.

"I was in the closet, uh, checking the furnace. Remember, I said you needed a new filter? Anyway, I heard somebody sneaking around and I chased them out the back."

"Pshaw." Ruth pulled cans of beans, kraut, and corn from the bag, carrying armloads into her pantry to stack on the shelves.

"This sounds like what happened to Woody Reese the other day." Dallas peeled a newly bought banana. "Woody thought he heard somebody sneaking about his loft. Didn't see nobody, but next day he finds his chainsaw gone. Brand new saw don't just walk out of a man's barn."

Ruth came out of the pantry. "You think Wanda's to blame? Royce saw her on the Frozenhead just the other day."

Dallas took a bite of banana. "Wanda wouldn't need a chainsaw."

"I don't know why you take up for that woman." Ruth gathered more cans to her bosom for the pantry.

"Listen, I'm telling you, I heard somebody in the house," Royce insisted.

From inside the pantry came a loud crash. A can of pork and beans rolled across the linoleum floor.

"Mama!"

Ruth sprawled on the floor inside. "Sugar," she mumbled. "My sugar."

He helped her to a chair. "Did you faint? Where's your medicine?"

"My five-pound sack of sugar, it's gone from the top shelf. Someone stole my sugar."

"First Woody's chainsaw, now this," Dallas huffed. "Bet it's them drug people. Remember, Junior Gudger caught them growing dope on the old Wilson farm?"

Ruth whispered, "Lord, where's Dean?"

Royce hurried out the front door, but his voice was louder than he intended as he screamed from the porch. "Dean! Get in the house. Now!" And he waited until the ashen-faced boy with the red-stained hands came through the barn gate.

In the kitchen, Ruth was wailing. "I'm a poor widow woman who can't lock her back door."

"Mama, we'll fix the door before we go."

"No, you can't go. You stay here tonight."

"Dallas can stay."

"Boy, if there's drug people poking around folks' houses like you say, I best go guard my place."

"Dad! You didn't say we had to stay tonight," Dean whined.

"I'll make up the sofa so you can sleep downstairs," Ruth insisted. "It's decided."

"It's going to be fine," Royce tried to calm Dean down.

"No, it ain't going to be fine," Dallas said solemnly. "Things are going to get worse. Last days, last days, like the preacher said Sunday. It'll come like a thief in the night, but if you ask me, seems like tribulation's done arrived."

22

"Why, Eva Wilder, is that you? It's me, Lucy Gudger from Beaverdam!" Stopped on the city sidewalk in broad daylight, Eva touched her fingers to the side of the sunglasses that hid her eyes, then smiled, tight-lipped, controlled but with that slight hitch of a sneer that even Lucy could catch. "Why, Lucy, of course. What brings you to town?"

Sweet as all get out and thin as a fence post, with a flash of barbed wire in her manner, Lucy couldn't make out what Royce had seen in the likes of her. "Oh, I'm just headed to the library. A research project for church," she said. "Fancy running into you right smack in the city."

"Oh, Altamont is still a small place."

"Nah, this is the big city to me. My granddad used to tuck all his money in his brogan when he came to town, afraid he'd get robbed blind." Lucy couldn't help herself, let alone shut herself up. She saw herself, or two smaller versions of herself, reflected in those fancy sunglasses, just flapping her gums, making the biggest fool of herself. "How's Royce doing and your boy, Dean? He's a smart one all right. I wish he'd come back to the Sunday school class. We had an interesting discussion when he was there." The words flew out her mouth faster than her mind could think. She was nearly breathless filling the air between them so that that uppity city woman wouldn't edge in a cross word against her.

"Yes," Eva said. "Listen, I have to..." She pointed down the sidewalk. "I'm helping out at the soup kitchen here this afternoon. I need to talk with the father."

"Say hi to Royce for me," Lucy called after her. *Father?* she thought. *She's talking to God now?*

Lucy Gudger didn't come to Altamont all that often. Although she seemed like any other citizen, she was an alien. She walked from the parking deck to the Altamont Public Library, tightly clenching her fist so no city slicker could count her fingers. Oh, sometimes she daydreamed of bumping into Royce in town, but the last one she wanted to see was his skinny rail of a wife.

In the library, she headed straight to the regional collection. The librarian, a thin, spectacled woman who looked like another Episcopalian, brought the right box of papers, but held her intact finger to her thin lips when Lucy twanged out too loud, "Much obliged."

She tiptoed with the box to the reading room table and spread out the mimeographed papers. Notes from the annual meetings of the Three Forks Baptist Association, of which Beaverdam was perhaps the second-oldest congregation, founded in 1893. It wasn't entirely her fault that she had burned the church's only copy of the historic papers. It was in her blood; her people had always favored a fire for purging out the old and the underbrush with the first of spring. So she'd done the same that day at the church; spring-cleaning wasn't complete without a fire. She had hauled out the box of used Sunday school quarterlies and chucked them in the oil drum out back where they burned refuse, then another box of correspondence, and before she knew it, she'd torched the collected archives of the Fellowship meetings of the Three Forks Baptist Association going back a century.

Lucy would have never known better until the preacher was asking one day: "Seen a box with some envelopes inside? I was looking for it behind the pulpit. Some real old paper, church minutes, books, too."

"Never seen 'em," she lied straight out.

That had been last spring, and she believed she had gotten away with her deed until Ruth Wilder, that weepy old widow, started harping on the hundredth anniversary and wouldn't it be something to put out a program like she remembered at their diamond jubilee, way back in 1967. And Lucy had smiled and pulled at the half knuckle of her right hand, hidden in her left hand, and said, "Bless your heart. Of course we can."

Lucy copied as best she could. Once she had had the best of handwriting in a Palmer script, but after her middle finger had been lopped off,

110

her stump of a knuckle had been too sore for the pencil to rest against. Her handwriting went all to hell.

She was tempted to slip the book into her handbag, but they had these newfangled alarms at the front counter. She had seen the buzzer go off and a stern-looking man in a blue blazer with a security crest inquire: "Is there a problem here?" The same mean voice that Junior could muster when he was dealing with a ne'er-do-well. So she copied by hand, and in that way she felt closer to the poor soul of that saintly secretary who had penciled the plodding proceedings of the church's governing body, the pastor and the deacons who met every Sunday afternoon, long after the preaching was spent and the sinners and the saved had gone home to chicken dinners across the cove.

But Lucy's sharp eye soon saw names of the living and not the buried, crossing from dead history into what was more like gossip.

Dallas Rominger, Junior's own great-uncle by his aunt's side, had been the mailman driving every curve in the cove, with one long right arm on the wheel of his Ford Fairlane and reaching out the passenger window with his long left arm to shove circulars, bills, letters from distant family, Sears & Roebuck catalogs, and other items into the fat farm mailboxes on the Rural Free Delivery route. Like Santa himself six days a week, excepting federal holidays.

Everyone knew Wanda McRae, that witch who lived on the raw dirt road up George's Gap. She never came down the mountain except to throw stones at the doors of Beaverdam Baptist. Everyone knew that story and Dallas Rominger was sure to show every kid in the church that secret with the holes left in the wood. She remembered how brave Royce had been, walking straight to Wanda's house and throwing rocks right at her.

But she had never seen this written out in black and white. Dallas had always been single as far as anyone in the cove or church had known, but go back forty-five years and under a double asterisk, his name coupled with Wanda McRae's. Her eyes fell to the bottom of the page for the asterisked footnote: W. McRae was "churched" in 1947, examined by the elders and her membership officially revoked in the winter of that year as well as her legitimate Christian union with Rominger. It was all in the records, sealed in the book no one had bothered to read in decades.

Her eyes widened at what came next. A box falling under the dash of their two names, broken off by the annulment, which seemed to suggest

111

the unfortunate union had borne some particular if unnamed fruit, marked only by a question mark. Wanda had herself a woods colt?

"Excuse me, lady, can I ask you something?"

Lucy was so caught up in her copying, she didn't realize she was being addressed until she got a noseful of the unwashed stranger. Lord, he smelled to high heaven, a blast from both breath and body, unwashed and marinated in wood smoke and maybe whiskey.

"You work here? I'm looking for—"

She snorted. "Me, a librarian? I ain't even from around here." She shook her head fiercely. *Go away,* she prayed.

"Sorry, you looked like you worked here."

But instead of wandering off, the stranger rounded the table and took the chair on the other side. He wasn't much to look at, all bony with no flesh to pad out the stiff and outcast clothes that draped from his poor frame. Lucy kept her head down, like she was still reading, but she could still feel his cold blue eyes boring into the top of her head. She brushed her bangs and shielded her downcast eyes, then glanced through her fingers at this nosy stranger. He had a piece of paper unfolded in front of him. Tongue dangling out of the side of his whiskered mouth, he kept licking the nub of a pencil he'd swiped from the card catalog.

"Writing a letter to my girl." He blushed underneath the sunburn and grime, a delicate red.

"That's nice." She breathed through her mouth, trying not to gag.

"You doing research or something?"

"Yes, for my church." Honest to God, she felt she was going to be sick with the smell. She gathered her papers to go, but left the books scattered on the table. Let that uppity librarian earn her taxpayer-backed paycheck.

"Good luck with that church," the man said.

She could have wished him well with the girlfriend's letter that wasn't going well, but she needed to be getting home and she was already afraid of walking into the gloomy parking deck where she had parked the pickup, and she was even more afraid a man like this might follow her into that concrete cave.

23

Hurry," Father Michael said. "It's almost showtime."

Her potholder slipped and the heated steel of the baking pan burned the heel of her hand. She nearly dropped the institutional lasagna on the tiled floor instead of the table, but she didn't cry out, kissing her hand.

Father Michael followed with the second pan. "You didn't hurt yourself?"

"I'm all right." She didn't need to appear too needy. She was here to help, perhaps win some wages in doing so, if Michael was impressed enough with her volunteer spirit. She was, in fact, the only volunteer aside from the paid priest, just two of them tonight to feed and house the strangers who might be Christ in disguise.

"There's some ice in the fridge. I do that all the time, burn the hell out of myself when I'm cooking."

"Thanks." Eva found a limp bag of frozen peas to lay on her wound. "You know, I'm not trained to work with these kind of people," Eva suddenly admitted to herself, to Michael, back in the kitchen for the limp lettuce they would serve as a salad.

Michael paused. "What kind of people would you say they are?"

"Poor. Crazy. Out of luck. I don't know. There just seems to be more of them everywhere you look nowadays."

The banging at the door made her jump again. The priest glanced at his wristwatch. "Showtime."

Eva wasn't ready for this. "Is there a prayer or something we should say?"

"God help us. Amen. That sometimes works." Michael winked. "Don't worry. Remember the rules we went over and you'll do just fine. They're all God's children, but you have to be firm with some of them."

The priest unlocked the door of heavy oak and iron, like the entrance to a medieval dungeon. On the other side, a woman was slamming a grocery cart full of garbage bags like a battering ram against the barricade.

"My goodness, five o'clock. Time to open up, isn't it, Suzanne?" Michael's voice remained pleasant but he exaggerated his inflections as if speaking to a child.

She was an obese woman made even rounder by layers of sweaters, jackets, and a raincoat. Over her mouth and nose she wore a cotton mask, filtering the steady mumble of megalomania. Eva caught a strong whiff of body odor. No wonder the woman wanted to wear the respirator.

"Who's she?" the woman's eyes narrowed at Eva.

"My name is Eva. I've volunteered to help out Father Michael tonight." Eva extended her hand, hoping the smile on her face seemed sincere. But the homeless do not shake hands, or perhaps Suzanne was afraid of germs. She only stared at Eva's outstretched hand.

Behind the woman and her shopping cart crowded some two dozen men. Eva had never seen a more pathetic group of people even if they were all God's children. What had happened to them, what had they done in life to get so beaten down, so broken? They edged through the open door, burrowing weak and stubbled chins into upturned collars that afforded little protection against the cold. One by one, they passed between Father Michael and herself, who greeted each man warmly, even as they sniffed the breath and searched for clear eyes. The rules were no alcohol, no drugs, no weapons. Everyone had to be clean and sober. Crazy did not count.

"God bless. Welcome. Good to see you again." Father Michael patted their slumped shoulders and squeezed their skinny arms. They filed through the door, their heads bowed, not in reverence, but from fatigue.

"God bless you," Eva parroted the priest. She worried Father Michael would turn someone away. The priest said that when the temperature dropped low enough, the city's shelters filled up. Packing too many into an old church basement violated city fire codes. The homeless knew this and took their place in line early. Eva had lost count now of how many she had let in. At the back of the line was a bearded man with a bedroll and a stick. Could that be the one who had made off with her TV? All unwashed and unshaved, color of red clay, the homeless looked much alike in their donated clothes. "Welcome." She waved to him. She didn't even know her visitor's name. In her mind, she called him the TV man.

She wasn't saying "please" now, and she breathed through her mouth so she didn't have to smell them, so ripe and fermented in their rags and ill-fitting cast-off clothes. Michael stopped the last in line, the TV man. "Sorry, my friend, you can't take that inside."

"It's a good stick." The TV Man clutched his staff.

Anyone could see the end of the stick had been blackened over a fire and crudely sharpened into a point. The man waved the stick in the priest's face and Eva was afraid he might suddenly jab it through Father Michael. "No weapons," the priest said firmly.

The man hurled the stick into the street like a javelin. It clattered on the asphalt and rolled to the curb.

"There better not be any trouble from you or you're out tonight, understand?"

Minus his stick the man stalked inside, past Eva at the door. "Welcome," she said, but he didn't act like he remembered her.

The line turned to a horde, yelling and talking and pushing toward the food on the counter.

"Wait, wait everybody," Michael insisted. "This is a church. Please, we have to say grace."

Eva closed her eyes. What to pray for? She could hear their stomachs rumbling. They wanted food, not empty words.

"Our Father..." Michael began.

Some of them actually knew the words. The homeless haltingly prayed for sustenance, forgiveness of shortcomings, and deliverance from evil. She even heard Suzanne mumbling under her mask.

"Forever and ever, amen." Eva opened her eyes, blinking.

The TV Man was staring at her. "Do we eat now?"

24

Kyle stared at the steam pipes knocking overhead while the rest bowed their heads and prayed with the priest and the volunteer lady. The words blathered on about trespassing and forgiving trespassers, but at last he was in line and the lady was ladling the food onto plastic plates.

"Much obliged," Kyle said.

Her face flushed from the steaming food, she smiled. "You're welcome."

The cabbage was watery, the beans mushy, but Kyle would call this home cooking if he knew what home was like. Up and down the tables came the sounds of slurping and chewing, but no dinner conversation. The meal took only a few minutes as everyone got their fill. The homeless threw their plates in the trash and pulled thin mattresses from a pile to spread across the concrete floor.

Kyle got the last mattress. He flipped it over, checking for stains or vermin, and then found an empty space near the door. He propped the mattress against the wall for a backrest and settled down. A smoke would taste good, but he saw "No Smoking" signs taped to the walls. He took out the book he'd pinched from the library, the one that the lady had been cribbing from. Something about the cover had caught his eye, the tintype picture of an old-time country church, whitewashed clapboards and rows of serious-faced men and pale, frowning women. He'd flipped through the mimeograph papers, and when no one was watching, had slipped the papers into his burlap sack. Inside, he'd caught a familiar name, Beaverdam

116

Church, and some of the names he seemed to recall from that country his mother still inhabited or haunted.

"Excuse me, you don't remember me?" The volunteer lady loomed over his mattress. "You came to my door the other day. You asked to drink from my faucet then you took a television set."

"It was broke," Kyle said.

"Never mind that. I don't think we've been formally introduced. My name's Eva. What's yours?"

"Kyle," he said warily.

"Pleased to meet you, Kyle..."

She hesitated like he might supply a last name. When he kept quiet, she kept on talking. "So what's that you're reading, Kyle?"

He turned the cover over. "Minutes of the Three Forks Baptist Association."

"Sounds interesting," the lady lied to him. "You like history, Kyle?"

"It talks about Beaverdam, where I'm from."

"Really, my husband is from there, too. Small world," she paused in her small talk.

"I ain't been there in years," Kyle said, not wanting to go there or much of anywhere with this woman and her nattering conversation.

"Well, I'm glad to get to know you, Kyle. I'm glad you found your way to St. Thomas'. Remember you can always come here, Kyle."

He nodded, and waited for the woman to take her sorry feeling elsewhere. Kyle was too tired to read tonight. He unlaced his boots and pulled them off, wiggling his toes through the holes in his socks. He hid his plastic bag of snakeweed in his right boot. No trusting anybody here tonight. He stretched out and studied the steam pipes knocking overhead.

Finally, the priest called out "Good night" and the lights went out. Kyle kept his eyes peeled to the ceiling. He listened to the night sounds around him: coughs, snores, whimpers. One guy in the corner sounded like he was dying from the rattle in his ribs. Soon the basement was filled with the steady breathing of people too tired to dream. Kyle rolled over, muffling his good ear against the mattress. The human noise haunted him. After about an hour, he decided he couldn't sleep. He needed a smoke to settle his nerves. He sat up and checked his boot. The plastic bag crinkled as he opened his stash. Rolling a fat joint in the dark was no problem. Lighting it might be.

117

Joint between his teeth, boots laced around his neck, Kyle stole toward the door past the huddled bodies of the homeless. Behind a battered hospital screen slept the women. Suzanne sprawled on her back, arms outstretched, blubbering under the mask she wore even in her sleep. Beside her lay the volunteer lady, one hand clasping the collar of her nightgown. Her arm squeezed the pillow over her face against Suzanne's stench.

She rolled over and her eyes opened wide at him standing over her. He pressed his finger to his lips. "Just me."

"What..." she lowered her voice, steadied her tone. "What do you need, Kyle?"

"Go outside for a smoke."

"Once you leave, you can't come back in. It's the rules."

"Lot of rules around here. 'Course, you could hold the door open for me."

"No, I can't do that."

"I won't be long. Just a few tokes to help me sleep."

"I'm sorry."

"Yeah, there you go again."

Kyle closed the heavy door behind him. He slipped on his boots on the icy sidewalk. He walked outside and sat on the stonewall by the church. He struck the match against the rock and lit his joint, the seeds popping inside the rice paper. The smoke slid easy all the way down. Exhaling, he felt the snakeweed slither up his spine, right through the top of his skull. He was instantly, pleasantly stoned. He banged his heels against the wall until he couldn't feel his feet. Leaning over, he spat a long strand of phlegm onto the sidewalk.

"Whoa." He leaned too far and fell off the wall, but kept his feet. He laughed. Quick as a cat, you always land on your feet. Arms out for balance, he danced along the length of the curb until he tripped on a stick lying in the gutter. This time he fell hard, bloodying his palms on the asphalt. His stick, he'd found his stick! He climbed the staff, hand over hand, until he stood upright. He looked around and laughed when he saw who was watching his antics.

Bathed in floodlights, the Christ figure spread marble hands, blessing the intersection. Below his punctured feet on their pedestal, signs pointed arrows east and west guiding the lost to the Interstate.

"Well?" There was no answer, no voice. All Kyle heard was the wind licking against the white statue. Shake the hand of the Man from Galilee tonight, you'd likely stick to the stone. The carved folds of the robe were discolored with grit and exhaust fumes. Night after night, the headlights of the interstate traffic washed over the muted whiteness. Maybe Jesus spoke over AM radios and in the dreams of dozing drivers.

"Which way?" Kyle poked the side of the statue with his stick. "Yes, you, I'm talking to you."

A gust tapped his shoulder. The pressure in his bad ear changed and Kyle could hear a sharp whistle. He could hear the blood pulsing in his neck. He could hear everything. Overhead, the traffic light changed from red to green. "Much obliged," Kyle thanked the statue.

He could hear voices no longer muffled. Noises were now amplified and perfectly clear. He heard the sound of rushing water. Down the street, he stepped over a storm grate. What he'd mistaken for the blood beating in his skull was actually a stream running underneath his boots—a creek buried under the city streets.

❖

Eva waited by the door, her arms crossed, trying to warm herself in the chill. The mullion window in the stone wall allowed no look outside at the modern night, but she felt like a medieval gatekeeper, waiting for what? To be rescued instead of doing the rescuing? Michael had been right. What was she doing here instead of in her warm bed with her husband and her son in his bed down the hall? She had her own life, her own to look after.

"Something wrong, Eva?" Michael was up now.

"He left."

"Who?"

She shook her head.

"Never mind," he said. "The important thing is you followed the rules. We have to follow the rules, Eva. We need the rules. It's so hard to get people to understand that, particularly these people." Michael patted her shoulder, that warm hand again on her skin. "Get some rest, Eva. I'm glad you're here."

119

25

Phoning home, Royce listened to the slow clicking of the rotary dial, then to the ringing miles away at 18 Chester Place. He imagined the chirp of the avocado extension in the kitchen or the jangle of the princess model in its brass cradle in the bedroom. "Pick up, pick up," he said. He wanted to talk to his wife, especially after what she'd said in bed the other night.

"We don't love each other anymore."

Royce's eyes peeled wide in the dark hovering over their bed. He had heard his share of mumbled memories, Eva calling for her dad (but never her mother), the half-asleep whispers as she drifted into uneasy dreams, letting go of the million mundane details that made her day, her duties. More often than not, he heard his own name, Royce, called out sharply as if in warning, not the husky voice she used when they made love, when Royce felt more in the mood.

He didn't take these ramblings too seriously. The next morning, when he asked at breakfast, "Bad dreams?" she would shake her tousled hair. "No, why do you ask?" But last night there had been a doubt in her dreaming voice that scared him.

After four rings, the answering machine clicked on.

"Hey, it's me. We're at Mama's. Something's come up, so we'll be staying. Don't worry, everyone's fine. Dean's okay. Mama fell. Nothing serious... Look, I'll explain everything tomorrow. We love you. I love you."

He hung up. I love you. Maybe he didn't say that enough in his marriage. Eva seemed so distant these days, so angry and untouchable.

"She was going to the homeless shelter, remember?" Dean said. He half lay, half sat on the couch. His feet on the floor, but lying slumped.

"Sit up, why don't you?" Royce gave his son's shoulder a little helpful shove, maybe harder than he meant.

"Was that Eva?" his mother called out from the kitchen over the rush of tap water.

"She wasn't home. I left her a message."

Ruth came to the door, drying her hands in her apron. She switched off the light to the kitchen. "Hope she won't be mad."

"Why would she be mad at you?"

"You know how she looks down on me sometimes."

"Mama, if there's anybody she's down on these days, it's me." He felt a twinge of guilt for this small betrayal of his wife to his mother.

Dean gave him a mean, furtive look and crossed his arms for emphasis. He was still irked at being left out of all the excitement, high on the ladder while burglars were ransacking the house and cutting their car's tires.

"Did I lock the front door?"

"Mama, sit down. It's okay."

"I'll just check. No need to make that burglar feel welcome to all my treasure."

"What treasure?" Royce laughed.

"When folks get desperate anything's a treasure. Don't forget in the Civil War my grandma killed a bushwhacker trying to make off with her garden. Shot him dead in the cabbage patch."

"Dead? Really?" Dean came back to Earth from whatever clouds he lived in whenever something bloody and violent caught his attention, Royce noticed.

"It's just a story, Dean." Royce had heard that tale since he was little. Whenever he saw cabbages in the garden, they reminded him of small green skulls with the rest of the bones buried beneath the dirt. "You don't have to shoot anybody, Mama."

"I still got your daddy's gun. I might not kill 'em, but I'd scare 'em half to death."

She scared Royce sometimes with her ideas.

"La me." Ruth's knees creaked as she collapsed into her rocker. She extended her chapped hands toward the stove, then got up again, jabbing the poker into the dying fire. "You about let it go out. Go fetch them sticks Dallas brung in."

Royce went through the dark kitchen to the back door where his uncle had piled a few seasoned splits of oak. He checked again the polyurethane sheeting he had tacked over the broken door. Something was moving outside in the dark. Night brushed against the opaque plastic like a beast rubbing an itch in its fur.

When he returned with three big splits, Ruth was by the window, fidgeting with the curtain. "Did you hear anything out there?"

"Just the wind," he said. "Bad out tonight."

Royce fed the logs into the woodstove. Flames licked greedily at the bark. He closed the small iron door and took his seat on the sofa, the vinyl cushions sighing. The room was silent except for the creak of the rocker, the popping of the fire. She kept glancing toward the window. Royce kept looking at the closet behind her.

"You want to watch the television?" asked Ruth. "Go ahead and turn it on."

This far from Altamont there was no cable, and aerial reception was terrible wedged between the Buckeye and the Frozenhead. Ruth only got one snowy channel and Friday night did not favor this network. He tuned in to an inane sitcom he'd never seen before, about several unmarried people living together in a big city. Precocious kids rolled their eyes at the grownups' childish behavior. There was some crisis about walking the dog. A laugh track roared in the background, but Royce saw nothing funny about the situation. Every joke was smarmy, every innuendo pointed to what went on in your crotch. Royce didn't think he was a prude, but society had gone sex-crazed, it seemed. Madonna, that pop star whose music you couldn't avoid on radio or TV, was releasing a book called "Sex," posing nude with homosexuals and sado-masochists in leather. From pop to porn, the whole culture had coarsened. Add in a teenager soon about to be fifteen, and it was hard to watch or listen to anything that didn't embarrass you to the bone.

But even as he felt his blood pressure rising and his face blushing, a chill draft was creeping up his pants leg. The closet door behind his mother's rocker was ajar, and every time he looked, it seemed to yawn wider. Finally, Royce went to close the door.

"It don't shut good," Ruth said. "Warped years ago. I'd just as soon nail

122

it shut if it weren't for the furnace. While you're up, can you hand me that sweater inside."

Royce unhooked the cardigan, a tattered gray sweater that had once belonged to his daddy. He peered inside at the furnace. "I need to check that filter."

"Thought that's what you were doing this afternoon."

"Uh, it needs a new one," Royce quickly lied. "Maybe me and Dallas can bring one back tomorrow when we get the tire fixed."

"Turning colder." Ruth draped the sweater over her shoulders. "You best sleep down here on the couch. It's warm next to the fire. I sleep out here myself sometimes when it turns real cold."

Royce imagined his mother shivering under quilts by the faint glow of the stove. Would he drive up one day to find her stiff on the sofa? What if the furnace really did need a new filter? The television show and its fake laughter grated on his nerves. He switched it off.

"Hey!" Dean said.

"You weren't watching that."

"I got some pencil and papers. I know how you always like to draw."

"Mama, he's fine. Don't go to such trouble."

Ruth rummaged in the next room and returned with the half pencil and a sheaf of stationary. "Here you go. Why don't you draw something nice, like you used to?"

Dean blushed, but still he took the paper and blunt pencil with appreciation.

"Jake was the same way," Ruth observed. "Didn't care much for the television, just liked the radio. Said he liked the sounds a fire makes best of all. Just watching a log burn was enough for him."

Royce recollected his father sitting by the fire for hours on end, tending to its appetite like a beloved pet. Sometimes it seemed he liked the flames more than family. His father always seemed cold. His thin lips nearly blue, a tremor in his hands that he kept rasping together. Turns out that the old man was just waiting for them to go to bed so he could tipple from his supply kept in the crawlspace.

"Once Jake stayed up all night," Ruth recalled. "There was something wild on the loose. A panther, maybe some big old dog, picking off stock. Nobody was sure, except it ate half of Wanda's skinny cow and we figured that thing must be mighty hungry. Jake sat all night by the fire with his gun."

"I don't remember that," Royce said.

"This was way before you were born. Nothing came that night. Next morning I got up, he was sound asleep with his gun. Fire died out."

She gazed fondly at the horsehide chair where no one sat out of respect to the memory of Jake Wilder. The cushion was still imprinted with his absent weight, as if he'd just stepped out of the room. "He wasn't much of a talker, your grandfather, but he thought the world of you, Dean."

"Huhh," Royce heard his father's voice in his throat, the guttural exclamation of a ghost.

He could remember the body in the casket, the last time he'd seen that face wearing the rouge and powder of the mortician's art, the thin lips clamped shut, the eyelids betraying no flutter. That's not the man, not my daddy, he'd thought. But then a different image came to mind—the photograph he'd found upstairs in his daddy's coat pocket, now in his own shirt pocket. He could show his mother. He wanted to throw open the trapdoor and let out all the secrets. Here was my father, your husband, the man you never knew.

"Tell me about him," Dean said. "What was he like when he was younger? Did you know him when he was a boy? I mean, my age."

"What was he like?" Ruth's brow wrinkled. "He wasn't from Beaverdam, originally. Your granddaddy was always the same all the while I knew him, though I heard he lived up to his name before me. He was wild."

Royce had to laugh. Wild the way his mother meant the word covered anything from drinking to card playing, dancing to consorting with Methodists, all those sins Jake Wilder had stood foursquare against as a deacon.

"I didn't notice him until the Sunday he repented," Ruth said. "First time he'd sat in a church in ages, I reckon. He came right down front and took Jesus as his personal savior. It was only March and still winter, but he insisted on getting baptized in Beaverdam Creek. I watched him go under a sinner and come up sputtering, a new man. I walked him home all wet, his hair just curled like a baby's at the back of his neck. Sunday after that, we began courting."

Ruth fell silent. Her rocker ceased its creaking rhythm. The fire popped inside the stove, the clock ticked on the mantel, and a wind knocked slowly upstairs.

When she spoke again, her voice was husky. "Look there at his pipe."

Royce took the straight briar from the mantel, its stem still impressed with the clench of his father's teeth. The bowl stank of Prince Albert, the wadded pouch that had always bulged at his back pocket.

"You don't know this but I still buy his tobacco at the store. Sometimes I light it, just to remember."

Royce bent and kissed his mother's tightly permed hair, still smelling of the chemicals from her beauty shop this afternoon. "Go on to bed, Mama. You look beat. Me and Dean will sit up a while."

Ruth trudged into the bedroom then returned with a spare quilt. "You might need this." She stacked the cover on Jake Wilder's empty chair, and underneath the quilt she had a shotgun, which she leaned against the arm. "Good night."

Royce aimed the old Remington out the window and fingered the trigger. The safety was on. He snapped open the breech and saw the round brass shell in the chamber. "No need to worry," Royce said to Dean who seemed surprised his old man knew his way around a real weapon. "You can go on to bed."

"You mind if I stay up a while longer. With you?"

"Sure. You're not getting too bored?" Bad TV, no cable, no music videos, no computer games, far from all the comforts of home in Altamont. Royce wouldn't blame him if he were. When Royce was his age, he couldn't wait to be free of this cove, break out of Beaverdam. He'd only gotten as far as Altamont, but that was a brave step.

He imagined his father sitting in this same room, with this very gun, waiting for a strange beast at the back door. Now it was his turn. Not only was he on guard against someone wandering the night with an ax or worse, but maybe against an invisible gas seeping through the floorboards or just the bad luck braided into his DNA. "You scared?"

"You?" Dean asked in return.

It was Royce's turn to shrug. "That woman is plenty scary, and if she's slashing people's tires, that's not good. But she's always been like that."

"What made her that way?" Dean asked.

"Maybe she's just crazy, or Alzheimer's. Maybe just mean and crazy too." So many half-told stories, whispered truths—then that time he went to her house and saw that lassoed boy. He couldn't tell his son that secret, that shameful moment when he'd turned tail and ran home. "Wickedness, I reckon," Royce heard himself drawling out Dallas' wisdom.

"You believe that?" Dean asked.

Royce cleared his throat. "Doesn't much matter what you believe in the long run. You have to make the best of it."

26

Under the hum of the mercury streetlamp, the woman waited on the corner. Leaning against a trash container, her hands burrowed into the pockets of a thin suede jacket, cut for looks more than for the cold. She wore jeans too tight for her heavy thighs, fuzzy acrylic leg warmers pulled over stocky calves. A car crept toward her, flicking its headlights. She shook her hair, bleached blonde combed out into a frizzy come-hither cloud. The car drove by for a look, accelerated. Tires screeched around the corner. She sagged against the trashcan and waited.

Kyle was stoned, but he knew this woman. Her hair wasn't the same, but the slouch of her shoulders gave her away, how the flesh rounded down her back. "June?"

"Jesus!" Startled, the woman turned on him.

"Remember me?" He stepped into the light.

"You scared me." June shook her blonde hair again and he could tell now it was only a wig. Underneath was probably the same mousy cut she'd always had. He remembered the startled look she gave him. She'd been rocking May in her arms at the time. Look what you done, her look said without any words.

"How long you been back in town?" Kyle asked.

"Few days."

"You saw they tore down the Windsor?"

"That rat hole? Good riddance." June lit a cigarette, cupping her palm around the flame for a little warmth.

126

"May liked it all right. Said it was romantic."

"That was May's trouble. Romance."

Maybe that was Kyle's fault as well. Looking for romance in the ruins, digging up mummified memories from what should have stayed buried in the rubble. Kyle had waited until the demolition workers took a lunch break before he broke into the Windsor last week. Overhead he could hear a faint ticking in the joists and beams. He took the stairs cautiously, testing each squeaking step before trusting his full weight on it. His foot tripped on a riser pitched higher than the rest with the settling of the house. He fell against the banister, felt the old spindles give way. The section of railing fell like a harp through the empty air and shattered into kindling below. Kyle breathed deep the dusty air, which set off a coughing fit that echoed along the empty halls.

The Windsor was used to such sounds. The former hotel had been built at the turn of the century, catering to tubercular tourists coming to the Blue Ridge as if the haze on the hills could clear their choked lungs.

"Sometimes I wonder who lived in this room before me, if it was a woman with a cough. Maybe she spit up blood in a handkerchief." These previous guests had fascinated May. She believed in reincarnation, insisted she may have already lived and died in the third-floor flat she shared with June. "Don't you ever feel like there is a moment when you're standing on the street and you blink or turn your head and suddenly you know, you just know you've been here before? Long ago when the street was cobblestone and there weren't any cars, or maybe longer still when the street was just a path in the woods and there weren't even buildings, just trees, but it's still the same you, a thousand years old?"

"I reckon so." Kyle had never seen such an excitable girl as Maybelline Carter. But he knew exactly what she was talking about. He had felt it himself, back in Beaverdam. Suddenly he was shivering out on his mama's porch, not from the cold, but from a thrill that had come over him, a knowing deep in his bones. He could reach up and scatter the stars in the night sky. He could scratch his back against the spin of the planet. He was a million years old, immune to the rush of time and space above and below. Then that secret moment hurtled by, the knowledge faded, and time resumed its place again: a small boy tied to a porch post with a half-rotten rope. But he still held to the memory of feeling like forever.

At the end of the dim hall was May's door, across from Kyle's room.

Here he had learned the hard way to knock first after he had walked in on May and a client. She was lying naked on the bed, her legs aimed at the ceiling, open for business, waiting for a short balding man in gartered hose and T-shirt who was one step too slow out of his boxers.

"Don't you ever knock?" May cried.

"Oh, Lord," said the little man. "I didn't mean nothing. I didn't touch her. Oh, Lord." His erection bounced smaller and smaller and he hopped on one foot trying to step back into his shorts.

"Who the hell are you?" Kyle demanded.

"I'm nobody, mister, nobody. You won't ever see me here again. It's my first time. I swear it's my last, too."

"Kyle, we're kinda busy." May sat up, her small breasts drooping as she pointed to the door. "Out now! No, not you!"

But the balding man had already gathered his pants, his coat, his shoes. He threw a roll of cash in May's lap, then retreated. "No, sir, you won't see me here. Y'all stay here and I'll be long gone in just a second."

The door slammed shut. They could hear the man running down the hall. Kyle stared at the greenbacks on May's white thighs.

"Shit, I was only charging him twenty. There must be a couple hundred here." She started to laugh so hard, the bed began to bounce. Kyle laughed too.

June came in about that time, took one look. "What the hell?" Then they were all laughing and rolling on the bed, across May's legs and the greenbacks and the rumpled sheets. It was as happy as Kyle ever remembered himself, arms full of money and women and possibility.

They had worked the scam for a few months. June pimping for May, hunting out the john on the street, opening the door to May's room for a full eyeful of the joy to come, then collecting her finder's fee. After the sap went inside, Kyle would make his entrance as the angry boyfriend. All of the johns would surrender the rest of their wallets, along with watches, rings, sometimes even their clothes, anything to get out alive. It worked well until the last john pulled out a badge and a gun.

June blew a stream of smoke from the red corner of her mouth. "So where've you been staying?"

"Woods for a while. Then it got cold."

"Tell me about it, honey."

June burrowed her chin in her coat, eyeing the Interstate Motel across the way, where a neon sign signaled "VACANCY $24 Rms."

"I've been waiting for a date to pick up the tab. I'd do the whole night if they wanted, just to stay inside, but the only ones out are looking for other guys. Don't nobody want a straight time in this town." She considered Kyle. "You got twenty-five bucks?"

He turned out his pocket. Nothing but a handful of lint and woodchips.

"A place tonight?" she asked.

He glanced up the street toward the shelter. "I did, but I didn't like all the rules. They don't let you smoke what I like to smoke."

Kyle relit his joint and offered it to June.

"Mean stuff." She coughed.

"You'll feel good soon enough."

"I've got nothing against feeling good."

Kyle hesitated before asking what he needed to know. "May? What happened to her?"

June handed over the joint. "You know junkies. You were in the Windsor long enough to know how it all ends."

"All I know is y'all went off to Florida."

June laughed bitterly. "Weren't no vacation down there."

"So tell me," Kyle leaned on the trashcan.

He wasn't sure she was going to say anything. She kept blowing smoke into the cold night, her breath coming in exasperated sighs. She dropped the cigarette, crushed it under her boot heel. "Scoot over." She slid one buttock on top of the trash container, leaning into Kyle for a little warmth. "Least it was warm down there."

"Go on. What about May?" He put an arm around her, rubbed her back.

"I had to hold her. I held her all the way down. She kept shivering in my arms. 'I'm cold. I'm cold.' But her face was like to burn up."

May once wrapped arms and legs about him, clinging like a summer vine, skin so hot and dry. Her tongue slipped into his ear. She begged him for a needle, for him to cook the works for her.

June was still talking. "Old car I had made it as far as Jacksonville before it overheated. Leak in the radiator. May was dead to the world in the back seat, about to burn up herself. She kept raising her head. 'Is it Florida yet?' 'Yes, almost honey, almost,' I'd say. She spied the first signs welcoming you to the Sunshine State, but it was overcast in Jacksonville and that's as far as we got. I used to dance down there in the clubs and I thought I could make a little money, get May some of that shit she was al-

129

ways, always needing. But she was so far gone, she wasn't even worried about that. She wanted to see the ocean."

Kyle could hear the water roaring under the street, under his boots, rising now through his stoned mind. "I was gonna wrestle 'gators," he murmured. "May was going to swim as a mermaid in the show."

"She couldn't swim! There wasn't hardly enough fat on that girl to float, just skin and bone, but I took her to the beach anyway. No swim suits. We waded out in our underwear. I carried her in my arms into the waves."

Kyle imagined the water as far as the eye could see. He could feel May in his arms, the waves lifting her, letting go. His arms suddenly empty, water sliding from his palms. "She drowned?"

"No, you dumb shit. She was too sick to drown. I took her to the emergency room when we got to town. Left her sitting in the waiting room. I took her pocketbook so they wouldn't know her name, but they would have to take her. They can't let nobody just die in the waiting room, insurance or not. She wasn't even Maybelline Carter at the end, just Jane Doe when I called the next day, one of three they admitted, the only white girl to die of hepatitis that morning in Jacksonville General, and when I knew, I just hung up. They buried her, I reckon, down in the swamp somewhere, city expense. Fucking Florida."

Kyle sat next to June on the trashcan, putting his arms around her to warm her. They said nothing. He felt her trembling and he held her tighter. "Enough of that." June smeared the mascara under her eye with the heel of her hand. "This is business."

She slid off the can and knelt between his boots, pushing his knees apart. Unzipping his pants, her hand was cold, and then her warm mouth took him in. Her head bobbed between his thighs. He touched her wig, winding blonde ringlets in his hand. Whose hair was this, he wondered. He closed his eyes and thought of May's long hair streaming in the waves. The water in the storm grate grew louder. He raised his face. He held his breath. When he could hold back no longer, he cried out, shuddering.

June tucked him into his pants, zipped him up, patted his crouch. Her knees creaked as she stood and spat on the sidewalk, wiping her mouth. "I never had much use for you, but Maybelline thought you were something special. Consider that one on the house."

27

That night saw the first hard frost in Beaverdam. Clouds blotted the sky and crescent moon, streaming south until the sky cleared and the blood-red mercury dropped in the rusted thermometer hung on the side of the barn. The last of summer withered and died back overnight, vines blackened, and each blade of grass was etched in crystal. The only one awake, watching, was Royce, all through the small hours.

Dean had kept him company until the adrenaline finally drained and his head drooped. Royce pushed him upstairs half asleep, guiding him along the drafty hall to Royce's old bedroom. There he tipped Dean onto the high bed, pulled off his sneakers, and covered him with the counterpane to sleep the sleep of the young, the fearless, those who knew no better.

Royce returned downstairs for the night guard. Not that Wilders were known for bravery; none of his forebears had ever fought in a war. His father somehow slipped out of service in World War II; his grandfather had sat out the century's first fight in France. Royce's pride in being the first in the family to attend college was muted by simple self-preservation, buying him a draft deferment during Vietnam, while the likes of Junior Gudger had answered the call of his country. The only blood shed by his kin belonged to the bushwhacker blasted away in the cabbage by his great-grandmother.

Royce dozed off a dozen times, head wobbling until chin poked chest, and he'd jump in the dark, jerking the trigger of the shotgun. If the safety hadn't been on, he might have blown buckshot into the closet, fatally wounding the furnace. He knew no one was really there but he still coughed loudly to warn any would-be intruders that he was on guard. He stared at the closet until his eyes grew heavy and his head nodded once more.

Royce awoke to the clatter of pots and pans in the kitchen, the familiar scent of bacon frying. A radio voice drawled out the day's weather and yesterday's burley prices.

"Rise and shine, sleepyhead," his mother crowed from the doorway, snapping on the overhead light. "Chickens are already awake."

"You don't have any chickens." Royce rubbed the sleepy crust in the corner of his right eye. "What time is it?"

"Five thirty. Your daddy would have done half an hour's worth of chores by now. You used to get up early too when you were little."

And hated it, to tell the truth. Royce had his own version of Ben Franklin's maxim: early to bed, early to rise makes a man tired and dumb as dirt. Royce rose stiffly from his father's chair. His left shoulder was sore, his neck had a crick, and his dorsal muscles were cramping over his kidneys.

"Dallas will be by directly and he's not one to lollygag. Let me cook some eggs and sausage. I'll make biscuits, too. And grits, unless they stole my grits. La me, I didn't close my eyes once, waiting for them to break in and kill me all night long." His mother chattered into the kitchen.

Royce opened the closet door he'd been guarding all night. Nothing inside but the hulking shape of the furnace, no Shadow Man in sight, but the trap door that led to the underworld, the realm of radon. How much had seeped up during the night? He didn't dare look. He emptied the chambers of the shotgun, propped it inside, and shut the door.

In the bathroom, a cinder-block extension that felt like a walk-in freezer, Royce did not need the light; by force of habit, he aimed at the toilet. He was semi-erect. If he'd been at home he wouldn't have minded slipping back into bed with Eva, make a little morning mischief that would have brought a slight smile to his face the rest of the day. But last night she had been sleeping with that priest in a roomful of shiftless drunks. So much for love. Flushing the toilet, he shook himself and zipped his trousers.

He sat at the kitchen table, eating the last of his fried eggs and grits when the knock came at the back door. "There's Dallas now. Running a bit late," said Ruth.

"Doesn't he remember that door's broke?"

"Best go remind him."

In the walkway between the kitchen and the springhouse, Royce swatted the darkness until he found the twine pull to the overhead light. The bare bulb shone against the filmy plastic stretched across the broken door. Beyond his own distorted reflection, Royce could make out the shadow of a man on the other side.

"Door's broke, remember? Go around front."

The shadow said nothing but turned and disappeared.

At the front door, Royce found Dallas scuffing his brogans on the sisal welcome mat. "Fifty years of coming round to the back door is a hard habit to break. You about ready? You sure did pack a lot here." Dallas kicked the pair of floral suitcases inside the door.

"They ain't mine," Royce said.

"Looks like somebody's going on a trip." Dallas lifted one and listed to one side with the weight. "Feels like a long trip."

"Wait," Royce said. "I'll be right with you."

Ruth was washing his dishes in the sink. "Mama, why you got your suitcases packed?" he asked in what he hoped was a reasonable voice.

"I'm not spending another night alone in this house, not with that crazy woman out there breaking in to murder me."

"Mama, nobody's going to murder you."

"You bet they're not. I've got the shotgun. You get them tires fixed and you're going to drive me down to Altamont."

The telephone rang. "That will be Eva. You best get it," she said.

Just from the shrill ringing, he could already tell his wife was mad.

"What in the world is going on, Royce? I get home from the shelter and neither one of you are here. You about scared me to death. Is Dean okay? Ruth?"

"He's fine. She's fine. She had a little fall, but she's okay. We had a little scare, is all."

"You're not telling me something. I can hear it in your voice."

"Uh, someone tried to break in the house."

"Oh, no." Eva's voice faded to a whisper. "So why didn't you come home last night?"

133

"I've got a flat tire and the air's all leaked out of the spare. Dallas will give me a ride to town first thing this morning. We'll get the tire fixed, then drive it back and put it on the car. We'll be home this afternoon. Mama's coming, too." He could hear her sigh through the static on her end and he braced herself for the angry blast, but there was nothing but silence. "Eva?"

"You're sure about all this?" she said.

"What else can we do? She's my mother."

"I know. Just remember she's not my mother."

Here it comes, Royce thought, but she said nothing. He could hear voices, conversations bleeding into their line, unintelligible like a foreign language. "Look, I love you," he tried, but it sounded forced.

"Sometimes I don't know. Sometimes I wonder if you and I are doing all right." She sounded farther off than just forty-five miles away.

"Trust me. We've been married a while, we're doing fine."

After they hung up, he checked again in the kitchen. "You and Dean will be all right until we get back?"

"Sun's shining. We'll be just fine." Ruth plunged her wrinkled hands into the soapy water. "Go on now. Quicker you get going, quicker you can get back and take us on to your house."

Dallas crouched by the car, inspecting the flat. The dirty fleece lining his denim jacket scraped the gray stubble of his chin. "There are tracks all around. Dog's been sniffing in the middle of the night." He wrinkled his nose. "I believe it peed on your tire."

"This is going to be my day, I can tell." Royce zipped his windbreaker but the thin nylon offered little protection against the cold.

"I brung the tools." Dallas lifted a large clawed jack from the bed of his pickup.

"This isn't a tractor, Dallas, it's a Mercedes. You'll tear the bumper off with that thing."

Royce opened his trunk, before he remembered his spare tire leaned against the wall of their now tidy garage over in Altamont. It had been weeks since the fateful yard sale, and he still hadn't replaced the tire in the trunk. At least he hadn't removed the compact hydraulic jack and short iron rod that served as jack handle and lug wrench.

"That tiny thing?" said Dallas. "That don't look like it could lift a baby off its butt."

The cold seeped through his trousers into his stiff joints as he crawled under the car, positioning the jack against the frame.

Dallas watched in amusement. "I'm glad you gone to college. That looks tricky."

Rather than leveraging a series of ratchets, the Mercedes-issued jack used hydraulic pressure. Royce fitted the handle and pumped the jack. The slashed tire puddled on the ground as it lifted into the chill air.

Dallas crossed his arms and studied the light over the Buckeye. "Reckon we'll make it to town about the time the garage opens if you hurry."

"Hunh." Royce pried off the hubcap with its triangular logo then fitted the wrench socket over the first lug. He pulled but the nut refused to give. Get your tires rotated and some idiot always uses an air wrench. The first lug finally relinquished its grip with a metallic squeak. Royce went to work on the next. Sweat formed on his forehead and he was breathing harder. He got the second loose, then the third, but he couldn't crack the tight seal of the last lug nut. Royce squatted like a weightlifter, both hands flexing the end of the iron. On a mental count of three, he strained upward, eyes bulging, blood coloring his face. "Come on, come on, come on."

The wrench slipped. As he fell, Royce felt his back go, the same muscle he'd pulled waltzing with the television the other weekend. He sat and licked his bloody knuckle where his hand had scraped the fender. "Just resting," he said. "I about got it that time."

"Lemme give her a try." Dallas grabbed the tire iron in the grass. He tapped the metal against his palm, studying the situation, and then he positioned the wrench at an angle opposite of Royce's attack. He pressed a boot on the end of the rod. "Yep, that's on there all right."

Balancing against the quarter-panel, the old man stepped on the iron with one foot, then all of his weight. Dallas bounced up and down until the metal arm moved, wrenching the nut free. He rode the rod down until the tip dug into the ground. He stepped off, repositioned the wrench, and repeated his acrobatics. "Some things you can't force. Got to outthink them." Dallas winked and pulled the wheel from the axle and rolled it to the bed of his truck.

Royce scrambled to his feet, brushing the cold seat of his pants. Dallas grabbed his wrist and, grinning, inspected his scraped hand. "Want to run in and let your ma kiss it before we go?"

135

Royce tried to jerk his hand free, but Dallas held on. Royce shoved at him with his left, but the old man caught his wrist. "So you want to Indian wrestle, eh?" Dallas grinned.

"I've no time for this foolishness. Let me go!" Royce sounded like a little boy to his own ears and he was getting angry now. They did this kind of horseplay when Royce was a kid and Dallas in his thirties, matching strength against balance. Royce slid his slick-soled loafer, braced himself against Dallas' brogan. He pushed, then pulled, trying to topple the old man while keeping his own balance.

Dallas was tightening his grip on Royce's scraped hand, grinning his yellow teeth. "Come on, you city slicker."

"You old hick, let go."

"Make me, mama's boy."

"I don't want to hurt you."

"You couldn't if you tried."

They were breathing hard, snorting angry clouds in the cold, and starting to cuss.

"Goddamn it, I said let go, old man."

"Damn yourself."

This was no game, but bad blood that boiled up between them. If he could wrest his hands from Dallas' tenacious grip, he'd no doubt wrap them around that skinny throat. Royce shot their locked hands and arms overhead, leaning hard into the old man, bumping him with his chest, and they were falling. Royce landed on top, felt the scrape of the gray whiskers, heard the stale tobacco breath leave the ancient ribcage, and saw the startled look in the old man's eyes as he banged his head on the frozen ground.

"What are you two doing?" Ruth hollered out the door. "Dallas, are you all right?"

Dallas lay still, eyes rolled back in his pale face. Royce sprang to his feet, suddenly afraid he'd killed his kinsman.

"Nah, just resting." Dallas sat upright. "Hard work changing these durn foreign tires."

"Well, it's taking a mighty long time for two grown men to change one tire." Ruth stomped into the house.

Royce extended his hand to his uncle. "You sure you're all right. I didn't mean—"

"Reckon I'll live." Dallas slowly, stubbornly got up by himself.

"Good." Royce shoved his scraped hand into his pocket.

"Great." Dallas prodded his bruised ribs.

Sheepishly, they piled into the pickup. The old man turned the key and a twang of country music blasted from the radio while oily air gusted from the heater. The gears made a grinding noise as Dallas wrestled the stick shift into reverse.

They rode in silence, worn out from their wrestling, surprised by an old intransigence that wouldn't release its grip. As they headed toward George's Gap, Dallas kept looking over at his nephew. He wouldn't let it go. "I believe you got the smallest hands of any man in the family. Take after your daddy, I reckon."

"Shut up."

"You always did take things too seriously. Just horsing around and you turn it into do or die. Just like your daddy."

"Quit saying that. I'm not him. I am not Jake Wilder."

Dallas gave him a sideways look. "No, you're not Jake, not by a long shot." The old man could still cut him when he wanted. They rode on in seething, stubborn silence. They passed the high roofs of a farmhouse set below the curving road and Royce looked down on worn shingled roofs and crooked chimneys with their old-fashioned lightning rods.

"Leonard Landrum, you talked to him lately?" Royce asked.

"Oh, that fat feller? We talked a spell the other day, but no, haven't seen him since."

"I had lunch with him."

"Lunch, huh? Don't know if I'd want to watch that fat feller eat or not."

"Look it, he told me about your deal. What were you thinking?"

"Got enough to pay off them taxes, didn't I? Well, your mama's property at least. I don't need your advice. I've been doing land deals since before you were born."

"I know," Royce snorted, "but all that talk about radon gas, how it was supposedly higher out here than just about anywhere? You didn't let him talk you down?"

"You never know. If the price is right..." Dallas pulled his stubbled chin with fingers.

"You don't need his money, do you?"

"Never you mind."

The two kinsmen stared out the windows, fogging the glass with their heavy breathing, their angry musings. They were climbing the gap now, out of the last stretches of farmland and pasture and up into the woodlots, second- and third-generation timbered long ago by the Romingers, Greenes, and Gudgers, and years away from any decent harvest. The wind had stripped the trees of the brightest leaves, and when it had died last night, the frost had killed whatever green was left in that world.

Royce was exhausted from lack of sleep and having to wrestle with the tires, then his uncle. A great yawn overtook him.

"I ain't boring you now, am I? Old unlearned hillbilly riding around with a college graduate, a big-city appraiser."

Royce didn't rise to the bait. "Nope, I didn't sleep good last night."

"Sleep?" Dallas snorted. "I would have gotten up on the wrong side of the bed if I'd bothered to go to bed. I sat up all night, just in case them prowlers came along."

"See anything?"

"No, but I sure heard more things go bump and boo last night than since I was a boy."

"Me too. I was up all night with his gun."

"Lord, she didn't get out Jake's old scattergun, did she? If you take after him, you couldn't hit the broadside of a barn and that's standing inside the barn." Both men laughed. They were all right now, the wrestling and argument behind them. "I don't believe I ever saw such an unsteady shot in a man. Probably a good thing me and him were 4-F and didn't get drafted to go fight them Germans."

"I heard about your flat feet, but what was wrong with Daddy?"

"They said he had a weak heart, but I never believed that. Not after our share of scrapes down in Fontana in the Triple C."

"Triple C?"

"Civilian Conservation Corps. That was with FDR, WPA, TVA and all the rest of the alphabet back in the Depression. Got a shovel, work clothes, three hots and a cot, which was a sight more than most folks was getting in those days. We marched into the Smokies and damned the rivers for electricity."

"Mama was saying last night you and Daddy were kind of wild back then."

It was Dallas' turn to squirm. "Well, some of them boys down there were right rough. Lots of cussing which I never could stand—blaspheming and profaning left and right, blankety this and blankety that. There were cards and liquor, lots of liquor, when we weren't digging all day, and a few of the fellers liked the kind of girls who don't make you like yourself the next morning." Dallas rubbed the grizzle on his cheek that was blushing bright red.

The khaki uniform in that old photo yesterday made sense now. Royce could still see the cocky grin of his father with the cigarette dangling from the corner of his mouth. Couldn't have been more than twenty at the time, still boyish despite a three-year stint with a CCC shovel rather than a GI's rifle, his man-hours spent moving mountains and damming rivers as evidenced by the wiry muscles under the rolled-up shirtsleeves. And the woman, only half seen in the torn photo, probably just some floozy down at Fontana, making her living like all loose woman have made their way since time out of mind. And was she on the mind of Jake Wilder who played a stern Baptist deacon all those Sundays, grimly hung over from Saturday nights next to his trapdoor of temptation.

But Dallas had his own terrible thoughts. "Yes, this might've turned out for the best. Lord knows what might have happened if you'd scared off them burglars yesterday. They might have made off with more than a sack of sugar, done more than just slit your tire. They might have slit our throats when me and Ruth came in. You'd have found us in pools of blood, two old defenseless people."

"No, I wouldn't go that far." Royce tried to quell his uncle's rising fancy, but too late.

"Yes, sir, we are living in terrible times. The bowels of hell are just yawning for some what walk the Earth. Preacher will tell you that every Sunday. Turn on the radio every other day, you'll hear about a brand-new evil." As if warding off such evil reports, Dallas reached over to switch off the radio. The truck rounded the curve, drifting across the faded yellow line. Dallas jerked the wheel, stomped the brake. Royce was flung against the dash as the truck skidded to a stop.

Only a few feet from the bumper a mangy cow stood in the roadway, chewing her cud, mournfully considering the two men in the truck.

"Oh Lord, don't look now." Dallas shielded his eyes with the flat of his hand.

Wanda McRae was hurrying up the road, arms flapping. "Bossy! You Bossy!"

139

Dallas shifted into low gear and crept around the cow.

"Damn your eyes!" Wanda slapped the windshield with her bony hand, glaring through the dirty glass. "You hypocrite! You old pharisee!"

Dallas accelerated, hunkering down behind the wheel. Royce turned and watched Wanda flapping her arms as if trying to lift her skinny body into flight. The cow lowed and Wanda kicked the beast in its belly.

"That woman's crazy."

"Crazy or just plain mean." Dallas' knuckles were white on the steering wheel.

"What's she doing in the middle of the road?"

"She uses the right of way for pasture. It's a wonder that poor cow hasn't been hit. Sorry thing deserves to be shot."

"Wanda or the cow?"

Dallas didn't even crack a smile. "Law frowns on shooting a woman no matter how mean."

"You wonder about folks like her," said Royce. "You see lots of them around town, just talking to themselves. Homeless, I guess, but a lot of them are just plain wacko. I tell Eva you can't help them when they're like that."

"It's a mystery, all right," Dallas nodded. "You try to do for some folks and they never forgive you for that."

"What did you ever do for Wanda?"

"Give her a place to live for one thing. That cabin on the Buckeye was built by Rominger. You look at the original deed and see whose name's on that land."

"What? You own the witch woman's cabin? Why did you let her stay all these years?"

"Christian thing to do. Young, scared thing, no people of her own, her home in Fontana all flooded out when we built the dam down there."

Royce turned in his seat, but Wanda was hidden around half a dozen curves. The tire bounced in the truck bed, showing its gaping wounds. He faced the road ahead and tried to speak his suspicions, what he knew was on Ruth and Dallas' minds as well, and had always been, the whispered adult conversations always just out of childhood's hearing. "You don't think—"

"No," Dallas cut him off. "Some days it don't scarcely pay to think."

28

A commotion came from the yard below, dim male voices, clucking woman's worry, the clang of metal. An engine coughed and cranked to life, but upstairs Dean was dead to the world, his head nested softly in a feather pillow. A thin thread of spittle trailed from the corner of his mouth with his steady snores. The engine faded down the cove, the creek kept up its crazy babble out the window. The caw of a distant crow flew through his dreams. His eyes fluttered open. He cried out, then caught himself. The red barn looming all night and a wild-eyed woman chasing after him with a bush ax—they were just dreams.

It had been pretty scary last night sitting around the fire with his dad, and pretty cool with the shotgun, waiting for some intruder to return, to slaughter them all in their sleep. He didn't remember his dad leading him upstairs and putting him to bed. Dean was still wearing his jeans and his shirt, one sock twisted half off his cold foot. He climbed out of bed, the cold linoleum sending a shock through his bare heel.

He thumped down the stairway slipping his head into his hooded sweat-shirt, and nearly tripped over the pair of floral suitcases at the foot of the stairs, waiting by the door as if someone were going on a trip. He opened the parlor door carefully. "Dad?" he called, but the room was empty, the fire going in the stove.

He was relieved when he found his grandmother at the kitchen table, sipping a cup of coffee. She was studying his drawings from last night that he had stupidly left on the sofa for her to find. He'd drawn a cartoon, caricatures of all of them. He'd accentuated his father's high forehead, his thinning hair, his crooked teeth, the way he held his neck with the palm of his hand, like he was perpetually rubbing at some pain. His grandmother he'd drawn with gnarled, farm-woman hands clenched in the lap of her gingham dress, an old woman with a prunelike face, permed hair, and breasts sagging like watermelons in a feed sack.

"Oh, it's you." She started in her chair. The shotgun his father had cradled all night leaned again against the stove, in ready reach.

"Sorry," he said. "Where's my dad?"

"Oh, he went off with Dallas to get those tires fixed. They'll be back before long."

He tiptoed around the table, hoping to collect the criminal cartoons.

"I've been looking at your drawings. You're a real artist. This is me?" She held up his rude caricature.

"It's nobody." Dean winced.

But she wouldn't let it go. "But it sure looks like the way I feel after last night. La, I didn't sleep a wink."

Dean didn't know what to say. She seemed about to cry, an old woman wiping her fingers behind the dusty lenses of her spectacles, her pursed, wrinkled lips trembling. "Grandma, it's okay. It's not you," he mumbled.

"What? What did you say?" She brightened at her name. "I didn't hear you?"

"Uh, Grandma," he said again and winced. Dean of course thought kindly of the old woman who gave him cookies and money at Christmas and always argued that Eva wasn't doing enough for him, her favorite and only grandchild, but just saying the word "Grandma" made him feel like a little kid. He hadn't called her "Grandma" in years, generally addressing her as "uh, you."

"You must be hungry. You like eggs, bacon? How about I fix some biscuits?"

"Sure," he mumbled, taking the opportunity to stuff the incriminating drawings into his pocket.

Ruth waddled around her kitchen on stout ankles, purple veins zigzagging down doughy legs, wheezing in her heavy bosom as she busied herself at the stove.

He couldn't keep his eyes off the shotgun. "Did your grandma really shoot a man?" he asked.

142

"Why, yes, I believe she did. Least, that's what she told me when I was a little girl. She was the oldest and most wrinkly person I'd ever seen and she scared me."

Dean had always thought of Ruth as the oldest person on the planet when he bothered to think of her, but behind all the wrinkles and age spots, he suddenly saw another person, her real self, the little shy girl, speaking.

Ruth's hand clasped his, but he pulled away from her surprisingly powerful grip.

"I can cook you eggs every morning if you like, now that I'm coming to stay with you. You won't mind me coming to stay with you for a while?"

Dean's mouth fell open. He didn't know what to say, but he could imagine what his mother would say.

"I talked to your father. I mean, what with Wanda out there. We agreed it would be for the best."

Dean sat there. Was he supposed to nod? Maybe he should say something. "Is this Wanda really crazy?"

Ruth sighed. "Some people just have too much devil in them. She might not ever been quite right in the head. Some folks say she might've had a child along the way, but mistreated him so bad, the county people had to come take him to foster care, but that's just talk. So don't you go repeating that."

Dean wasn't sure who he would share that with.

"Just wicked," Ruth went on. "She was into moonshine way back when, probably into the pot now. Dallas says Junior Gudger arrested a few folks over on the River Road with a sack full of seeds. I wouldn't be at all surprised if they was coming from her place."

"You mean marijuana?" Dean asked.

"World has changed since I was a young'un and about all a body had to worry about was getting into the liquor. Now there are all these drugs. TV news makes it sound like just about every child in Altamont is smoking marijuana." His grandma gave him a sidelong, suspicious look like she wanted to ask him a sharp question, but then her thin lips pursed even more primly as she thought better.

Dean kept his head down, poking at the greasy sausage patty on his plate. Bad enough his mother grilling him about drugs, he didn't want to be having this conversation with a sweet but irritating old woman like his grandma.

She loaded his plate. At home, his mother was glad when he downed a

143

glass of OJ and peeled a banana. Here, breakfast was a full meal: bacon, sausage, scrambled eggs, grits with butter, and biscuits with butter and jam. She poured him cups of coffee and didn't even worry the caffeine would make him hyper like his mom did. "I do like to see a man eat. Back in the day, we used to eat pork chops and steaks, pancakes, eggs, all in one sitting. If you didn't eat breakfast you were likely to wilt by midmorning with the sun sitting on your shoulders."

He pushed away from the table, stuffed and ready to return to bed. He laced his fingers behind his head and sighed. She smiled when she cleared the dishes. "Full, eh? Maybe that will last you this morning while you're out there painting."

"What?" Dean hadn't planned on work.

"Royce said you need to finish painting before he and Dallas get back. Go on now, get your job done."

And he realized that without his mom running interference, his grandma could order him around. He wasn't a special guest to be entertained. He was expected to pull his weight, and strangely enough, he felt good about that. At last here was an adult trusting him to be responsible. And painting wasn't bad.

The air was crisp and he could see his breath steaming in the cold as he trudged to the barnyard. A sheen of ice coated the rickety wooden ladder where he'd left it against the side of the barn, but his sneakers didn't slip as he climbed the rungs with the paint bucket.

Damn barn from hell, he would paint it all red. He trembled half from the cold, half from the fear. What if Wanda was out here watching? She roamed the woods at will, jumping out at his dad whenever his back was turned. Yesterday, he had been on the ladder, when she came running through the open bay of the barn, a flash of red plaid coat and gray hair under a battered hat, like a scarecrow in the neighbor's field come to life. For an old woman, the same age as his grandma, she sure could move. He'd heard the wheezing before he saw the crone come at a slow run, swinging the bush ax at the empty air. "Damn your eyes, damn you to hell," she kept cussing. All she had to do was look up and she would have seen him, but she didn't.

It was his secret. They had all been so rattled, his dad and Grandma and Uncle Dallas, he didn't think it wise to worry them further. Besides, Wanda was gone so quick into the woods with only the green leaves of the laurel waving in her wake, Dean wondered if he hadn't dreamed it all.

144

29

Is this Royce Wilder?"

"Yes," Royce said, his ear to the receiver.

A man's voice, with a strong twang, a familiar voice out of the sticks, deep in the holler. "Royce, it's me. Remember me?"

"Umnh, yes?"

"You don't have a clue who this is?"

"No." He thought of hanging up. "Junior?"

"Lucky guess!" Junior Gudger laughed. "How long has it been, twenty years?"

Not long enough. Junior was kin he'd never be shed of, a second cousin once removed in that web of bloodlines that only his mother could trace and untangle. Ruth's oldest sister, Ada Rominger, had married into the Gudgers, over into Bethel, other side of George's Gap. Junior had been a couple of years behind Royce in the grades, a gangly kid with big teeth and jug ears.

"How's the appraising business over in Altamont?"

"Junior, I'm kind of busy here. Is there something I can do for you?"

"You're right, this ain't a social call." Little Junior shifted into his adult self as Sgt. J.R. Gudger of the Zebulon County Sheriff's Department. Royce could almost hear the creak of the leather belt with its holstered gun across the khaki belly.

"Your mother called, wants to swear out a warrant against Wanda

McRae. Says she broke into her house two weeks ago and stole her sugar. Said you knew about this."

"I heard someone in the house."

"If that's true, why didn't you report it two weeks ago?"

"We thought it might blow over. Be best if Mama moved in with us until her nerves settled."

Junior made a ruminative sound, like he was sucking his back teeth. "You're putting me in an awkward situation. I don't see any proof, any evidence it was Wanda. Your mama's word against Wanda's."

"Who do you believe, Junior?"

"Ain't up to me, it's what a magistrate might believe."

"If it wasn't Wanda, then who?"

"Might be some gang activity. I seen graffiti on the backside of your mama's barn, driving down the road the other day."

"Is that still showing? That was no gang, but my son. Don't worry, he's going to paint a second coat over it."

Junior chuckled. "Kids, they can be a handful, I tell you. Our oldest has about caused me and Lucy a couple of heart attacks. Just last year he rolled his Jeep off the side of George's Gap and got flung into the creek. Good God, I was thinking the worst when I came driving along and fished him out of the creek. Thought my boy was dead, but he lifted his head out of the creek where he'd been baptized. 'I'm sorry, Daddy,' he tells me. 'Don't be mad.' Hard to be mad at a broken arm, three busted ribs, and a ruptured spleen."

"He's all right now?"

"Oh, completely recovered, and completely useless. Going out and hanging out at the Altamont Mall. You know a teenager. Maybe him and Dean can get together?"

"Well, fortunately Dean doesn't drive yet. Not looking forward to the day."

"Yeah," Junior agreed on his end. "Now look, Wanda McRae is one mean old lady. Ain't nobody going to argue with that, but I'm not sure meanness is against the law. Besides, she might have some bone to pick with you. Lucy tells me you once snuck up there and pitched rocks at her house."

"Oh, yeah, well, once," Royce hemmed. What else had Lucy told him?

"Maybe you can talk to your mother. Get her all calmed down. Like I was telling Lucy, neighbors ought to be able to sort things out before the law gets all involved."

"I'll talk to Mama and I'm keeping an eye on Dean."

"Good talking with you, Royce. Stay in touch, now, you hear?"

Daylight savings had ended. Bedraggled bed sheets masquerading as ghosts still hung from neighborhood porches, the jack-o'-lanterns losing their fleshy grins as the Halloween pumpkins turned to puddles. On the drive home he fretted, unable to get Junior's twang out of his ear. Why had Junior told him that horror story about his boy's wreck? He couldn't help imagining Dean behind the wheel, hurtling down the streets toward home, taking the curves too fast.

Eva always said they hadn't spent enough time together, father and son. Fact was fathers and sons don't like each other's company. Jake Wilder always made him fidget and he recognized that same restlessness in his offspring. Didn't they try the Scouts once, that father-and-son camping trip with the Webelos, that intermediate rank between Cubs and Boy Scouts? Dean had come home that Friday with a mustache, a miniature Snidely Whiplash curl on his upper lip. He had been on the school bus, clowning around with some twerp kid who talked him into drawing his own facial hair. Dean of course never bothered to check that the marker was permanent ink. Eva had scrubbed at his newly haired lip with a washcloth until his nose started bleeding.

So Royce and Snidely ventured out into a damp October weekend. Saturday morning, after a miserable night on surplus army cots in the bunkhouse, they tried to build a fire from the wet woods. Dean put the bacon strips into the tin frying pan and broke the two eggs with plenty of shells over the cold meat and began to burn their breakfast over the small flame. "No, that ain't gonna work," Royce groused. He saw a twitch in the little boy's cartoon mustache. Then the rain came down. They headed back to the bunkhouse and ate a couple of candy bars. It had been their last real outing.

He wheeled round the corner at Chester Place and pulled slowly into the drive, waiting for the remote garage door to open like a drawbridge into one man's castle. The paneled partition rose slowly as his headlights played over Eva and Dean inside the empty garage, frozen in a pose, their eyes wild at his approach. He switched off the diesel engine and heard Eva light into Dean again. "You're in trouble now, mister," she blessed out the boy, her voice bouncing off the concrete slab and the drywall now that they had tossed out all of Royce' rusted and molded treasures.

"I told you it wasn't me." Dean raised his hands in futile surrender.

"What happened? What's wrong?" Royce was out of the car, wading into the crossfire, not sure who needed protection and who prosecution.

"I'll tell you what's wrong. Your son here has defaced St. Dunstan's property. How could you? Where your grandfather was headmaster!"

"Damn it, Dean."

"It wasn't me."

"Let's go inside and discuss this."

Eva balked. "We can't. Your mother."

'Like she can't hear us out here?" Dean said.

"I've had about enough backtalk from you." Eva shoved his shoulder, pushing him toward the car. "Get in!"

"Hey!" Dean staggered backward, then lunged forward, his own fists clenched. For a second, Royce was afraid he was going to hit Eva.

But Eva didn't back down. "I said, in the car."

They got into the Mercedes, slamming the doors, Royce behind the wheel and Eva in the front, the prodigal slouched in the back.

"So tell me again what happened," Royce said.

"The assistant headmaster called to say our son defaced the chapel. You know that low stone fence around the outside, the one with all the green moss? It now evidently has red and yellow graffiti."

"Those aren't even my colors," Dean argued.

"You have colors?"

"Usually red and black. I don't like yellow."

"Usually? You're still spray-painting after what you did at your grandmother's?"

"Why can't you chill?" Dean said. "It wasn't me."

"Chill?" Eva shrieked. "Don't tell us to chill, mister. We're still your parents."

Royce hadn't seen her that pissed when Dean went to town on the barn in Beaverdam, but put a little paint on Episcopal property and she went ballistic. "Who then?" Royce demanded. Dean's small chin ducked, the bravado sinking with him. "Names. We need names, mister."

"What about those boys you've been hanging out with at lunch?" Eva asked. "Tucker somebody, right?"

Like interrogating a stump or a stone. Royce resisted the urge to reach over the seat and shake some sense into him. "Speak up."

"Do you have any idea what kind of trouble I'll get into if I snitch?"

"Do you realize what kind of trouble you're in if you deface school property?" Eva said. "This is not a public school where they're just going to suspend you. St. Dunstan's can kick you out and press charges for vandalism to private property. Do you want a criminal record?"

Royce's mind raced with all the possibilities. Dean wasn't even old enough to drive. Here he was talking colors, like he was in a gang. What was next, drugs?

"Why don't you go ahead and get divorced like most parents and quit taking everything out on me?" Dean jumped out of the car, slammed the door, and ran inside the kitchen.

Ruth poked her gray head into the garage. "Everything all right? Why are you sitting in the car?"

Royce shooed her inside with a wave of his hand. "Give us a minute, Mama. We're just talking."

"She's driving me crazy, Royce. What are we going to do?"

"It's just been a couple of weeks."

They sat in the garage, listening to the soft knocks of the diesel engine cooling under the hood.

"I've got to go. I'll be late," Eva said.

"Not the shelter again."

"It's a good cause. Besides, Michael is still talking about hiring a full-time staffer to head the soup kitchen. I think that could be me. We need the money."

"Not if they kick Dean out of St. Dunstan's. There's always public school, that's free."

"Don't say that."

The cooling engine knocked under the orange hood. Royce suddenly had a terrible thought, and worse, let it out into the open. "That priest, you're not fooling around with him?"

"Good God, Royce. Is that what you think of me?" She got out of the car, then ducked down, issuing her last orders for the evening. "There's a lasagna in the freezer you can microwave. The salad is already in the refrigerator. There's not much cleanup involved, but if Ruth insists on washing the dishes, let her. She doesn't know how to operate the dishwasher.

149

I'll be back in the morning. Don't think this is over." She slammed the
door and left by the garage, headed out to her SUV and her appointment
with the homeless.

He hated an argument that would last through the night. He hadn't ever
seen her so angry, but he had just accused her of adultery. Now what? At
least she had said that it wasn't over. Meaning what? Their marriage. Yet?
He stared through the cracked windshield of the Mercedes at the back
wall of his garage, now bare after they had sold off all his loot at the yard
sale. He missed his hoard, his home, the way things used to be.

30

They resumed their argument the next morning. "I can't live like this," Eva restated her position, hands clasped around the thick, white coffee mug, trying to wring out the last warmth.

"What?" Royce was still chewing the last of his bacon.

"Are you listening?" She put down the mug, a tremble in her hand. Too little sleep last night at the shelter: she had been up since six, shooing the homeless out into the streets, into the bright light and low possibilities of Saturday, before she returned to her own unhappy home.

"It's only for a little while," Royce tried to argue.

"Two weeks is a not a little while."

"It's like a vacation. A chance to rest her nerves."

Through the glass door, they watched Ruth slowly rake the leaves from the oaks in the backyard. Royce usually got out his leaf blower and blew them all down to the curb for the city to collect, but Ruth missed her chores. There was no garden to weed, no chickens to feed, no wood to chop—not that she was capable of those chores back home. The first frost did away with her garden. Her chickens had all gone years ago, a few feathers and pellets of shit and feed left in the cold coop the only reminders, and Dallas took care of the wood for her last summer.

She complained that she was cold at their house, that she didn't care for their heat pump and missed her woodstove that she could fire to a tropical eighty degrees when she wanted. She'd made the mistake of leaving

151

behind Jake's old cardigan, so she had commandeered Dean's black, hooded sweatshirt, just as she had taken over his room, banishing him to sleep on the pullout bed in the den where he watched TV late into the night or listened to his music with the headphones. It was like having two difficult children now at different ends of the spectrum.

"She's driving me crazy," Eva said.

Just the other day, Eva had come home to find that Ruth had defrosted the refrigerator and thrown out most of the leftovers, scrubbed the inside with warm soapy water, doing her country best, but forgetful of the carton of ice cream she had taken out of the freezer, placing it on top of the refrigerator to melt in chocolate dribbles down the door. "I was just trying to help out around the house," Eva mimicked her mother-in-law. "You know that little voice she gets? 'Don't,' I told her. 'Please don't.'"

Royce pushed his plate aside and rested his arms on the table discouraged with the day's direction, his Saturday turning surly. "She's not going back up there, not while Wanda's on the prowl. She called the law on her."

"She did what?"

"I got a call from Junior Gudger. You know, Lucy's husband."

"Oh, Lucy, your long-lost sweetheart."

"Eva, that was a long time ago."

"What did he want?" Eva sipped her cold coffee again.

"Mama had called him about Wanda McRae. Wanted to take out a warrant against her for trespassing. Junior said he couldn't do anything without proof, and since no one ever saw her in the house, there's nothing he can do."

"So Ruth won't ever go back, is that what you're trying to tell me?"

"It's really not safe," Royce hesitated. "I didn't tell you or her or anybody, but I put radon tests in the house. That's what I was doing inside the house when Wanda broke in and stole the sugar."

"Radon? As in radioactive?"

"I wanted to see if Landrum was telling the truth. He said all the properties up there were off the charts as far as radon contamination, which means they're not worth a dime for residential resale."

"So there's no money?"

"Maybe on Landrum's terms. Who knows?"

Ruth had a long barrow of the leaves arranged and was pulling loose leaves from the tines of the rake. She was a peasant at heart, used to shoveling, hoeing, mucking, digging. She stopped only to pat her red nose with a wad of tissue she pulled from the sweatshirt pocket, then started again. Royce suspected she was singing, as she usually did when she got caught up in work, likely a hymn about bloodshed and repentance rather than grace. She loved those bloody Baptist anthems from the Broadman hymnal. Life was short in this vale of tears, reward elsewhere in rumors of heaven, as dead leaves flew around her in the brilliant blue here and now.

"What about a nursing home?" Eva said.

"We can't afford that. I'm not sure she can."

"You can't keep putting off the inevitable. You did this when your father died. Acted like a good little boy when you had your talk with Dallas. He was the executor and you still don't know what that estate is worth. You don't even know what Dallas is doing with all her money."

"For God's sake, Eva. This is Dallas you're accusing. He's her brother, family. If you can't trust your own people, who else is there?"

"What about your wife, Royce? For once in your life, what about your wife, your child? Not just your parents, your childhood, all your guilt. For once, can you think about us?"

He licked his lips, wiped his mouth, folded the napkin again on the plate. "I'm always thinking about us."

"We never make love."

"That's hard to do when my mother is just down the hall." That and talking constantly about his mother didn't put him much in the mood.

"Royce, you can't live in fear of your parents all your life."

Just then there was a flash in the backyard that caught the corner of Eva's eye. "Oh my God."

Royce was already out the door, running down the steps, across the yard, where Ruth had set fire to part of the grass and a small pile of leaves that was gusting over the yard, flames everywhere.

"Mama, what the hell?"

"Son, don't you cuss at me."

He grabbed the rake from her and swatted at the flames, stomping on it. Burning leaves were spitting across the yard, hurled by the breeze, embers flying against the side of the house.

Eva called 911, "We're on fire, please hurry," then ran outside for the hose and turned on the faucet. She held the spray and soaked his legs as he danced about.

"Not me. Aim at the fire!" he screamed. They had everything out when they heard the sirens.

Royce was as red-faced as the truck that pulled into his driveway, the firemen in their turn-out suits and vulcanized boots. The fire marshal followed in his pickup after the crew had called in the false alarm. Tramping through the yard, looking at the damage done, wearing his official look of concern, chewing a corner of his brushy mustache. "There's a burning ban in effect, Mr. Wilder. You're fortunate, you know."

"I know." He waited for the marshal to rip the pink citation from his clipboard. A fine for one hundred dollars, plus court costs, a grand total of $212.50.

"Thank you," Royce said, his face on fire.

31

You actually had to call 911?" Michael laughed. He was enjoying himself, reclining in his leather chair, his hands laced behind his curly hair, that smile growing wider as she told her story.

"It's not that funny."

"I'm sorry. That's really awful." He came back down to earth and, with a squeak in his priestly chair, put on his concerned look. Michael had his mannerisms, but he was easier to read than Royce, whose face grew blanker as their troubles piled up. It had all started with the yard sale, it seemed, trying to clear away all the clutter of their marriage, but she hadn't expected to discover such an empty space between them.

"My door is always open to you, Eva, but you might need professional help. Have the two of you ever tried counseling?"

"He won't go. It's bad enough that he thinks I come to see you," she sighed, then breathed deep. Here in his office, in his sweater and khakis, his tweed jacket, he was just Michael, not Father. He kept his collar in a desk drawer. The smell of a man, a priest—the incense from the sanctuary clung to his stole hung on a hook on the heavy oak door together with a cassock back from the dry cleaner, shrouded in crinkling plastic, sleeves pressed like wings, a deflated angel.

"So why are you here, Eva?"

She had no idea. Maybe a confession? She had had a dream about Bill Clinton, the new president, of all people, and he had been very smooth.

But she couldn't very well admit that to Michael, could she? Not with his pious look, his hands clasped with his index fingers pointing to the dimple in his chin. Did they have a course at seminary how to look so serious? She laughed.

"What's so funny?"

"Nothing," she said and her eyes teared up. "I'm sorry."

"I know things have been difficult." He leaned over and patted her knee. "Have the books helped?"

All the right books on the shelves, just the ones her father would have had, but then more eclectic titles reflecting Michael's mind: Buddhist sutras, Merton, of course, *Course in Miracles*, Castaneda. He had lent her books he thought would speak to her situation. Nouwen. Underhill. Julian of Norwich.

"All shall be well and all shall be well. Right?" She daubed at her eyes with a tissue from the ever-present box on the desk. She was supposedly seeing to her soul, but reading mystics of the Church, with all their platitudes of faith in things unseen, did little good with all the things seen in her home since her mother-in-law had moved in. "If you ask me, the dark night of the soul sucks."

He laughed, that warm sound that warmed her as well.

"Royce went so far as to accuse me of flirting with you," she watched the quick cloud in his eyes, but he didn't blink. "The real reason, though, I've been coming around is not you, but the work. My job is winding down at Keep Altamont Beautiful. I thought there was a paycheck in helping the homeless. Maybe Christian charity would pay, but then it really wouldn't be charity, would it?"

Now it was Michael's turn to look out the window of his study. The bright leaves slipping away from the trees, already half naked in the November blue, fled with last month's tourists. Only the homeless remained behind.

"I'm sorry. I didn't mean to mislead you about the job. It was part-time only, and I'm still arguing with the diocese about funding any staff for the soup kitchen and the shelter. Work in progress."

"I like the work. I like you," she admitted. "Being around you reminds me of being with my dad."

"He was a priest too, you said."

"It reminds me of home, all this." The smells of men in robes, the incense, the burnished wood, the slow motes of dust falling through prisms

156

of afternoon sun shot through stained glass in deserted sanctuaries. "It makes me feel closer to God, somehow." Then she added, "If he still exists."

"That's all right. I'm not so sure at times either. That's why they call it faith. Doubt is often healthy for one's faith. In Zen Buddhism there is a saying: 'Great faith, great doubt, great enlightenment.'"

She nodded, having no idea what he meant. Michael was a beautiful talker.

Then he asked a far too pointed question. "How's your husband handling all this?"

"Badly. I don't know. He's always been prone to dark moods, but lately, it's just like talking to a stone." Eva held her breath, then admitted, "We're not intimate much these days."

At least Michael lost his smirk. "Could be depression. Has he been to the doctor?"

"Of course not. He's like his whole family. They'd rather die than go see someone."

It terrified her that her husband was turning into his father. A sullen, stoop-shouldered man, furrows plowed into his forehead, the widow's peak thinning, hair growing in his ears, his paunch thickening. He actually flinched when she touched him. He was so cold, like a distant planet orbiting far from her.

"You're somewhat distant, Eva." Michael seemed to read her thoughts. He rose from his chair and stood in front of the window, blocking her view of the trees that she had been staring at again as she talked. "Do you love Royce?"

"Yes, of course..." her voice trailed off. "Nineteen years is a long time." She was slowly shredding the tissue in her fingers, confetti of confusion in her lap.

He walked behind her, his hands on her shoulders, gently kneading the tired, tight muscles. Such a grip she kept on herself. She felt herself melting every time he touched her. "You have needs. It's all right, Eva. It's biblical to be heartsick, lovelorn—but you have to communicate them." He took a Bible from his deck, sat down, and thumbed through until he found the passage he wanted. "'O that you would kiss me with the kisses of your mouth. For your love is better than wine...'" He turned the thin onionskin page with a rattle. "'Your lips are like a scarlet thread and your mouth is lovely. Your cheeks are like halves of a pomegranate behind your veil. Your two breasts are like two fawns, twins of a gazelle that feed among the lilies...'"

She closed her eyes and heard his soft voice. "'My beloved put his hand to the latch, and my heart was thrilled within me. I arose to open to my beloved and my hands dripped with myrrh, my fingers with liquid myrrh upon the handles of the bolt. I opened to my beloved, but my beloved had turned and gone. My soul failed me when I spoke. I sought him but I found him not: I called but he gave no answer. The watchmen found me as they went about the city; they beat me, they wounded me, they took away my mantle. I adjure you, O daughters of Jerusalem, if you find my beloved, that you tell him I am sick with love.' The word of the Lord," he said, and she heard him close the book.

"Thanks be to God," she whispered by rote. The silence was worse in the close office than in the sanctuary. Her skin was flushed and it was hard to breathe. "Shouldn't we pray or something?" Eva said. Anything to fill the silence, that ache inside her.

"Prayer is two hearts in communication. It's not words. It's...it's..."

Their heads moved closer, touched. She could feel his brow touching hers, the scalps mingling, and his luxuriant head of hair. Amen, she heard the whisper. Eyes still closed to what they were doing, they raised their heads, bringing their faces together. His mouth met hers hungrily. Her mouth fell open in sweet surprise and his tongue darted in.

32

Realty Ranch, can I help you?" Royce answered automatically, his ballpoint pen poised over his paperwork on a thirty-acre farm property he was appraising. Not that anyone wanted the barn, or shed, or even the farmhouse, or the mile or two of good fencing that surrounded the property. The farm would likely be scrubbed off the face of the Earth, down to the red clay, and refashioned into a subdivision of townhouses and apartment complexes within sight of the Interstate.

"Royce, that you?" He knew that ingratiating drawl as soon as Junior called his name, and Junior Gudger was the last person he needed interrupting his day.

"I'm kind of busy, Junior. This better not be about Wanda again."

"No, listen, you better get over here to the hospital. There's been an accident."

In the emergency room Dallas and Junior sat in the rows of chairs like they were just waiting for a ride. But Dallas was missing his boots for some reason, his shirt was torn, and one side of his face had turned blue with a bruise. His uncle wasn't sitting in a four-legged chair, but in a wheelchair.

"You look like hell," Royce said.

"I'm sorry, Royce. You didn't have to come all the way over here for me."

"How else were you going to get home?" he asked, then turned to Junior for the real news. "So, how bad was it?"

"He ain't dead, but that's just a miracle once you go sailing of the side of the mountain below George's Gap. He about flipped that old Ford down the mountainside. If he hadn't hit a big tulip tree with the grille, he would have gone all the way down to Beaverdam Creek. I'm telling you, Royce, this old boy here is real lucky." Junior slapped the old man's knee, and Royce knew it must have been bad, how they were fanning Dallas' spirits that had come close to being snuffed out like a match in a windstorm.

"We still need to fill out a report." Junior held up an engraved ballpoint pen and the sapphire in his community college class ring flashed, but the marks he made were heavy and crude. He had an associate's degree from Altamont Tech in Criminal Justice, four semesters learning how to do all the paperwork and the protocol for criminal investigations. He drew the curve of the road with arrows pointing the truck's direction of travel. A branched figure represented the tree, a rectangle was the truck, a toppled stick figure stood for Dallas thrown from the vehicle.

"So you were headed west over George's Gap at approximately 3:35 p.m.?" Junior asked.

"Reckon so." Dallas pressed a thumb to his loosened dentures. Dried blood blackened the split lip where he'd hit the steering wheel. "Lord, I drove that route for thirty years as a mailman. I could about do it with my eyes closed: every twist, every curve, slide right up to the mailbox and poof, in goes the catalog, the *Progressive Farmer*, the rural coop bill, the letter from the grandchildren moved off to the city. I've driven that road so long, I reckon I've done it in my sleep a few times."

For God's sake, Dallas. Don't say that to a deputy, even if it is Junior.

"So you crested the gap, heading towards Beaverdam. Then what happened?"

"I must have missed that curve. Blue sky is all I remember. The view opens right up and you can see straight to Tennessee. Took a wrong turn."

Of course he hadn't been wearing the seat belt in his truck when it went over the side of the Buckeye. What if the car caught fire, I couldn't get out, could I? Dallas always argued. The only thing that saved him was his hard skull bouncing off the web of shattered windshield.

Junior flipped through his paperwork, looking perplexed. "We're about done, but I'm gonna get a pop from the machine. Anything for you, Royce?"

"I'm good."

160

Dallas waited until Junior had walked off, then waggled a crooked finger for Royce to come close. "It was Wanda again," he whispered. "She took a swing at me with the bush ax, busted the window." He felt the side of his hair. "Think I got glass in my ear, it rings so bad."

"Did you tell Junior?"

"No, keep it under your hat."

"He's the law, you need to let Junior know."

"That's nobody's business but me and her. Don't you tell him a thing, swear!" He held him close, his bloodied mouth and old-man breath, the hard, veined hand clutching at him. "Swear now, son."

Junior returned, sipping a Diet Coke, nectar of law enforcement, sugar substitute and caffeine, to sub for the cigarettes they wouldn't let you smoke anymore at Altamont Memorial, now a smoke-free campus. He gulped his soda, his Adam's apple rising and falling in his throat, like he was parched. "Okay, here's the awkward part. Did you have anything to drink this afternoon? Anything alcoholic in nature?"

"Junior, you know that Dallas doesn't drink," Royce said. "He's been a deacon about all his life."

"I've got to ask. It's part of the report here."

"No, sir, I signed the pledge years ago," Dallas bristled. "You can look it up in our family Bible."

"Any medication that might cause you dizziness or blackouts?"

"Well, I do have high blood pressure. Doctor makes me take pills, eat bananas for potassium. Ruth says sometimes my medicine makes me kind of foolish."

"You're not going to ask if he's got Alzheimer's or if he's crazy, are you?"

"I'd probably forget the question," Dallas joked.

"I believe that will be all, Dallas. Sign here."

"You're a good boy, Junior. It was my fault, so if you have to write me a ticket, well, you're just doing your job." Dallas cocked open his one unswollen eye, scrawling his name, holding his tender lip between his yellow teeth, then handed over the clipboard.

A nurse in a floral smock crept up in her silent sneakers and squinted at her own clipboard. "Mr. Rominger? You care to join me?"

"Why, that's the best invitation I had all day." He tried to wink, but it was hard to do with a black eye swollen shut. He made as if to rise up out of the wheelchair.

161

"No, hon, you just sit still. I'll wheel you on back."

"I can walk."

"I know, but we want you to ride. You've been in quite a spill from the looks of you."

"Bet I have to pay extra for all this."

"Oh, honey, you better believe it. We're not a cheap hospital," said the middle-aged nurse, knowing how to flirt with old farts and how to slap away their too friendly hands. Anything to keep the customers from believing the worst, that maybe half of them that were rolled upright through those automatic doors wouldn't come back out, except feet first.

Junior was flipping through his paperwork, no longer smiling. "This is not good. Dallas hasn't had his license renewed. I was going to let him slide, but you get them sumbitches at DMV involved, it gets sticky."

"He's still a good driver. He's only seventy-two. Maybe he doesn't see or hear as well as he did, but he's sharp as a tack."

He was lying, of course. Dallas' driving had terrorized him when they took the slashed tire to town to be fixed. Dallas negotiated every blind curve down the yellow lines. "There's something else you ought to know," Royce was breaking whatever silly solemn oath he had sworn to his uncle, but he had to tell the truth. "He says it was Wanda what caused him to go off the road. Did you ever talk to Wanda about the break-in?"

"No," Junior sighed.

"Look, that woman's crazy, and I'm afraid she's after my family now. You better do something about her before somebody gets killed."

"Calm down, Royce, and don't be telling me my job. I'll go talk to Wanda."

"I appreciate that." Royce never wanted to be beholden to his old rival, but he was grateful.

Junior took his papers to Zebulon County and Royce waited in the waiting room, checking his watch, slowly going through back issues of *U.S. News & World Report* he'd already read. Dallas was taking an awfully long time for what he thought was going to be routine tests. "Um, where's my uncle, Dallas Rominger?"

The receptionist called on the phone, and Royce could tell something was wrong as the corners of her mouth pulled downward and her eyes squinted. Her voice was colder now when she talked to him over the receiver. "He's in surgery now. They had to rush him to the OR."

162

"He was fine just a few minutes ago."

"I'm sorry. You better sit down. The doctor will be out to see you when she can."

❖

"Mr. Wilder?"

It was probably dark outside, not that Royce could tell from the windowless waiting room they had sat in for what felt like forever. Eva drove Dean over after school, picking up Ruth at the house before they headed to the hospital.

The surgeon came out, her mask down to show a serious Asian face. Dr. Kim explained they had put a stent in his skull to relieve the swelling on his brain. The words washed over Royce with his family, what was left of them, all huddled in this antiseptic hallway. Dean looked pale, Ruth haggard, Eva held herself, arms crossed under her breasts. They leaned in, listening to the petite woman, no taller than a child, who had held Dallas' life in her small hands, under her delicate scalpel, and brought him back from darkness.

He was lucky was what they repeated to themselves after the hallway consultation with Dallas' surgeon. From what they were able to decipher among all the medical terms—edema, hemorrhage, cranium, stent—that rough ride down the brushy mountainside, the scrape with Wanda, might have saved his life in the end, or at least put him in the proximity of the hospital when the hemorrhage in his brain began. Could he have hit his head against the wheel or even the windshield? Could that have caused the tiny clot inside his thick head to suddenly explode? He was in a drug-induced coma for now. There might have been some brain damage, Dr. Kim couldn't be sure. "There might be some decisions that have to be made down the road."

"What kind of decisions?" Eva dared to ask.

Dr. Kim shook her head sadly, sincerely, to suggest these were only the hardest choices to be made and all in Royce's hands. She had the paperwork Dallas had filled out in the ER naming Royce Wilder, his nephew, as holding power of attorney in all of his medical care, entrusted to keep all his secrets as well. But all he could hear were Dallas' last coherent words to him: "Don't say a thing, swear!"

163

33

Hunched over the handlebars of the stolen bike, pedaling slowly up the grade, Kyle tottered on the bicycle and headed for what was once home. In the afternoon the highway gleamed like it was paved with diamonds. If he had his bearings right, Beaverdam lay twenty miles away as the crow flew, probably twice that by this road that corkscrewed to the county line, over George's Gap, and down into the cove before branching right into a dirt lane winding back to a cabin he had left as a boy more than thirty years ago with not even a look over his thin shoulder.

One by one, a car or truck or trailer sailed by him. Kyle clamped his hat to his head, but the bike wobbled in the wake. He'd never owned a two-wheeler those first few years in Beaverdam, where there wasn't any flat ground for a body to learn to balance. He'd done better at foster homes along the way, but had fallen more than a few times this morning.

The road grew rougher. Pavement crumbled off into a gravel shoulder running by a deep ditch and the red clay bank. Kyle rode the edge of white paint as traffic whipped around him. A mufflerless Mustang rumbled alongside. Kyle eyed the primer-coated door a few feet from his left knee while wrestling to keep his wheel on the white line. A beer bottle exploded on the pavement. The car roared away, trailing drunken laughter.

The bike veered off the road, skidded over the gravel, jumped the ditch, and headed halfway up the embankment. Kyle felt himself suspended in midair, the wheels shooting out from between his legs. Then hard ground

164

buffeted all breath and thought from him. He landed on his back. Trees and clouds reeling overhead, he believed he might throw up, but he couldn't turn his head to the side. There was a catch in his throat, yet nothing came out. He gasped; no air would go down.

Last time he fell this hard, he had seen swirling constellations, bright lights. He could make out his mama's face, her fist, and a frying pan. His head hurt so bad, she must have walloped him with both. Face and jaw had no feeling. A finger touching his earhole came away red and wet. He could see her mouth moving, but he could hear nothing. Only by the look on her face could he tell she was screaming.

He sat up very gingerly. The bike lay on its side, spokes still spinning, but the gears were wrapped with the broken chain. Kyle cradled his head until it and the wheel both stopped going around.

"Caw. Caw." A large black bird settled on the roadway and commenced to poke its yellow beak at a flattened carcass.

That could have been me, a red spot on the road. Kyle gathered himself gingerly. Nothing broken, just bruises along his backside. The bird squawked, then flapped away to watch from a nearby pine. He squatted by the road kill. No telling what it once was—possum, small dog, maybe a rabbit. All that was left was a dark smear of blood, fur, and bone on the blacktop. Its dinner interrupted, the scavenger had left behind a black tail feather. Kyle twirled the vane under his nose. The faint smell of shit turned his stomach. He hadn't eaten anything decent in days. Kyle kept the feather for a souvenir, thrusting it into his hatband. He tipped his hat to the former owner cawing in the pine tree.

"Caw. Caw. Caw." The crow launched into the air, following the sweep of transmission lines that marched from tower to tower up the hillside. Beaverdam lay in that direction, a long day's hike cross-country. He turned his unbroken neck up and down the highway. No car had passed since he'd landed in the ditch. He could stick out his thumb but he doubted any Samaritans would stop for a bloodied man. The only thing traveling this stretch of road was a wind that raised a flap of fur from the roadkill.

Kyle untied his gear from the handlebars. Some other scavenger would be along to pick its frame, and at least the wheels had gotten him halfway home. He leapt the ditch and climbed the bank, boots kicking footholds in the crumbling clay. He grabbed a hold of a sapling at the top but fell backwards when the roots pulled free. He tapped the dirt from the roots and stripped the green shoots. A good stick would come in handy for the walk ahead.

He set a slow pace uphill, flailing a path through the tall grasses beneath the electric whispering of the wires. Rabbits and titmice flushed from under his boots, a sudden burst of fur bounding away, a blast of feathers in the warm air. Chicory and dock, pokeweed and marigolds raised a last green stink before winter. He swatted through clouds of gnats, smelling and hearing and tasting them. He passed through a bramble of blackberry. Mindful of briars, he popped the juicy buttons into his mouth, staining his chapped lips and raw fingers. He rested in a bed of broom straw trampled by deer. The sun was warm and he closed his eyes. He awoke to white clouds slicing through the black wires.

He crested the hill shortly before sundown. Hard enough to catch your breath when the view was so breathtaking. The electrical pylons crossed the ridge and descended through poplars and maples turning red and gold. The sun barreled over the far ridge, burning the horizon. After all this time, the outline of the mountain still loomed in his mind, dimly recalled like the shape of the suckled breast. He was drawing closer to home. Behind the Buckeye, one day ahead, lay Beaverdam.

Kyle spread his blanket over the concrete footing of the pylon. He heard the wings flapping overhead. "I know you're there."

"Caw. Caw. Caw." Then silence.

The sun slipped over the Buckeye and its shape was lost in the night. Stars came out one by one, the bright planets to the east and west, then overhead the constellations, names he never knew. He gathered a pile of twigs, dead pine and birch, and lit a small fire. He rubbed his hands over the flames. Tonight's clear sky promised to be cold with frost by dawn.

Kyle listened to his stomach rumble. His throat was so dry, he could scarcely swallow. The climb had dehydrated him. He would need water tomorrow if he were to make it much farther. There was nothing to eat and nothing to do but shiver.

Nightlife commenced in the shadows: eyes shining in the dark, high-pitched yelps, deep growls, sudden screeches. Prey fled from the pounce of claws. Scents were in the air. In the night, everything got confused. Feeding and breeding sounded the same. He'd heard long ago that a scream could mean pain or pleasure. How many times had he heard his mama cry out when the Shadow Man showed? He wanted to cry too, but kept his fingers jammed between his teeth.

She used to make him sleep out on the porch, always tying his leg when putting him to bed. "I can't be keeping my eye on you all night long, so you get into any mischief, this rope will let me know."

She bound him other ways too, scared him with her tales about a bogeyman rising through the planks to snatch little boys unless their mamas kept them roped in. Actually, she was the one afraid he would leave her. When he grew old enough to know the Shadow Man wasn't real, that the rope was unnecessary, he found she had other lies, other lines cast into the darkness.

The soft tread on the floorboards woke him, not on the porch, but inside the cabin. Kyle slipped from beneath his blanket and went to the window. Inside, he could see his mother's narrow bed. She sat on the edge, her shoulder blades pale as wings. Then, in the corner, he spied a shadowy figure slouching toward her. At first, it seemed to creep on all fours, then crouched, then stood erect. As the figure crossed into a shaft of moonlight, the shadows dropped away from a naked man.

Wanda lay back, her loosened hair spread over the white sheets, pulling the Shadow Man down on top of her. Kyle wanted to turn his head, to close his eyes, but he also wanted to look, to see what he knew dogs, cats, chickens, cows, and the rest of the barnyard did without compunction, what seemed horrible between humans. His mother's eyes rolled to the whites and bloody roots, her mouth opened on yellow teeth and full of darkness. The Shadow Man rode her hard, his skinny butt bucking. His naked limbs glowed like luminescent Indian pipe in the gloom of the woods.

And as the boy he was watched, his penis blindly stirred. Afraid, he tried to push it down but the unruly erection kept growing in his hand. He couldn't help himself. His knees trembled. Something was about to break inside him. Her head banged against the bed, her face tilted upside down. She spied his contorted face in the window. She screamed his name.

"Caw. Caw. Caw."

He stirred stiffly under his blanket crusted with a faint frost. The hoarse bird cry woke him. Dark wings circled overhead. "I ain't dead. Can't have me yet." His knees popped as he stood and stretched. He kicked the metal tower to get feeling in his feet. The only way to get warm was to start walking. Shouldering his bedroll, he started down the slope.

167

The frost burned away under the morning sun, but the sky stayed overcast. The leaves that had glittered like gold and rubies yesterday rustled brown and dead in the woods on either side of the meadow. A mile down, the power lines crossed a stream seeping through the tall grass. Kyle knelt, pushing aside the brown stems. He pressed his lips to the dank earth and slowly lapped the water.

The black bird spiraled over the pylons, then shot over the treetops, winging its way toward the familiar ridge.

Kyle wiped his mouth. Time to leave the path cleared by the power company and start bushwhacking up the Buckeye. He remembered when Wanda took him to these slopes to dig for ramps for eating, sassafras for spring tonics. In summer they had sought out the ginseng prized by Chinamen. In fall they picked huckleberries on the rock faces and galax at a penny a leaf for the Christmas wreath trade.

Sometimes in these woods she'd played a scary game of hide and seek with him. Kyle must have been no more than six or so and ordered never to leave her sight, but the rules didn't apply to her. Turn his back for an instant, and she would be suddenly, mysteriously gone. He called her name and panicked when he realized she'd left him here, alone. He'd run from tree to tree, frantically searching, his voice rising. When he passed the right trunk, an arm would shoot out, a hand clap over his crying mouth. "Gotcha. Scared you, didn't I?" So she did. Wanda still scared him.

The soft carpet of needles sunk under his step and the point of his stick. Ground gave way to granite. Soon, Kyle was scampering up and over boulders and barriers, walls and cliffs that rose out of the hillside. Scaling one shelf, Kyle pulled himself up by the gnarled branches of a rhododendron. He pushed through the thicket and into a clearing. In the weak light, a stand of plants shuddered in the breeze. Their stalks reached tall as a man with jagged leaves and heavy buds. The air seemed to buzz with their green musk.

Kyle unsheathed his knife and severed the top. He sniffed the sap on his blade. Potent marijuana. Snakeweed. Just one whiff made him dizzy. He shook his head, but rocks, sticks, leaves commenced to crawling underfoot. The buzzing began at his feet, a vibration that rose through his legs and spine and clutched at his heart. Coiled in brown and dusty rings about the stalk only a foot from his foot, a timber rattler sang its deadly warning.

He retreated slowly. Around the base of every pot plant slept a snake. Here was a harvest that would keep a street of dopers high for a month, not by accident surrounded by sidewinders. On these slopes, Wanda had kept her still, cooking a whiskey as deadly as snake venom. The Buckeye was legendarily too snaky even for the bravest of revenuers to come bust her operation. When sugar grew dear and the rain had rusted away the metal tubing, Wanda must have happened upon another, more lucrative market.

Kyle stuffed the buds of the marijuana into his bedroll, watching for an opening in the slither of snakes. The largest rattler flicked the air with a black tongue. With half its six feet coiled around the pot plant, the poisonous patriarch raised its blunt head, ready to strike. *Run, fool, run.* It was like his head telling his feet what to do, but they were frozen in his boots, his toes curled tight. The snake struck at the same time he hurled his walking stick, and the riled serpent scraped its fangs against hard wood rather than sinking into soft flesh.

Kyle didn't quit running for twenty yards and stopped to rest against a tulip poplar tree, bent over, trying to catch his breath and trying not to puke. His hands were still shaking. A little more warmth from the sun today and that cold-blooded reptile might have been quicker to strike. Kyle found himself another suitable stick, long enough to rustle the leaves at least five feet in front of every step he planted uphill. Slow going this way, but he wanted to make sure to meet no more of his mama's fanged friends.

The summit was deceptive. Rise gave way to another rise as he kept climbing. But after the sun had gone over the top, Kyle saw the mountain's namesake ahead. A buckeye spread its canopy where forest gave way to high pasture. A few strands of rusted barbed wire marked the county line and the beginning of Beaverdam.

A sign nailed to the tree trunk gave notice of no trespassing. But Wanda paid no respect to property, coming and going as she pleased. Out of mischief or pure meanness, she used to cut fencing, pull survey stakes, and yank such warnings from trees. The nails she kept for herself. She especially hated the signs telling her not to set foot on private property, not to trap game or dig plants on public domain. "Who do they think they are? Animals can't read. They go eating each other and rooting for plants, but let a body come do it, they put up a sign saying no." Of course she never came across such a sign unless she had a sack of ginseng dug from the National Forest or a few rabbits slung over her shoulder.

Rain had faded the posted sign into an illegible yellow patch, like a fungus grown into the bark. He couldn't tell to which side of the fence the warning applied, and like his mama, he wasn't about to pay any mind. With his stick he lowered the top wire of the fence and stepped into Beaverdam.

The sun was sinking into the clouds massed over toward Tennessee. A single shaft of light struck the floor of the cove, glinting from the tin roofs of houses, barns, and sheds. The hillsides were dotted with grazing cattle. Beaverdam Creek below was a shiny ribbon plaited through stands of timber and the bottomland of tobacco and cornfields. Beside the bright water, a pickup traveled the winding road. Kyle imagined a boy standing in the truck bed, face in the wind, beating his fists raw against the roof of the cab, hollering for joy to be leaving this place.

His boot slipped on the fallen buckeye littering the ground. Kyle picked one up and split the green hull with his thumb. The tender brown nut popped into his palm. The nut was fragrant enough to eat if you didn't know it was poisonous. But buckeyes were good luck. Pocketing his find, Kyle thought maybe his luck was bound for a change after so many years. He headed downhill toward home.

34

Dean was tired. His hand was cramped and slick with sweat inside the heavy rubber gloves two sizes too large, as the excess flapped on his fingertips like loose flesh on small bones. He scrubbed away with the bristle brush that the janitor had lent him, the lye solution starting to dissolve some of the paint deep in the pores of the rockwork that separated the campus green from the chapel. His eyes watered from the fumes in the bucket. He sloshed more solution onto the rock, then he bent and scrubbed harder. He thought he had been through an hour ago, but then the assistant headmaster suddenly loomed over him, pointing out the inadequacy of his efforts. "There, I can still see it."

Dean worked steadily, his blazer folded on top of the rock wall so he wouldn't get any telltale spills on that at least. Last thing he needed was his mom to go crazy over buying a new blazer. She was in a grumpy mood ever since Grandma had moved in.

His mother had banished Ruth from the kitchen, forbidding her from cooking, since she had burned a pot. It was the second trip a fire engine had made to their house in less than a month. Grease fire in the damper scorched the tiles. Insurance, his father said, was sure to cover it. None of the adults seemed to be talking to each other. When he came up for the adult air, unhooking his headphones from his ears, there was nothing but a soured silence in the room, like milk gone bad they had all drank but refused to spit out.

"Nice elbow grease there." Tucker hopped up on the wall for a seat, kicking his feet only a few inches from where Dean was working.

Perry was on the other side, leaning over, hanging his head down. "Say, you missed a spot."

"Thanks."

"So what did old man Smoot want?" Tucker asked.

"Nothing," Dean said.

"You seem like best friends now. You were in his office a long time the other day."

"He was asking about the piece we tagged at the fish house. Said the cops had called."

"Yeah, what did you say?"

"Nothing."

"You're a good man, Wilder. Keep up the good work." Tucker hopped down and slung his book bag over his shoulder. "You coming, Fairy, I mean, Perry."

"Go to hell, Fucker, I mean, Tucker."

Laughing, the two strolled off to their dorm room, leaving Dean behind to clean up their doing, their handiwork. He hadn't ratted them out. In fact, the rest of the school thought he was the tagger. Each afternoon this week, the other boys had watched him after class carry out the scrub brush and the bucket and set to work. Their nods were curt in his direction, but admiring, all except for Tucker, the one guy he wanted desperately to notice him.

35

Royce drove up the weed-cracked drive to the peeling Victorian that housed his appraisal office. He had company. Lawrence Landrum sat in the porch swing, the chains creaking ominously from the bolts rusted overhead, swaying his three-hundred-plus pounds and the heavy black satchel on his lap with pushes from his surprisingly small feet in their alligator-skin loafers. "Mr. Wilder, I was afraid I'd gotten the time wrong."

"Sorry, I'm running late. Had to drive over from Beaverdam."

"Not to worry. I've just been watching your neighbors go by." Landrum hoisted himself from the swing, which jerked back and forth on its suddenly slack chains.

Royce wouldn't have wanted to be sitting out in the cold for the last half hour, and not in this neighborhood, which was marginal at best in the realtor's euphemism for seedy. Royce suspected a crack house in the vicinity, given the low, rusting sedans circling around the bad block, where men in hooded sweatshirts and backwards caps loitered at all hours on the corners. But at least he'd never had a break-in after he added the iron bars over the ground-floor windows.

"I've also been admiring your architecture. Queen Anne, I'd said." Landrum patted the newel post, waiting for Royce to fit his key into the front door.

"Old is all I know." Royce suspected a sad tale attached to the rambling story with its milled fretwork, the dry rot under the gabled eaves, the rounded turret ready to lock up an addled aunt or crazed uncle. "I once heard the original owner lost everything in the stock market crash. Committed suicide, they say. Drank lye in the kitchen."

"Haunted, huh? How quaint."

"Nothing to be afraid of. Come on in." Royce snapped on the lights, and everything was as he had left it, the same paperwork and problems awaiting him. He shivered. The antiquated furnace in the basement hadn't kicked on since he'd dialed down the thermostat. He hadn't been in the office since Dallas took a turn for the worse, busy between the hospital and home.

"Nice," Landrum politely lied.

"A regular pack rat's trap," Royce repeated Eva's constant complaint.

"No, you've quite an eclectic collection." Landrum studied the mounted longhorns, the tattered Navajo rugs, the bronze Remington replicas of broncobusters and defeated warriors.

"You can take it all off my hands if you want. It came with the business."

Royce didn't share the kitschy western taste of Jimmy Fink, his previous boss. Half snockered, old Fink would rock back bowlegged on the rounded heels of his cowboy boots, which together with a bolo tie and a white Stetson made up Fink's marketing scheme for Realty Ranch. After Jimmy marinated himself into an early grave, Royce had bought the business from Jimmy's widow. He'd kept the name, but dropped the corny motto. "Home on the range where no discouraging word is heard." He couldn't bear to throw out Fink's cowboy memorabilia, though.

"Some of these items are quite valuable if you find the right collector, of course. Ah, I recognize this." Landrum turned the radio dials and ran a fat thumb along the sleek bevel of the cherry console. "You're still enjoying your trophy from the auction?"

"Doesn't work. I probably paid too much for it."

"Nothing to be ashamed of. Nostalgia is a weakness of mine as well," Landrum said.

"I wouldn't call it nostalgia." Royce settled behind his desk into the cold, loud leather of his chair. "I like to think of it as just respect for the past. Everything's changing so fast."

"My point exactly. Change is good. We live in exciting times, even as we speak," Landrum huffed in that breathless voice of his, warming up to the idea. "I think the coming decade will prove more transformational

174

than anyone can possibly imagine. We're watching the analogue age passing into the digital. The Internet is in its infancy. Think of every home with a computer connected to the wider world. Department of Defense is talking about opening the satellite system to commercial use. Imagine being able to pinpoint your location anywhere on the planet. Imagine making a phone call from your car or walking down the street. It's all coming, and soon."

"Sounds like Big Brother, science fiction. I kind of like the way things are, the way they used to be. Progress is not all that it's cracked up to be."

"Yes, progress." Landrum's chair squeaked as he shifted his bulk on its spindly legs. "Mr. Rominger used to mention progress a lot in our discussions. How is your uncle?"

"Hanging in there, even with the ministrokes he keeps having in the hospital."

"Did he get the flowers Mr. Matsui and I sent?"

"Yes, thank you. They were very nice. Uh, I thought Mr. Matsui might join us."

"Matsui had to fly out early for the Thanksgiving holiday. A family gathering. I believe his father may be dying."

"I'm sorry to hear that."

"Yes, sad, I suppose. It happens."

Royce thought better of asking about Landrum's own family. Had he been raised by hippos or a herd of circus elephants, was his uncharitable thought. He glanced at the time, then rubbed his bony wrist where the watchband itched his skin. Eva always said he wore his watch too tight. "Look, I don't want to take up your time. The reason I called, I'm having second thoughts."

"For the radio?" Landrum's plump fingers drummed the top of the useless radio. He smiled to let Royce know he could take this as a joke.

"I was talking about my property in Beaverdam."

"I made you an offer that you refused. What changed your mind?"

Royce laid out the radon tests recovered just an hour before from his mother's house.

"Pretty bad, huh?" Landrum said.

Royce had been late because he kept going over the instructions trying to decipher their meaning. The chart that came with the instructions showed the risk of lung cancer at various levels of exposure. At four pic-

175

ocuries per liter of air—the acceptable level approved by the U.S. Environmental Protection Agency—the mortality rate ran between one and five in a hundred. The chart illustrated the number with a phalanx of identical smiley faces, except for three grinning skulls. At 20 picocuries the chart pictured about a dozen death's heads. At 200, the chart was divided almost evenly between smiles and skulls. All of Royce's readings were off the scale.

"This is what I need to know. What is the worst that could happen in Beaverdam?"

"Worst-case scenario?" Landrum smiled. "The statistical blip of Beaverdam's abnormally high cancer rate draws attention from the Centers for Disease Control. They call the EPA. Lo and behold, they discover the place is contaminated. Everyone exposed to radon is at risk for lung cancer. I would anticipate another Love Canal, but all natural. No big company to blame, no dumping of toxic chemicals. No one at fault except Mother Nature. Federal government condemns the land, evacuates the residents who get a paltry something. I negotiate with the feds and get the land."

"What's our best-case scenario?"

"I buy the land directly from Dallas Rominger, Ruth Wilder, you, and any other property owners. Skip Uncle Sam as the middle man."

"Then what? Turn Beaverdam into one big uranium mine?"

"You're right that uranium is the source of the radon, but we have all the uranium we need. Beaverdam is the perfect site for long-term ground storage of radioactive materials. They've been manufacturing warheads over at Oak Ridge for decades now. In the final analysis, I'm in the trash business, trying to bury what nobody wants in their backyard."

"But it's home," Royce said.

"No. Home is where you can safely live. Beaverdam is not that place, never has been." Landrum rummaged through his briefcase. "Here's something else I came across in my research. The Cherokee used to call Beaverdam *atsilu anitsasgli-yi*—the place of ghost fire."

"Ghost fire? The Indians knew about radon?"

"I'm sure that they didn't grasp the physics of the problem, but they understood that something residing in the earth made any inhabitants of that valley grow sick over time. Ironic, isn't it? Oh, here's something else that's interesting." Landrum slid over a sheet with graphics. "The logistics

176

can be mind-boggling given the time scale we're talking about. Uranium has a half-life of a half million years. The problem will be with us for quite some time to come. How to warn future generations that a dangerous substance has been buried on the land? What happens if they don't speak the King's English? Some post-historic anthropologist has been doodling these in his spare time."

Royce studied the drawings. A skull and crossbones. A stick figure flinging up his arms in distress at the wavy rays emitting from the ground. How many visual representations for poisoned ground could carry the message into the millennia ahead as the radioactivity decayed, the atoms bombarding any trespassing flesh? Ghost fire was as good as any.

Royce pushed the drawings across the desk. "Radon or not, that land is still worth more than what you were offering Dallas or me."

"I'm not sure your uncle is in much of a position to negotiate."

Landrum shuffled through a sheaf of files and folders in his satchel. He had all the data at his fat fingertips. "I see he took care of your mother's tax bill before the accident, but there are still some outstanding liens on some of his properties. If your uncle recovers, God knows we're all rooting for that, he faces some rather serious costs, beyond what Medicare would cover. Let's be realistic, an old man living far from a hospital on a mountain farm might present difficulties. But then nursing care can eat you alive."

"I'm not sure that's any of your business. It wasn't even mine until Dallas put me in charge of his living will."

"Wait, you hold the power of attorney for your uncle?" The fat man didn't know everything about Dallas' private affairs.

"Yeah, he signed me up." Royce coughed. He still wasn't over the crud that Dean had brought home. Either that, or the cancer that had claimed his father was wracking his lungs. Crawling in that deadly dust beneath the house, collecting the tests, he'd had a strange tickle in his throat and a gnawing at the pit of his stomach.

"That's a nasty-sounding cold," Landrum leaned back.

Royce blew his red nose on a bandanna. "Sorry. That's why I didn't shake your hand." Royce wished he had a neat white, starched handkerchief instead of this red rag waving in the fat man's face.

Landrum dug through his portfolio of briefs, cases, deeds, sales agreements, and tax records, and produced a series of documents he laid out on the desk now. "Mr. Rominger was coming over the mountain to close on the deal when he met with his unfortunate accident. With your power of attorney, you can sign these for him and make sure Mr. Rominger gets his money."

Royce flipped through the papers, squinting at the fine print. He had seen enough property transfers and contracts to spot the red flag buried in the legalese and boilerplate. "Eviction? Who are you trying to evict?"

"We understand a woman has been living there for a number of years, with some question as to what kind of claim she has there. We need the title free and clear."

"Wanda McRae. What happens to her?"

"I'm sure the county can take care of her, social services, someone. It's not like she's your family."

The papers were crisp and orderly, adorned with tabbed arrows showing where he should sign or initial. But his familiar pen, which had signed off on a hundred deals, resisted, the ink running dry as he scratched out his name, carved it into the binding document. "Is this really legal?"

"Oh, I think we can argue that it is if it ever comes to court. I don't believe it will." Landrum tore a voucher from his leather checkbook and handed over a check made out to Royce.

"What's this for?"

"Oh, it probably would be illegal if it were ever proven to be a quid pro quo in our discussion here today." Landrum drummed his fingers on the radio. "Let's just say you sold me a five-thousand-dollar collectible."

36

Eva daydreamed in front of the window with an open book on her lap. Nouwen saying something inspired and depressing. Words for a sad time. Trying to understand God's will. She had read over the sentences again and again, but found no consolation. Instead she watched clouds float by in the blue sky beyond the slotted window as she absentmindedly ran the slender gold necklace across her lips, chewing on her mother's old cross.

Dallas snorted, bringing her back into the small hospital room where he lay leashed with an array of dripping tubes. His head was swathed in gauze and looked enormous, inhuman, like they had somehow transplanted a watermelon onto his shoulders during surgery. The stent was buried deep into the bone, nearly touching the brain, while along his arms, into his nose and mouth, and down between his legs hoses and tubes fed in and out of him, filtering in clear fluids, siphoning off colored discharges. They wanted to put a feeding tube into his stomach. That was the next step, the next decision.

At times he expelled a long breath that sounded ultimate, a rattle that seemed to climb out of his thin ribs like a ladder, lingering in the sterile air overhead and then lost in the glow of the TV that was always on, flickering its bright images of happy lies over their wan faces, repeated room by room, floor by floor, through a hospital of sick and dying people. But he lived, and Eva and Ruth and Royce took their turns by his bedside, waiting for what was next. There was no job at Keep Altamont Beautiful to worry about. Eva had plenty of time on her hands.

There was a soft knock at the half-open door. Eva was surprised to see it wasn't the nurse on her hourly visit, but Michael.

"May I?" He closed the door behind him, but not completely, a clergyman's crack there, a little privacy from anyone passing in the hallway.

She put her book down. "What are you doing here?"

"I was over making my rounds. There are always some hospital stays among the parishioners. The nurses at the station said you were in here."

She stood but kept the bed between them, the broken old man between their warm bodies, just in case. "You shouldn't be here."

"Why not? It's what I do," Michael tried to strike their lighthearted, ironic tone from their Fridays together. "What we're all called to do: visit the sick, the suffering."

He approached the old man in the bed with more curiosity than compassion, Eva thought. It was a textbook problem for a seminarian. Apply comfort to the afflicted with sufficient pressure thusly. Secure with prayers on either side. Wait for the divine will.

"So how are you doing?" He did not look at her directly, but kept his warm eyes on Dallas. "I've missed you on Friday evenings. I've missed you, period."

"Don't."

"I'm sorry if I was too forward, if I misinterpreted your signals in any way."

What signal was it she had given that caused a priest to lean over and kiss a married parishioner in his church office? Her mouth still burned. Sometimes she closed her eyes and fingered her lips. Just then, Dallas, what was left of him in the bed, made a noise, a moan that startled the both of them. "He does that sometimes," Eva said. "It's a good sign, the nurses say."

They watched the steady rise and fall of the caged life pumped by the ventilator. It was easier to talk without looking at each other. "I wanted to beg your forgiveness if in any way I offended you, moved too fast, was too forward." He finally dared to meet her gaze, holding his mouth in a neutral line without a flicker of the ironic smile. "I may have thought you had certain feelings. I may have been mistaken."

"Oh, hello. Am I interrupting?" Royce came in, running a few minutes later than he had said he would, as usual. He had stopped downstairs in the hospital cafeteria for coffees, one black for him, one with cream for

180

her. He set the coffees on the tray that went unused by the bedside and wiped his hands on the sides of his pants, then reached out for his handshake. "Royce Wilder. Glad to meet you."

"Father Michael Donovan, St. Thomas'."

"Glad you could stop by, though he's not Episcopal," Royce pointed toward the patient in the bed. "If he woke up, you'd scare him to death with that collar. Eva has said wonderful things about you, feeding the homeless and all."

"Eva has done wonderful work herself at St. Thomas," Michael said. "They all miss her."

"Too bad that job as a grant writer didn't work out," Royce said.

"Yes, as I was just telling Eva, maybe we can get some funding for that position sometime in the new year."

"God's will and all, I reckon," Royce rubbed it in.

"I just wanted to stop by, see how everyone was." Michael edged toward the door.

"We still get that prayer, don't we?" Royce blocked his way. "We could use all the help we can get."

"Certainly." Michael held out his hands.

Royce stood his ground, bowed his head, clasping his hands before him to signal this should be a straight-forward, stand-up-straight Baptist-type petition with none of that Episcopal kneeling or laying on of hands, no group hug.

Michael got the message and flipped through his Book of Common Prayer: "O God, o lover of souls, bless and hold in your hand the heavy hearts of your children. Lift up your healing arm, o Lord, and make our brother Dallas whole if it be thy will. Keep and protect and comfort your children, Royce and Eva, and show them the way, Amen."

Michael couldn't resist the flourish of crossing himself afterwards, a little Episcopal touch, Eva thought.

"Amen," Royce said. "That was a good one."

"Appreciate your visit, Father," Eva said.

"I can stop in again next time I'm over here," Michael said brightly. "Unfortunately, we have a lot of parishioners here as patients."

"That really won't be necessary," Eva said, showing Michael to the door.

"So that was your friend?" Royce asked.

"No," she said, leaning her weight against the door, her arms crossed behind her. "Just another priest."

37

The mailbox at the highway had no name, but everyone knew who lived on top of the hill. The patrol car turned up the rutted road, spitting gravel beneath its worn shocks. Junior Gudger rounded the last curve of rhododendron and saw the cabin perched on the hillside. Where the road ended, he parked next to the rusting hulk of an old Ford up on cinder blocks. Kudzu grew through the windows of the wreck and sprawled in and out of the open trunk. Frost had burned back the shoots, but next summer the green would swallow the car and claim the side of the unpainted shack.

Chickens pecked in the dirt yard. The flock clucked at his approach and retreated under the porch. The bowed steps groaned under his shiny oxfords. Junior's lip was moist, the film of fear he could always smell when he walked to the speeding car he'd just stopped, wondering if the driver had a gun under the seat. But he hated this even worse, the eviction notice on his clipboard.

Junior felt it just above his paunch, that hollow hole where the wind blew right through and the cold crept up the nape of his neck. Lucy had said she'd seen only one boy brave enough to go to Wanda McRae's front door and throw a rock right at it. Royce always was braver than him, older and better. He'd made good his escape to the other side of the mountain, over to the big city, raking in the big bucks appraising fancy houses.

Even Junior could appraise this door looked like trouble. Rattlesnake hides six foot long hung from either side of the frame, their dried tail buttons scraping the porch. Faint initials GTT were carved in the wood, but the door had seen more recent abuse—a white gash from some sharp blow. Junior blew on his knuckles before rapping them against the hardwood. No one answered but the chickens clucking beneath the porch. He was about to knock again when he heard a metallic ringing in the air echoing up the mountainside.

Around the cabin in back, underneath the trees, he found a man chopping wood. The man was using a bush ax, with its pointed blade shaped like a can opener, better for hacking kudzu than splitting kindling. The man balanced a poplar log on the ground. He swung the ax overhead, right hand sliding down the shaft to meet the left. The blade split the grain, the poplar popped in half. Kicking aside the kindling, the man positioned the next log.

"Beg pardon," Junior Gudger said.

The blade fell, but the log splintered rather than split. The woodcutter scowled at this interruption. With his bearded face and long hair tied under a bandanna, the man looked like any of a dozen composite sketches of wanted fugitives Junior had on his clipboard.

"I'm looking for Wanda McRae."

The woodcutter said nothing, but swung his ax again, ripping the unseasoned wood. His arms were lean but muscular under the torn sleeves of his T-shirt. Underdressed for the weather, he had to keep moving to stay warm.

"And you are?" Junior asked.

"Kyle McRae."

A thin splinter of wood landed on the toe of the deputy's shiny oxford. He noted that Mr. McRae chopped wood with an attitude like he had a grudge against trees. "Related to Wanda McRae?" Junior pressed.

"Her son." The blade fell. Kyle's boot steadied the log as he wrested the ax free.

"I was born and reared here in Beaverdam. I never knew Wanda had any children. None I ever met in church or school." Lucy came back from the library about to bust with the news. No one remembered Wanda with children, none that ever showed up in school or Sunday school, but plain as day in the print, and now here in the flesh.

"I got sent to foster care when I was about seven or eight. I don't rightly remember."

"And your mama, she's inside?"

"She is, but she's feeling poorly. Not up for company, I'd say."

"I'm afraid I have bad news for her." Junior held out the envelope embossed with the state seal. "Eviction notice. I'm sorry, but this property has been sold and must be vacated within thirty days."

Junior pushed the letter toward Kyle but he still wouldn't take it.

"She ain't sold no land."

"Legal owner is the power company now. They've bought the north end of the cove, I understand, from a local family."

"She's always lived here."

"Maybe you should talk to your mother about this."

Kyle glanced over his shoulder at the cabin. Veins worked on his temples. "You said a local family sold it?"

"Mr. Rominger."

"Dallas Rominger? I thought he was dead."

"No, Dallas ran off the road and hit a tree. He's down in the Altamont hospital, still hanging in there, tough old cuss that he is." Then Junior added, "Your mother, she wasn't out by George's Gap that day, was she?"

"Like I said, she's been feeling poorly." Kyle set the next piece of poplar. "I've been up the last couple of nights tending the fire. It's like to wear me out." He split the wood with one blow, not at all like a worn-out man, the deputy noted. "Why you asking all this?" Kyle said.

The deputy hemmed. "Uh, it didn't go into the accident report but Dallas claimed your mother was at the scene, waving an ax at him, running him off the road." At Kyle's angry look, he quickly added, " 'Course now, he did suffer a concussion and he's getting on in years. And your mother, she must be what? In her seventies?" Kyle shrugged. "Well, I didn't think it sounded right for a lady that old or sick to be running a truck off the road. None of that made it into the official report."

"You mean you didn't have any proof." Kyle dropped the ax. He wiped his hands on the sides of his low-slung jeans, then bent to gather the split wood. Junior remembered the long slash along the passenger side of Rominger's truck, but he said nothing. Kyle rose with his arms loaded with wood. "Could you get that ax for me? Don't like to leave things outside to rust."

He headed toward the cabin, leaving the deputy to pick up the ax and check the blade's edge. Kyle was waiting on the porch when Junior

184

brought the ax slung over his shoulder. "Just lean that right there." Kyle nodded toward the bottom step. "If you don't mind."

"You need to take this." Junior held out the eviction notice again. Kyle lowered his arms still full of wood. The deputy slid the envelope between the kindling.

Junior glanced toward the door decorated with snake hides. "Those are some real monsters you got nailed there."

"They grow big under the porch."

"GTT," His eyes traced the initials carved into the door. "My granddad told me about that once."

"Been there as long as I can remember."

"Gone to Texas. They used to carve that as a sign to let the neighbors know where they lit out for. Sometimes they just left in the middle of the night, running from the law."

"I wouldn't know," Kyle said.

"Yes, sir, that's one historic door you got there," Junior said. Then he added, "I'm sorry about all this trouble. Your mother sick, now this news. I'm truly sorry."

"I reckon sorry don't change the law."

"No, sir, it don't."

Kyle waited on the porch, still holding the wood and the eviction letter, until Junior got into his cruiser and drove down the road. His arms were aching when he turned and kicked open his historic door.

"You're letting the cold in! Shut that damn door!" Wrapped in a quilt, the old woman wore a fedora pulled tight over her skull. He pushed the door to with his boot. "I could hear you out there talking. What did you tell that man?"

Kyle said nothing, but went to the woodstove, dumping his load of wood along with the notice on the floor. Opening the grate, he fed kindling to the dying fire. He was about to shove the letter in the fire along with the wood. Damned cop telling them to get off the land, who did he think he was? He opened the letter and read over the fine print, legal mumbo-jumbo...last legal notice...thirty days...thereafter trespassing and subject to criminal prosecution.

"I could have hollered, you know," Wanda said. "He would have come running in, taken one look, and arrested you. You can't hogtie a body like this."

She spread her quilt like tattered wings. Coiled in her lap was a rope with one end knotted around her scrawny ankle, the other leading to the metal leg of the Franklin stove.

"He'd be glad you were on a leash." Kyle stuffed the letter in his hip pocket.

"What's that?"

"Nothing. If I showed it to you, you'd burn it like the rest. Why you think I had to tie you down?" He had come in from hunting squirrel yesterday, and she was feeding the fire with all sorts of old photographs and papers, even stacks of money, muttering that no one, not even Kyle, would find out her business. No telling what he needed to know had gone up the chimney in that rich smoke.

He untied the rope from the leg of the woodstove and pulled it over to a cane-bottom chair. He straddled the chair backwards, propping his arms and chin on the ladder-back. He gave the line a little tug. She glared balefully. With her neck wattled with wrinkles and that fierce beak of a nose, she looked like a buzzard ready to peck his eyes out.

"You always were the sassy one. I never wanted you. I took all sorts of roots and herbs hoping to flush you out, but you just kept growing inside. I never wanted you one bit."

Kyle ignored this nastiness. "You were wrong about Dallas Rominger. He's in the hospital, but he ain't dead. Not yet, at least."

"Son of a bitch." Wanda laughed, a sound that flew out of her throat like a flock of starlings. Moments such as this he wished she were dead. Soon, very soon, she would be, she would have to be. But he didn't know how he would feel if she were to fall over right now.

"It's growing late, I best fix supper." He played out a length of rope into the kitchen and tied the end to the refrigerator handle. He didn't want her slipping out while his back was turned. He knew whenever he wasn't looking, she was working at the knot around her leg. Good thing her knuckles were swollen with rheumatoid arthritis, her teeth too loose to chew through the binds.

The squirrel soaked in a cast-iron pan, vinegar tenderizing its tough muscles. He rinsed the meat under the hand pump in the sink. Flour had gone bad with mites, so he couldn't fry it, but he did find a yellow onion and a shriveled potato. He diced the vegetables into the pan with the squirrel, added salt, pepper, water. At least the stew would be something to eat to keep flesh covering bone.

Wanda might be dead now if he hadn't happened along when he did. As it was, she'd nearly killed him. He had followed the flapping crow home, the bird laughing in the laurel hells along the road. In the dusk, he'd stumbled up the road in ruts washed deeper than he remembered, and around a curve of rhododendron, he'd seen the cabin. The glass panes of the still unbroken windows burned with the last fires of sunset. She was sitting on the stoop, scratching briar scrapes on her arms and legs. The bush ax propped beside her. She was smaller than he recollected, her hair gone white under the man's hat she wore. "He's dead," was the first thing Wanda said. "I killed him."

"Killed who?"

"Why, Dallas. I killed him. Just like this."

The last light flashed off the blade as the ax swung through the air. He felt a faint wind brush his throat. She swung the ax on around until it bit into the front door right over the initials.

"You killed him?" Kyle stepped back as if she had cut his head off and he didn't know it right yet.

"I said so, didn't I?" She pulled at the ax head wedged in the door.

"Oh, mama." Kyle shook his head still stubbornly attached to his neck.

Her eyes widened with recognition. "You!"

"Yes, it's me. I've come home." He climbed the steps and helped pull her battle-ax free.

Luckily, she hadn't greeted him with the shotgun he found leaning inside the door. The cabin reeked of unwashed clothes, spoiled food, urine, and the sweet smell of marijuana. The seeds of her harvest were scattered everywhere, dried beads that popped underfoot. Hardly any food in the house, or wood for the stove, but money abounded, layering the shelves of her pantry, inside her pillowcase, a plastic bag of bills stuffed into the oven with its burned-out electric element.

He carried the skillet with the squirrel meat out to the front room, careful not to slosh the broth on the floor. With an old rag he removed a lid from the woodstove and set the pan over the fire to cook. "It'll be a while." Kyle went into the kitchen to untie the rope. He came back and looped the rope around the rung of his chair, then sat down.

He stared at the iron pan on the stove. Suddenly he ducked, covering his head, remembering the blow after all these years. She'd caught him sitting on the porch, shutting out all the noise, not paying any attention,

187

probably staring at a cloud or a tree or some foolishness. But for a second, he had left the squalor of this place, the threats of his mother. She hit him from behind with the same pan she'd just cooked his dinner in. When he came to, he saw her face, her mouth moving. He knew she was screaming at him, but he couldn't hear her for the ringing in his ears. He raised his hand to the side of his head then gazed in amazement at the bright blood he found on his fingertips. "Do you hear me? Do you?" She'd shaken him until the words made sense to him.

Now the only noise in the cabin was the boil of the stew on the stove, the snap of the fire, the creak of Wanda's chair. It would seem almost peaceful if he didn't see the quilt moving, her hidden hand worrying the knot underneath.

Kyle dug a finger into his right ear, reaming out yellowed wax. His hearing was off since he'd gone hunting yesterday. He could still hear the echo of the shotgun off the mountainside, the drop of the squirrel from the treetop onto the forest floor. Taking the main road home, he had come across the wreck on George's Gap. He slid down the hill for a closer look. The pickup had come to rest against an old tree. The spider web of broken glass was flecked with blood. He traced the bright scratch along the door, like a white scar in the blue paint. Inside the truck, he found a bunch of unbruised bananas, a bottle of pills prescribed for Dallas Rominger. Wanda might find them useful so he carried them home.

He checked on the squirrel, poking his knife into the tough meat, the soft potato. Seemed done enough. "Careful. It's hot." He set a bowlful in her lap but she wouldn't eat. She rocked her chair, staring off into whatever world she saw, unconsciously plucking at that rope that bound her to the present.

Kyle bit into the squirrel's hindquarter. His back molar cracked against something hard. He fished with his fingers in his mouth, found the piece of shot under his tongue. Wanda wasn't eating. She stared at the fire in the stove, lost in thought. Perhaps he could sneak up on her like she did and hit her with a hard question she couldn't help but answer. "Why you want him dead so bad?"

Wanda squinted at the fire. "He was fixing to tell."

"Tell what? Tell who?"

But she pursed her lips. The bowl of food was growing cold in her lap. Kyle could see one hand edging down her calf, trying to reach the knot on her ankle.

"Remember," he held out the rope, "I'm always at the other end."

Whenever he left the room, he checked on the whereabouts of the shotgun, the ax. He couldn't even trust her with a fork for her dinner. He took her bowl of cold food, scraped the bones back in the pan, and set the leftovers inside the stove like a safe. When he returned, she was playing innocent, her hands idle in her lap. He gave her a banana. "Dessert."

After dinner deserved a smoke, but Kyle had ran out of tobacco leaf long ago. He still had the marijuana he cut on the Buckeye. "I nearly got bit by your buddies when I found this." Kyle rolled a joint and lit up.

"Huh," she grunted. "Snakebite would serve you right."

Leaning out of his chair, he passed the joint. She hissed between her teeth as she inhaled.

"How long you been dealing?"

"How long you been dumb?"

"So what happened to the rest of the crop?" Kyle took the joint from her, took another long hit.

"Sold it off to some Mexicans." Wanda absentmindedly peeled the banana. "Fools couldn't speak plain English. I saw how they crossed themselves when they seen the snake hides hanging by the door. Those fellers were too chicken to give me any trouble."

The smoke did funny things to Kyle's hearing. He rubbed his good ear, trying to stop the ringing. "Who? Rominger? He knew about the dope?"

"Hell, that old hypocrite?" Wanda snorted. "He knew my business all along. All those years, he brung me sugar and copper tubing I asked him for and he never said a word about what I was brewing back of the Buckeye. A Baptist knows all about sinning."

Kyle swallowed hard. The smoke had dried his mouth and his tongue felt like putty against his teeth. "I found out about you and Rominger."

"You know nothing."

In the corner where he'd piled his gear, Kyle hunted for the stolen library book. His fingers fumbled through the pages until he found the right passage. "Look, proof."

"Proof, piss."

"No, read it." He pushed the open book at her.

"Lies, all lies." Her hand clawed at the page, ripped it. He gripped her hand and rescued the torn paper, the only proof that might keep this land for them.

189

"It's no lie, is it? It says here you were married to Rominger. When you got divorced, he left you this cabin. That was the bargain, right?"

"Rominger never gave me a thing."

"But you were married, it says right here. He owes you."

"He owed me all right and he paid."

Kyle pulled the eviction notice from his hip pocket, waved it in her face. "Listen now, that deputy was here to throw us out. Unless you got proof that Rominger gave you this place, they'll make you leave."

Wanda raised her wrist bound with the rope. "I ain't going no place like this."

"Tell the truth," Kyle badgered her. "You got the land when you got married and you got to keep it when you got divorced."

"A divorce? Hell, they pretended we was never married."

"Never married?" Kyle smoothed the torn page on this thigh. The dope must have gone to his head. The words ran together across the yellow page.

"Listen," Wanda explained, her voice first a whisper in his bad ear, then louder. "Listen, it was a done deal when Dallas hitched up with me in the first place. And it was a done deal when he tried to get shed of me. Divorce, hell, they couldn't even say the word out loud in that place, that godawful holy place. You should have seen that place."

And as she talked, Kyle pictured the church. Although he'd never set foot inside the steepled sanctuary—still, he saw it in his mind. How hot the sanctuary was inside, so hot that sap still bled from the pine timbers in the walls. There was a stillness there that he'd seen in courtrooms in his own life, where jail time and parole and freedom were doled out by a judge in black robes. Wanda described the judges she faced, three old men sitting behind a table with Old Testament beards and burning eyes: the preacher with his King James Bible coming apart at the seams, the secretary with the minutes, the head deacon with the roll not to be called up yonder, but in the hellish here and now. And three of them sat on the other side of the table, waiting to be judged: Wanda, Jake Wilder, Dallas Rominger.

Preacher's hands cracked open that big Bible, pages rustled like a snake sliding through dead leaves. Baritone voice cleared through a knot of phlegm. "Repent, sister, and be baptized."

"Repent of what?"

190

"Consorting, fornicating, whoring, drunkenness, abominations that are a stench in the nostrils of the Almighty."

"You talk about stink. God must turn up his nose at the sweat rolling off this bunch come August."

"Backtalk like that will see you burn for eternity."

The air felt scarce in that shut-up room. Jake Wilder gnawed at a planter wart on the side of his thumb. Dallas squirmed in his seat with his new hemorrhoids. Both aimed to show these ailments as proof of Wanda's spells.

"Why do I have to be the one doing the repenting?" Wanda argued. "I'm not the one who set up the tent behind the CCC camp down in Fontana. I'm not the one who came night after night all liquored up for a little loving. What about him?" she fingered Jake Wilder.

"Brother Wilder has repented of his ways, confessed his sins, and professed his faith in his savior Jesus Christ."

"And him too? My husband?" she fingered Dallas Rominger. "He said he was going to make me an honest woman."

Redfaced Rominger protested: "That ain't true."

"No, truth is they flipped a damn coin and he lost."

"You deny the Holy Spirit? You have committed the unforgivable sin. Be ye not yoked with unbelievers. Annulment is granted, Brother Rominger. This union never existed in the eyes of the Almighty."

Wanda grew quiet. The wind whistled in the flue, guttering the flames inside the belly of the Franklin stove. Kyle had braided a curlicue into his beard, pondering his mother's story. "So there's no proof?" he said.

"Proof, piss," she said. "I'm still here, ain't I? Where else was I supposed to go?"

The wind died down and the fire burned high in the stove. Wanda's rocker creaked. "For a while, I waited for them to come tell me to leave. Dallas took off, went west for a while, just to make everything legal, hoping everyone would forget. I stayed put. I learned right soon that marriage or no, they wanted me right where I was. Dallas wasn't back more than a week, when he came sneaking on up here. He wasn't the first, but not the last. They all came this way in the dark."

As a young'un, Kyle watched through the window the succession of Shadow Men as they peeled off their dark clothes. Naked, they sometimes were short and bald, sometimes tall and lanky, other times with paunches and sloped shoulders.

"See, they thought I was the one bound for hell. That bunch of Baptists, what they really wanted was to take me out and drown me in the name of the Father. I tell you, it damn sure didn't save my daddy when the water rose over his head." Beneath the chair, Kyle felt the gentle tugging of the rope. He could see her hand moving under the quilt, and he imagined a rattlesnake coiled in her lap. "I got tired of them busybody Baptist prayers buzzing up the mountain," she said. "One Sunday, years after I walked out of that church, I walked down there and chucked a few rocks at the door. Called them all out by name. Dallas Rominger, you bastard, you! Jake Wilder, son of a bitch, you! They buzzed inside like hornets and directly they come flying out, stingers all ready. The whole bunch of them, preacher and choir and deacons, they all thought I was the whore of Babylon. They wanted a whore, well, fine, I'd give them a show. I went straight to Saint Wilder and smacked him a wet one on the mouth, that old Judas. I hitched my leg around his and rubbed up against and there was more to him that was stiff than just his spine, I can tell you."

Logs crumbled inside the stove. The fire was dying. Kyle stirred from his seat and fetched more wood from out on the porch. It had turned cold, but he lingered a moment before the weathered door, tracing the letters etched there. GTT, gone to Texas, gone to Timbuktu, gone to town. It meant nothing now, his childhood chant of leaving, his plans of coming back all gone to hell.

"Close the door," Wanda said.

He fed the stove and stoked the coals with a stick. His mother was silent. He saw the rope had worked loose from her leg. He knelt by her rocker. "Mama," he whispered. The story was long over but he still had one more question. "My daddy, which one was he?"

"Oh, you poor thing." Wanda mussed his long hair. Taken by this sudden tenderness, Kyle raised his face to her, hopefully. She dropped the noose quick over his head. He tried to shout, clawing his fingers at the rope cutting into his Adam's apple.

38

I can't sleep."

"Take another pill."

"I did."

Eva switched on the lamp by the bed. She checked the box of medicine on the nightstand, squinting at the fine print. "Royce, this is non-drowsy. You got me the daytime formula. I needed the nighttime. Now I won't get any sleep tonight."

"Sorry," Royce burrowed his head deeper into his pillow, away from the light.

She plumped her pillows and flipped through the paperback she was reading for her book club. "Close your eyes," she insisted.

He had dozed off, when the snap of the lamp brought the room to darkness again. Finally, he thought.

Eva punched her pillow, turned it over looking for the elusive cool to rest her cheek against, restlessly tossing, and then she lay very still. She sighed toward the dark ceiling. Royce's eyes popped wide open. After two decades of sleeping side by side, he could read her breathing and her eloquent silences. That slow seep of exhalation could mean annoyance or resignation, snorts of frustration or disbelief. But this was a new rattle from her thin ribs: the slow escape of despair.

"Royce, are you awake?"

"Yes." The clock on the dresser across the room flashed a red 1:00 a.m.

The night stretched ahead of them with all the small despairing hours. But daylight would bring no relief, all their troubles waiting for them. Dean and Dallas and what to do with Ruth. The money woes mounting. Royce found himself mentally sorting through all their accounts, shifting balances to meet the bills. Now with Dallas' tangled finances, he might have to pay an actual accountant to go through that mess.

Eva's last paycheck from Keep Altamont Beautiful would post to their account at the end of the month. There was no severance pay, no golden parachute for the executive director of a low-budget non-profit whose mission was being taken over by the Altamont Alternative Waste Energy coalition, or Altamont AWE, that wanted to turn the landfill methane into a power source. Who knew that electricity smelled so bad?

It was December, the longest nights of the year, but there was little sleep tonight. They had been married almost twenty years, sleeping side by side, night after night, making love when they were younger, now not so often, not really ever, as Royce faced a future after forty-five. They knew each other as well as people can know a body, a person. But there were chilly moments when they felt distant, perfect strangers.

With Royce bound by the genes and dispositions of the sulky, silent Wilders, Eva feared the inevitable night when her husband, growing colder day by day, grew stone cold to the touch under the comforter, passing silently in his sleep, while she woke up a widow with a dead man in her bed. She needed to say something before things got out of hand, beyond her grasp.

"Do you have secrets? Things you never told me or anyone?"

"I'm an open book. Unfortunately, what you see is what you get."

"Lucky me," she sighed, then paused. Eva evidently wanted to have one of her deep talks. "Listen. I think I have one. I think I saw my father cheating on my mother."

"You think? Did you walk in on him?"

"Sort of, but nothing flagrant. But there was something I saw that always bothered me. When I was little, I liked to go into the sanctuary, though they always warned me not to play in there. I went in and saw my father with a parishioner. Delores Smith. I still remember her name, isn't that funny?"

She had heard crying at the back of the church, beyond the doors to the side of the altar. The door to her father's study was half open; she saw nothing, but her father's hands and knees, next to a woman's bare legs beneath a skirt. His warm soft hand with the golden wedding ring resting on the woman's knee.

"You think he was fooling around?"

"I don't know. The way she said 'Oh, Father.' Isn't that funny? Just that inflection in her voice. Something about it was too familiar. It's not how you speak to a priest."

"You told your mother?"

"Never a word to anyone, but it was like a secret between my father and me. He saw me and his eyes widened like he had been caught at something. He sprang back and she was smoothing her dress, and they were both flustered."

"Why have you been thinking about that?"

"I don't know. I just have. I can't get it out of my mind now." She turned on her side, propped her head on one arm. "You don't have a secret like that. Something you've never told me?"

He hated this kind of conversation. "I don't know. I threw a rock once at Wanda's house."

"You've told me that story a thousand times. Lucy double-dog-dared you. I know all about that."

"No, you don't. I saw something that day. I never told anybody. Not Lucy. Nobody." His voice trailed off. Then he said it out loud, what he'd carried for more than thirty years. "A little boy tied up on her porch."

"Who? Who was it?"

"I don't know, but I got the sense that he belonged there with her."

Her hand brushed his shoulder, his cheek, and then left him. "Oh, Royce, that's terrible," she whispered.

"No, it's all right. I probably just dreamed it all. You know Beaverdam and how people talk. If it was true, someone would have said something."

The silence stunned them. They lay in the shadows of their bedroom savoring their secrets, the ones they had told and the ones they were still too ashamed to own up to. She chewed at her lips where she could still feel the kiss of a man other than her husband. And he clenched and unclenched his fist that had held a rock as a child, a rock that finally hit its target when he picked up the pen thirty-seven years later and signed the paper to evict an old, hateful woman from her only home.

39

Ruth made herself at home in Dallas' hospital room, directing Royce to move the reclining chair over by the window. She spread her quilting over her lap, pulling the bed tray over to hold her shears and needles. Dallas didn't need it since he wasn't eating regular food. The morning fell through the casement window, throwing a slab of light over the antiseptic surroundings, the tilted mechanical bed, the still legs underneath the thin, white sheet.

She talked like Dallas was listening, liable to sit up and argue like he always did. Doctor's orders. "He's comatose, but that doesn't mean he's not conscious on some level. He'll hear you if you just talk to him." This from a tiny, intense Asian woman who didn't look old enough to be poking old people with her stethoscope.

"I'm not so sure about her," Ruth confided in her brother. "Least, Royce said she wasn't Japanese. Korean." What was the difference? Hadn't they fought 'em both fifty years ago? But then doctors weren't Dallas' favorite folk. She couldn't blame her brother for avoiding their like for so long, but look where it got him, lying in a strange bed far from home with the spit drying in his slightly opened mouth, a faint gleam beneath his half-opened eyelids, the only motion the steady drip of fluids into his blue veins, the beep of the monitors that followed his heart climbing a steep mountain and dipping into a dark cove over and over, the journey of a lifetime. Quite a ride, Dallas might say, and Ruth would have to agree.

196

The conversation was one-sided, but she didn't mind. She knew all Dallas' arguments and retorts. "You remember that time?" she would say to herself as if he could read her mind.

Growing up in Beaverdam, in a time of kerosene lanterns and outhouses and hitching the bay to a wagon to go anywhere, Dallas had no patience with that past. Bring on the future. Let's hot-wire it. I much rather step out into a cold morning and turn a key to start my truck, rather than hook up one of them old plow horses to a wagon to go for a ride over to Altamont. Or give me a good gas-engine chainsaw and a can of motor oil, and that beats the gallons of sweat rolling off you when you're on one end of a double saw, trying to rip it through the soft sap of a heavy hemlock.

Dallas fancied himself an inventor. He'd cut out a picture of Mr. Edison from *Popular Mechanics* and put it into a frame he kept on his desk littered with the innards of radios he'd dissected and reassembled. At fifteen, he'd rigged a generator on his daddy's gristmill on Beaverdam Creek, then wired a red bulb across the road to create the community's first and only stop light. 'Course there wasn't much traffic then—mostly horses—and nobody actually ever stopped, but folks took to walking backwards down the road just to watch that light blink red off and on.

Dallas grew up to become a trusted civil servant, the rural carrier for decades, sitting midway in the front seat of a Fairlane, wheeling with one arm along the tight curves of the cove and with the other snatching open the farm mailboxes and stuffing them with the latest issue of *Progressive Farmer*, the box ordered from Sears & Roebuck, the letter from kinfolk off in the service or moved away to flatter parts of the world. "Look there," Dallas said. "I got one arm longer than the other to hook them mailboxes." And he hunched his shoulder so that indeed one set of knuckles hung a little lower than the other. "That's what Uncle Sam was looking for on the civil service exam."

Lord, how he always made folks laugh. He was the clown in the family, always aiming to crack smiles on those stern-faced parents, chasing after him with a switch cut from the apple tree. Ruth pursed her lips and slipped a finger behind her dusted spectacle to wipe the sudden tear in her eye. She set aside her bad quilting with the too big stitches and her mother's voice in her ear. "Lawd, girl. Pay attention now. You're getting sloppy." Ruth heard her mother more and more these days, almost fifty years since Ruth had nursed the harpy in her last days.

197

The nurse came in then and checked. "Hello there." A young woman, not much older than Ruth was at her mama's deathbed. No angel of mercy decked out in white like you'd think, these nurses these days had all these garish floral smocks with bright green or yellow pants and squeaky sneakers like they were about to run a race. The nurse checked the tubes, tapped them with a flick of her middle finger, listened to Dallas' barely moving chest with her stethoscope. Ruth shivered imagining that disk of metal cold as a snowflake draped on his bare skin.

"How's he doing?" Ruth asked as she always did each couple of hours they came in.

"Same as before."

"He's the only brother I got left, my last kin."

"Pray, dear. That's all we can do for him. It's up to him and Jesus." The nurse patted Ruth's arm.

"You believe that girl?" Ruth asked him after she left on her squeaky sneakers, but Dallas made no other sound than his breathing.

Families were bigger back then. There had been a mess of Romingers, now almost all gone. Grady, the oldest, the first to go, felled by the big chestnut he tried to fell. Hearts give out and Daddy keeled over. Mama never cried over any of her children. She set her mouth, made up her mind, and went upstairs to her bed to wither away and die, refusing every bite of food Ruth tried to bring.

Poor Houston, the men in the uniforms came riding to the house with the news. Tractor bucked and crushed Austin. Cancer ran hard among them, breast and mouth, Ada and Luella, the last to go. Just her and Dallas left these days, and they were just barely holding on.

"You still here, you old cuss?" The corner of her eye caught what she thought was some motion, a jerk of his bandaged head, or a leg kicking under the thin sheet. But nothing. Her little brother just lay there. She picked up the needle again and gathered her long thread. "You remember Fontana, and how full of yourself you were after you came home after that?"

That was the high water mark of his life, he always said, overshadowing the career as a U.S. rural mailman and a Baptist deacon. As a young man, Dallas had walked out of Beaverdam over George's Gap, looking for better luck, a larger world, then hitched a ride on a truck heading to Altamont and on to the Smokies. FDR needed boys down there to build the biggest dam yet. Other boys were fighting the Huns for the second go-round and the Japs what had snuck up on the fleet in Hawaii. He would have volunteered to go fight himself, but the draft board already told him he was flatfooted, not an arch at all in his boot, not that the Army could find one to fit his big feet. It was Uncle Sam's Armed Forces, not Ringling Bros. Circus. But national security needed electricity, juice to power the factories, the mills that made up democracy's arsenal. If there was one thing Dallas knew and understood it was electricity.

Dallas said when he first laid eyes on Jake Wilder, he was a skinny kid in clodhoppers clogging atop a plank table while a fiddler sawed out an untuned rendition of "Turkey in the Straw," but Jake didn't care. He was liquored up with the white mash being passed around in a fruit jar. His shirt half undone, holes in the knees of his pants and his boots untied, the laces lashing about his ankles as he pounded his own beat on the two-by-four, yodeling with his head thrown back, one dancing fool who clogged himself backwards off the table and fell flat on his ass. The girl ran to him and held his head, peppered his brow with soft kisses, but he wasn't coming to any time soon.

But Dallas saw electricity flashing out of the girl's eyes, looking up from the boy cradled in her calico lap. "Please," she said, though it was more of a command than a plea. Her eyes were green, her nose freckled, and her hair long and red. She was no beauty, too skinny, no flesh to speak of here, more bone than breasts. But when those green eyes widened, then narrowed, they pulled you in, like wading into a laurel hell down a mountain slope, a world of green you could just lose yourself in.

Dallas was no looker, he honestly knew that, the whole Rominger clan had the profile of potatoes just grubbed out of the garden, all eyes and knots and blemished skin. He'd stolen his share of kisses for girls in the schoolyard and felt new breasts on dares in haylofts. The one thing he could always do was talk, and here was his chance.

"Can you help me with him?" the girl asked.

"There's a spare cot in my tent he's welcome to."

"I'm Wanda. This is Jake. Jake Wilder," she smiled.

"Lives up to his name, don't he?"

"I don't believe he's good to walk," the girl said.

So Dallas slung his new bunkmate and future brother-in-law over one shoulder like a feed sack and put him to bed in his tent. And he thought Wanda was the most wonderful name as well.

There was no night and no stars or moon at Fontana, only the long day-light of summer and then an artificial day after the sun set. The government had mounted great floodlights and the project ran around the clock. You'd go into your tent, and the light would leak under the canvas. Dallas thought it fitting that they were going to flood Japan, the local village named for a flower rather than the eastern adversary. After what happened at Pearl Harbor, it felt good to just wipe Japan right off the map.

The boss put Dallas on one end of the cross-saw and little ole Jake on the other. It wouldn't have seemed even, but Jake Wilder kept up his end. And what did Dallas say to Jake as the woodchips flew and the sweat sprayed from their bare backs, their arms moving the jagged blade deeper into the virgin trunk? "That girl, Wanda? She's pretty sweet on you?"

"Sweet enough."

"I was just wondering—"

"Be better if you were working your end, 'stead of running your trap."

Dallas just grinned. "Sweet and sour, that's a good combination."

"Hunnh." Jake spat.

Jake could keep quiet, but he couldn't keep Dallas Rominger from talk-ing. Dallas must have talked his ears off that summer, bragging of Beaver-dam, how there wasn't a finer place in these mountains, how the farming was easier, the tobacco taller, the cows fatter, the corn riper, all the girls better looking. Did he mention Ruth, his older sister still ripe for the tak-ing for some studious young man? Did Jake just pull on his end of the saw and hawk out his hard noncommittal 'hunnh'?

Ruth had about given up on men, after all the boys in Beaverdam had paired off with the gals, had moved on or died off. At thirty-four, she was a spinster, a schoolmarm, still nursing the last bit of her mama, when Jake, not quite ten years her junior, came courting at the door with a sorry fistful of sweet William he'd pulled from some ditch.

Her fate was sealed after he swore off his drinking, signed the temper-ance oath in the Rominger Bible, and waded waist-deep into Beaverdam Creek to be baptized. He came up sputtering, with the water clinging to the short curls back of his neck, as he walked her all the way home, shiv-ering, a Christian gentleman. But along with Jake came Wanda as well. Dallas brought her into their once safe little community, but it was like slipping a snake into a hen's nest, waiting in the straw for all the eggs to hatch one by one.

200

She didn't ask when Jake was gone for days on end. Forget the bride and all that bother of trying to please a woman, Jake and Dallas would sneak off to go fish, or hunt, or just camp a few days back of the Buckeye, out in the woods like the Indians who once hunted here. Jake had some Indian blood in him, dark eyes and high cheekbones, and a taste for things that got him in trouble. Ruth didn't even say anything when he came home with no game, his head hung low, but the smell of whiskey still leaking out of his pores and another scent on him as well, if he'd let her close enough. She had caught that human reek, sniffing at his drawers left in a pile as he soaked in the tub of water, working up a lather on his back, as he rubbed himself raw with the long-handled scrub brush. Trying to clean himself once more. Oh, she knew in her heart. She had kept silent like all of them, nary a peep, another little chick who didn't see the red mouth striking, until much too late.

Ruth kicked aside the ring of hearts draped over her thick legs like a cocoon she had woven tight around herself so many years. She flew to the bed and shook his shoulder, jostling his hard head on the hospital pillow. "Oh, you foolish man, you foolish man, what were you thinking?"

The body in the bed wasn't thinking, nor breathing.

40

Hand me that joint." Tucker reached his left arm around the seat as he kept his right hand on the wheel and his eyes on the tightly twisting curves.

Dean placed the smoldering roach between his fingers, trying not to burn him. He coughed out the rich smoke.

"That's the last of it." Tucker quenched the ember on his tongue then ate the last of the stem, leaf, and burned rice paper, for every bit of buzz. "This better pan out like you said." Tucker's eyes narrowed in the mirror.

"Yeah, it's been an hour already." Perry threw his thick arm over the seat, turning to look at him. "You're not trying to get us lost, are you, Wilder?"

"It's not much farther."

Dean had taken the initiative. He'd gone straight to their table in the lunchroom, and said flat out. "I know where we can get some weed."

The word was that Tucker's usual sources had dried up. The rich boy needed him. "You're sure? Not much inventory in town now."

"This is a ways away, over in Beaverdam. Homegrown, I hear, but kick-ass." Dean was lying his ass off now, elaborating on the little crumb he'd gotten from Ruth.

"Meet us in the parking lot in twenty minutes." He had Mr. Spears' American Lit class in twenty minutes, but why not cut class? Live on the wild side. Just live. He just hoped he could remember the way to Beaver-

202

dam and could find the dirt road where Wanda lived. She was an old, crazy woman who couldn't hurt anybody as quick as he was, but maybe she could deal him some drugs. Wouldn't Tucker be impressed when Dean knocked at Wanda's door, and came away with a bag of the best buds?

"Man, this is Deliverance country," Perry said.

"Shoo-eee. Good God, banjos and geeks. Just don't bend over in these parts."

Dean didn't say a word when they passed by his grandmother's house, or the barn when he looked back and could see the faint POW of his tag on the side.

"Up there, take a right."

Tucker braked and swung the Camaro off the broken pavement up the dirt road. The road ran for almost a mile before it dead-ended at a clearing overlooking the cove. It didn't look promising. A car covered with the gray vines of frost-killed kudzu, a dirt yard littered with chicken feathers, stones, and rusted cans, but no sign of life. They peered through the dust-filmed windshield up at the tottering shack.

"I'll be back in a moment."

Dean had a pocket full of twenties he'd saved. Although he had no idea of what an ounce of dope was going for, he should have enough cash to cover at least a taste. Dean climbed the rotting steps onto the front porch. He knocked at the scarred door, turned, and waved to his friends in the car. The door opened and there was no Wanda, but a wild-eyed, bearded man who took one quick look, grabbed his arm, and pulled him inside. The door slammed and the dried ghosts of timber rattlers softly shook their translucent buttons.

41

What happens now? Eva sat at the desk in her office at Keep Altamont Beautiful for the last time. Her framed photos of Royce and Dean and her parents, the hand lotion, personal effects, a string of Mardi Gras beads and other silly souvenirs from past fundraisers were packed away. What a career comes down to at the end, a life. What happens now that your life has been exposed as a hollow lie? What happens when you wake up one day and find that this happy life you've been living, this solid home you've made, are nothing but illusions?

All the men in your life don't desert you in the end, but keep coming back, father, husband, and son, the same childish personality demanding: love me, nurture me, need me, feed me, fuck me, protect me. Your mother-in-law is a bother most days and a Baptist harpy from hell other days, but she's right when she says the past is junk that's cluttering the present.

She fiddled unconsciously with her gold chain, pulling it tight against the hollow of her neck, rubbing her chin and lips with the gold cross, pinching the meat of her forefinger and thumb into the metal, biting into her own flesh. It felt good, that slight pain, the heat of the metal warmed against her breastbone. She gave it no more thought than a charm bracelet or the wedding ring. It was a part of her, had belonged to her mother, and she wore it almost daily. Oh, there were pearls and other necklaces she wore on special occasions, but this was her usual attire.

Your past is full of pat answers that don't work. My husband loves me.

My son is a well-behaved little boy. My work fulfills me. I am happy with my life. I believe in the Nicene Creed. Things will turn out for the best. Had she dreamed all these things? Why did she wake up? What happened to make the dreams disappear? Had she simply opened her eyes to the strange life that was hers now? Or had Michael really kissed her?

At first she could not get the shape of his tongue, so soft, out of her mouth, out of her mind. But now she had forgotten the sensation. She could only taste bitterness, like trying to choke down a mouthful of dirt. She had opened her soul to a father-confessor, her priest, and the prick had tried to put his tongue down her throat.

She pressed her chin against the necklace. The clasp broke and the links slithered through her fingers like a snake. The cross was lost with a slight clink on the hard floor beneath her desk. She was on hands and knees beneath her desk, afraid someone might walk in and find her groveling, pleading for forgiveness. Oh God, please, don't let me lose this, not this.

She sat, breathing hard, the cross clasped hard now in her palm, pressing deep into the flesh, until she was about to bleed. A stigmata. Oh, don't be so dramatic, she told herself in her mother's tired voice. She poured the necklace into her purse and wrapped the cross in a tissue and put it in her wallet. It was time to pick up Dean at school, go home, and fix supper. It was all a lie, but what else could she do?

42

Dean's nose burned with the strange odor that seemed steeped in the wooden walls of the shack. He was afraid his nose would start bleeding. He crouched in the corner where he had landed. His arm was sore. When he was ten, he had fallen out of a tree and broke the tibia, freaking out his mom with the strange bulge on his forearm, and now he wondered if the man had wrenched it again when he had grabbed him from the porch, pulled him in the door, and flung him across the small room to the far wall, like in that kids' game he used to play, Snap the Whip, where a whole line of kids ran in a desperate circle, then flung you into space on the playground. But this was no game, and no one was playing.

When he hit the wall, he startled an old woman tied to a rocking chair. "Watch it, boy," she shrieked.

"Hush, the two of you," the man said. "Don't you move. I ain't going to hurt you none."

He stood by the window, the thick glass filmed with dirt, fogged by his hard breathing. "They're hightailing it for sure. Going for help, I reckon. It will be all over soon." The man cocked open the breech of his gun, loaded a shell.

"What have you done, boy?" The woman raised her groggy, white head, and her half-lidded eyes.

The man held a finger with a blackened nail to his chapped lips. "Hush. We're all just going to sit here and wait. He's bound to come this time."

206

Wait for what? For whom? Dean could hear himself screaming in his head, and it was all he could do to keep the words inside himself and not yell them into the intolerable silence.

Dean crouched by the wall. His thighs and calves were getting cramped and his left foot had fallen asleep, but he didn't dare move. He heard a tinkling of water and then he could smell the sharp tang. A yellow stream dribbled between the old woman's withered legs bound to the rocker and spread across the floorboards toward Dean's sneakers. The man paid no mind, watching through the window for whatever was to come up the dusty road.

43

Just three days before, Royce Wilder had traveled the slowest he had ever been over George's Gap, creeping in the long black limousine behind the hearse carrying his uncle's body, the last of the Romingers, to its final rest in the sloped cemetery behind Beaverdam Church. So slow, it felt he could swing the door open and walk the ten miles of twisted road, quickly outpacing the cortege, beating them all there to that gaping hole soon to be filled. And now like déjà vu on fast forward or his oldest nightmare rewound, he was flying over the gap, faster than he thought possible, his leg about to kick the accelerator through the half-rusted floorboard, trying to press as much speed as possible from the poor German engine that had already seen a quarter million miles, then through the curves standing on the soft brakes, fighting to hold the car on the asphalt as the treetops whipped by and the terrible yawning in his stomach grew worse.

"You best hurry," Junior had said on the phone. "We have, uh, a situation."

Junior had deputies surrounding Wanda's cabin. Shots were fired. A man down. But Dean was safe for now.

"Dean? He's supposed to be in school."

"Seems he's here at Wanda's."

"He's never been to Wanda's. How—"

"No time to argue, Royce. Just get your butt up to Beaverdam."

❖

Their blue lights strobing against the green hemlock, the patrol cars lined the pavement where the dirt road turned toward Wanda's place. All of Zebulon County's finest called to the scene. A deputy with the heavy gut of his khaki shirt overhanging a black belt stood in the roadway, trying to wave him on around. Royce cranked down his window. "Junior Gudger called me. I'm Royce Wilder. Where's my son?"

The deputy pointed him toward the impromptu command center. Junior and his men mulled over a series of topo maps spread out over the still ticking hood of the car. Other officers barked orders on walkie-talkies to men unseen moving up the mountainside, surrounding the cabin.

"Here put this on," Junior handed Royce a flak jacket. "Just as a precaution."

Royce felt his heart sink as he slipped the weight of the armored fabric onto his shoulders. "What's happening?"

Junior hooked his thumb at two ashen-faced boys sitting in the back of the cop car like they were under arrest themselves. "Seems Dean and his pals from school drove here, cutting class, maybe looking for trouble, they wouldn't say. Only that Dean knocked on Wanda McRae's front door, and when he did, he got pulled in and hasn't been seen outside yet. We're treating this as a hostage situation."

"I warned you Wanda was dangerous."

Junior held up the flat of his beefy hand. "Wasn't Wanda at the door, but a man. He might be holding them both hostage."

"Who?"

A voice crackled through the static. "Command one."

"Hang on," Junior spoke into the small walkie-talkie clipped to his shoulder. "Go, Sniper One."

"We're in position. We've got a sight on the suspect with a shotgun, clear target through the window. We also can scope a woman in a chair. No sign of the boy."

"Roger that, Sniper One."

"You're not going to start shooting? You said Dean is in there."

"We don't want to spook him," Junior said.

"Who's he?"

"Some scraggly feller, says he's Wanda's son. I met him when I served the eviction notice myself. You know that Wanda had a son?"

Royce said nothing, but he remembered all right.

"Wanda don't have no phone, but we got close enough to holler back and forth before he sprayed some buckshot in our direction like he means business."

"What does he want?"

"Talk to Dallas Rominger."

"Did you tell him Dallas passed?"

"No, not with him shooting at us," Junior said. "This sounds like one big misunderstanding."

Junior bent to the maps with his men, drawing their line of attack. Royce looked up the road. This was no dare, only what needed to be done. He started walking. He was already at the bend before a deputy looked up from the map and nudged his sergeant. "Royce, stop!" Junior hollered. "Wilder, come back here."

But Royce kept going.

"Hold fire, hold fire," Junior barked into his walkie-talkie. "We've got a civilian breaching our perimeter."

Royce hadn't been up this road but once, a lifetime ago, but every step of the way seemed familiar, inevitable, like a dream he couldn't wake from. The same breeze in the hemlock, the rustle of water in the laurel-shaded ravine, the background hammering of the blood in his ears, the catch in his throat he kept swallowing to no avail. No rock stuck to his sweaty fist; this time his hands were empty. No plan, no scheme other than to walk to the cabin and get his son out safe.

He rounded the last bend and stood in sight of the cabin, shivering in the late day. The door opened and a man stepped out, cradling a shotgun and a length of rope in his hands.

"Hey," Royce hollered, but the man made no acknowledgment.

Royce approached, holding out his defenseless hands, his knee grazing the fender of the old car, wading through the flock of chickens.

The man wore a dirty, white T-shirt and loose blue jeans tucked into the unlaced tops of his brogans. He kept looking past Royce down the road, as if expecting more company. "You ain't Rominger."

"No," Royce found his voice. "No, I'm not. Dallas Rominger is my uncle. My name's Royce Wilder, but I can speak on behalf of my uncle."

"Think you can, huh?"

Royce shrugged his shoulders in the heavy flak jacket. "I can try. I don't believe we've met. What's your name?"

"Kyle McRae." He propped the shotgun in reach against the porch post, then sat on the top step, running the rough rope through his hands.

How could a man sit outside in this weather with no coat, only a white shirt that made a sniper's aim easier? He kept his head angled, his eyes down, watching Kyle McRae from the corner of his eye, afraid to see that shirt suddenly splattered with red.

"It's all right. I know they're out there." Kyle said. "See yonder between them hemlocks, he's got us in his sights. And there, by that big rock, there's one with a bead on us too."

The wind picked up, tossing the branches of the hemlocks around the house. For a moment, Royce thought he saw a face in the woods. He shivered in the chill. Kyle's bare arms were goose fleshed.

"You go tell 'em I want to see Dallas Rominger."

"Dallas is, uh, was my uncle. He died." Royce swallowed, having to say this out loud for the first time since it happened. "We just buried him three days ago."

"Dead. How?"

"Ran off the road. He had to go to the hospital, but he had a stroke, then..."

"I'll be damned. Dead, huh?"

Royce licked his dry lips. "What did you want with Dallas?"

"I was thinking of shooting him if he showed his sorry face here." Kyle idly wound the rope between his two hands and jerked it tight. "Now you say he's already dead. Just damn."

"It's probably me you should be angry at. I signed the eviction notice. It's nobody's fault but mine."

"Nope. It's Rominger's fault."

"What did Dallas ever do to you?"

"You're his kin. You know."

"No, I'm afraid I don't."

"Then you're lying. People lied to me all my life, but I found out some things." Kyle pulled a folded paper from his hip pocket. "I found this."

Royce closed the distance between them, almost in reach himself of the shotgun leaning against the cracked post, but he took the offered page instead. The paper was soft to the touch, creased like old money, evidently a page torn from a book. "Where'd you get this?"

"Altamont Public Library, so it must be true."

Royce already knew what the paper in his trembling hands said, even though he could not focus on the words. He knew what Lucy and Junior had already whispered all around the community. Everyone secretly knew it but pretended not to. It was hard to think of Dallas as a liar, but here it was in black and white. All his talk of the Shadow Man and Wanda the Witch nothing but tall tales heaped over his secret shame. A good Baptist with a busted marriage and a bastard son to boot.

"I truly didn't know any of this. No one did."

Kyle waggled his fingers for the return of his valuable find.

Royce stepped forward. "Dean, you in there?" he shouted.

"Hey now," Kyle threatened. "Give me that back."

"Dean!" Royce shouted again.

"Dad!" came a small voice from inside the cabin.

"Come on out, Dean. It's okay." Royce held the paper aloft, something he could trade for his son now.

His son—still alive, thank God—slipped through the door, ashen-faced, shaky with fear, his ankle tied with one end of the rope.

Kyle looked to Dean. "You know him?"

"He's my dad."

Kyle scratched his scraggly beard. "All right, trade then."

Royce handed over the paper. Kyle took his knife and cut the rope. "Go on, git," he hissed.

"You all right?"

The boy nodded. Royce stood his son behind him, behind his flak jacket. They were all breathing hard, with no sound but the wind soughing through the hemlocks.

"Now what?"

"Let me think now." Kyle folded his paper and raised his skinny haunch to slip it into his hip pocket. The shotgun was only an arm's length away, but not close enough to reach before a sniper's bullet could run right through.

"You can let both of us walk right down the road, no trouble done. Nobody gets hurt."

"Shut up, mister, and let me just think."

Just then the severed rope came to life, and Royce could trace its path running across the porch, through the half open door. Rattlesnake hides guarded either side of the threshold, their dried tails scraping the floorboards. Kyle grabbed the line before it danced through the door. On the side of his neck, below the reddish beard, ran a raw stripe, as if Kyle had tried to hang himself with the rope he wrapped tight around his fist. "Sorry about that," he apologized for the interruption. "At first, I just had her leg tied, but she got loose and about strangled me. She's not right in the head." Kyle's finger drew a crazy circle against his temple.

"You tied her up?"

"Why she done the same to me." Kyle's eyes widened. They were blue.

"Wait, I know you. You're him, aren't you? You were a little boy tied up. I threw that rock. I don't know, I might have hit you. I heard you screaming and Wanda cussing."

"I don't recollect that. I know she used to tie me down when I was a young'un."

"I'm sorry."

"Reckon that's why Rominger came and put me in the foster home."

"Wait." Royce reached under the flak jacket for his hip pocket and his wallet.

"I don't want your money, mister." Kyle waved him away dismissively.

"No, this you need to see." Royce approached the porch and handed the photograph to the only one in the world who could appreciate it. He'd found the other half when they were going through the mess of papers at Dallas' house. Taped together, the torn halves reunited, the pretty young woman restored in between the two young bucks, looking hopefully at the future. "Remember Always."

Kyle's brow furrowed as he studied the sepia faces, turned it over and read the back and then looked again at the posed trio.

"That's my uncle Dallas there on the right, my daddy on the other side. I believe that's your mama in the middle." Royce was close enough now to grab the shotgun, but he just pointed out the people in the photograph.

Kyle gripped Royce's hand. His palm was calloused, rough as sandpaper. "You and me are kin, think of that." This close, face-to-face, Royce could see the strange feline eyes of Wanda in his features, but the sharp widow's peak of his receding red hair and those gapped teeth might have belonged to Dallas. Kyle squeezed hard, whether out of spite or friendliness, Royce wasn't sure. Then he let him go.

"You can keep that."

"Hunhh," Kyle jerked his head sharply to the side and spat, the familiar

213

derision of Jake Wilder for the whole world. He was the spitting image of all three of those young souls in the torn photograph.

The voice came from behind the door again, weak and pitiful. At first it sounded like a little boy from years ago, but it was a woman whimpering. "Boy? Where are you?"

"Here. Hush now. I'm coming in." Kyle wrapped the rope about his wrist. As he stood, his knees creaked and he staggered as if he might faint. He probably hadn't eaten or slept much keeping watch over his crazed mother. That and the dope had addled his brain.

"What happens now?"

"I don't know. I just wanted to talk to somebody before it does happen." He pointed to the shotgun. "You can tell 'em I'm out of shells. I may have shot Rominger if he weren't dead already, but I ain't going to hurt nobody else now."

Royce and Dean walked across the dirt yard, past the pecking chickens and the rusting car, toward the trees. He felt he should say something, but when he turned, Kyle had already shut the door.

The glass shattered in the cabin windows and fell in a rain of shards on the porch. Smoke billowed from beneath the cabin door. At first, Royce thought the place had caught fire, but then he was hit in the face by the harsh gas. His eyes watered. Bile rose in his burning throat. Royce turned and tackled Dean, feeling the breath knocked out of him as he fell heavily on his son, covering him while the gunfire and explosions echoed overhead.

Men in black fatigues charged through the fog. They did not have faces but masks that gave them the eyes of insects and the muzzles of animals. They swarmed the porch steps and crouched beneath the windows. At a signal, rifle butts shattered the glass and more tear gas canisters were lobbed inside. Two swings of a metal battering ram broke the door down and the men piled inside.

Kyle staggered through the chemical miasma, pushed through the doorway by a pair of SWAT men. Tears ran down his cheeks and vomit trailed in his beard. They made him kneel on the porch, twisting his arms until the shoulders threatened to pop from the sockets. "Down! Lie flat!" They forced him down on the shattered door. They read him his rights as they bent his arm behind his back, but they couldn't make him let go of the frayed rope. "Suspect subdued, over. We got a body in here, over."

Royce was on the ground, half blinded, his face pushed into Dean's unwashed hair with the taste of chemicals and earth on his tongue.

"I'm okay. It's all right. Get off me." Dean was still alive.

Royce slowly rolled off and raised his head, his stiff neck popping.

"You're bleeding, Dad."

Royce licked his lips, and tasted blood, then gingerly felt his nose. "I must have hit your hard head."

44

Through his tears and snot, the scrim of red burning his eyes and nose, Kyle wasn't just crying, he was bawling through his beard. It wasn't simply the pain, though they were twisting his arms until the shoulder bones popped. It was like a deep well had been struck and was flowing out of his face.

He couldn't remember ever crying. It had been years. The desert he carried in his face suddenly flooded, deluged. He had never seen the ocean, but had carried it deep within him. There was so much water he didn't know. May had dreamed of a distant sea.

They were muzzled like animals, goggle-eyed, their voices muffled behind protective respirators, helmeted. Down, down, stay down. Hands on your head, don't move, a series of commands and swift kicks. He felt the little cold mouth of the barrel pressed to the nape of his neck, the puckering of his skin sucked into that black hole. One wrong move, a pull of the trigger, and the hole would open inside him, straight through him, to hell. He lay still at last, rigid, saving his strength.

They were reading him his rights, that he could keep silent, he could talk to lawyers, that things would be used against him. He knew that much. He couldn't stop weeping as they chained his hands behind him. Then they had him up, marching arm in arm to the car. The yard was filled with cars now, the lights flashing against red clay and green rhododendron, blue, red, and green swimming in his watery vision. He kept twisting his

216

head over his shoulder, toward the fog rolling from the cabin's doorway. He wanted to call out for her, but he kept weeping and choking and retching.

"Watch your head."

He felt the hand on the crown of his skull, pushing him down to size, like a child once more. In the back seat, he felt the fight go out of him with the slamming door. It was all so familiar, and he was tired. The faces looked at him as the car drifted down the road, the heavy-bellied men with their guns on their hips, rifles at ready, all frowning as he passed by. It was getting dark away from the blue lights. He remembered when the Shadow Man had come for him. It was after dark and he was sleepy when the Shadow Man had put him into the back seat, filled with the brown sacks.

"Just go to sleep. Go to sleep," said the Shadow Man's voice from the front seat. He could see only the man's ear illuminated by the green lights from the speedometer and the dashboard. The soft curves swept around the mountainside.

"Where are we going?"

"To a place with a bed and three meals a day. You stay there, or I'll have to come get you again."

"What about her?" he meant the woman he could never bear to call mama.

"Go to sleep. Just go to sleep, boy. It will look different in the morning."

Kyle closed his eyes and rolled his head on the seat, rocked by the curves into the dreamless sleep of a tired child. *He drove me to a new house and left me there. Said they would take care of me better than I was used to. I ran away and they took me to a new house. The Shadow Man never did come back.*

45

Royce rubbed his bony wrist where the leather watchband had left a red welt. Eva said he wore things too tight, too snug, but at midlife he had accepted that about himself, all buckled up and buttoned down, too late for anything loosey-goosey. Pinched was the pose that fit a Wilder best.

The watchband had broken this morning of all mornings, and he fished in his pocket among the loose change and the penknife for the timepiece, pulling it out to check the hour. Five till noon. Royce reckoned that was right, even though there was no double-checking it against the courthouse clock that had stopped years prior at 10:32, like the whole of Zebulon county lost in time, stuck in the past, too cheap to fix itself and spring into the present. The courthouse was decrepit and dusty, termite riddled and rotting at the foundations, with a leaking roof and the stopped clock in its spire forever overlooking the brown-running river and the depressing downtown of boarded-up feed stores and bankrupted merchants. Royce's South, as familiar and awkward to him as fast fiddles on the radio, the place he had been running away from since he was a boy, looking for the bright malls and stately streets of Altamont.

A Friday in late March saw precious little trade on the mangy Main Street that ran between the railroad and the river. It was still cold and winter in the woods surrounding the town. There had been a few warm days the week before, but now the raw wind, sharpened along the rocks of the river and whetted along the long rusty rails of the Norfolk Southern, whistled like a razor past your ear as you pulled your stiff neck down into your collar, dug your fists deeper in the thin pockets of your polyester slacks.

The clerk of court came out with a clipboard and no hat, his hair blowing on his head above the horn-rimmed glasses that caught the March light. Junior shambled out behind him, with his ever-growing gut strapped in by his gun and shiny belt, his white Stetson trembling its stiff brim in the breeze.

Royce nodded at Junior, who pretended not to see him from behind the sunglasses. The chief deputy was here to provide crowd control. The wind seemed to blow up a last-minute crowd about the cracked steps leading to the courthouse on the hill. A sudden audience summoned by the unknown hour as Royce replaced the watch in his pocket. "By order of the clerk of court of the county, heretofore . . . "

Royce had seen enough foreclosures to know how the legal boilerplate was ladled out in any deal. Keeping his peace through the necessary prelude, he surveyed the curious crowd, a press of farmers in coveralls and fedoras, fleece jackets and ball caps, brogans and blue jeans. He appraised their profiles, chiseled faces and scrawny necks of Scots-Irish stock, crackers, rednecks, and rubes—faces you used to see in magazine photo essays about poverty and ignorance, but those native profiles were growing rarer in these parts overrun by retirees and transplanted Yankees. In the crowd he spied a green fedora and a plaid jacket and a gait not unlike his Uncle Dallas, and he felt the wind from the river lift his thinning hair from his head and raise goose flesh on his neck. The man turned and it was nobody but a rank stranger, like the song Royce once heard on his father's wooden radio, full of static and then silence.

"The auction is hereby open. Do I hear any opening bid?" The clerk blinked into the sun and shaded his eyes to see the crowd standing on the steps, a few stretching their legs, holding onto the rusted iron rails.

"Nineteen thousand, here!"

Royce didn't recognize the bidder at first, a gentleman in a business suit, not local. Landrum? He looked years older or younger, Royce couldn't be sure. He was so thin, wasted away, a frail fraction of his former girth. The suit hanging off him like a collapsing circus tent, the pounds of fat and flesh and greed flayed from his frame. He was eyeing Royce now, waiting for the opposing bid. Royce swallowed hard. He shifted his weight from the ball of his left foot to his right, rubbed his neck, but stood his ground, kept his mouth shut. The wind stood still like the time on the courthouse. Royce raised his hand only as far as his neck, but shrugged his shoulder and let his arm drop to his side, giving no sign to the clerk.

Parcel twenty-six on Plat 102 in the township of Beaverdam. Legal niceties—all that was talk for the Lord's house, the church where he'd spent an eternity of his childhood Sundays, baked his hard-shell Baptist soul on the hellfire and brimstone, beseeched Jesus his savior to come into his hard little heart so many times, sang the songs, the twanging hymns of blood, and the slaughter of mortal souls. He had sold out the Lord's house.

In a convoluted deal, vetted by several pinstriped Altamont attorneys and an Atlanta firm retrained by Landrum, it had been firmly and finally decided that Dallas was now dead, but that his estate was not exempt from taxes. He'd held the deed and had never proclaimed the church property as tax-exempt. Royce couldn't bear to sell the church outright, but allowed the county to foreclose and so let Landrum have his way. Everybody got their money: the congregation which didn't own the land settled for a tidy sum that helped them move on and set up in a storefront in a strip mall on the old Altamont highway. Their scraggly flock had actually grown, a whole parking lot on Sundays to themselves and paved so that no one tracked mud into the Lord's house. Most everybody had left the cove, moved on. Even Lucy and Junior took a place over in Bethel, a nice brick rancher with a two-car garage for his patrol cruiser. No hard feelings.

The price was low, only eight thousand per acre on average. He signed it all over, as the executor of Dallas' trust, most of the money going to pay for Ruth's new rooms at the Baptist Retirement Home on the Franklin highway on the outskirts of town. A trust for Ruth offered plenty for her to live out her days. Dallas had even seen to set aside money for Dean's college fund. Nothing for Royce but the hard work to execute the old man's trust in him.

"Do I hear any other bids?"

No flash, no quick yodels or fancy talk, just a pencil pusher, a county hack of three decades, saying, "All right, that's that. Parcel on Plat 102 in the township of Beaverdam is hereby sold for the bid of nineteen thousand and five hundred dollars."

220

The crowd dispersed. An old man spat tobacco juice to the sere grass growing by the broken sidewalk and limped away.

Landrum made his way over, a thin man who still carried himself like he was packing three hundred pounds.

"You lost weight," Royce couldn't help but blurt out the fact.

"Made good on my new year's resolution finally. Liquid diet for the past few weeks. Mostly protein milkshakes." Landrum waggled what had been his multiple chins and was now just sagging skin. He looked pallid, his eyes aglow with a fever, burning radioactive inside him.

"Where's your buddy, Matsui?"

"Japan. Three weeks visiting the shrines of his ancestors."

"Home, huh?"

"Actually, he's never been before. You have to remember he's a California kid. He likes potatoes more than rice."

What was there to say to this strange man who had barged his way into Royce's life, rearranged everything, and now was trying to slip out unnoticed? Landrum was smiling his wet teeth, but his cheeks were hollow. Royce had an urge to punch the man's gut, but it was as if Landrum had lost weight to shrink that target.

"You better take care of that cemetery," Royce warned, clenching and unclenching his fist.

"By law I have to. My Lord, there are more than enough laws about desecrating a graveyard, environmental impact statements when you start removing remains." Not just remains, but real people. His daddy, Dallas, grandparents, the whole clan that had staked claims in Beaverdam, their bones added to the rocky soil. "You can come out anytime, you know. Just let me know," Landrum paused. "You're quite the horse trader. Mr. Rominger drove a hard bargain before he died and afterwards. You do him proud."

Royce almost said thank you, this morsel from the former fat man.

"Oh, before I forget, there were a few more papers we needed to do. Dot all the i's, cross the t's. You know. Where should we do this?"

"Here is as good as any place," Royce said.

They stood over the shiny hood of the Lincoln Town Car and signed the flapping papers in the wind, initialing here and there, giving the devil his due, selling the house of the Lord. A million signatures for a million dollars, minus what the estate owed the county for taxes, then the proceeds.

Dallas had the lawyers in Franklin busy keeping his bidding from a grave in Beaverdam that now belonged to Landrum and the electric consortium, whoever they were.

"I once read a writer who said memory is the only real estate." Landrum stacked his papers. "It's business, nothing personal, you know. In fact, it's been a pleasure doing business with you."

Royce stared at the hand Landrum extended, that oily palm he couldn't bear to touch, then put his own hand to the hollow of his neck. Go ahead and say what you feel or carry it to your grave. "No, no pleasure. And this is personal. When I die, I don't know where they'll bury me, but wherever that first shovelful of dirt hits me in the face, I'll, I'll—" Royce choked up.

"I know," Landrum waved his hands. "But no need. Let's leave it at that."

46

As the bells tolled the dolorous noon hour, Eva sat with her knees tightly together in the pew, thinking wanton thoughts. It was the season of Lent, marching on toward a Resurrection. The season of giving up, and she had received her body back last night.

After so long, paradise again. She had felt his hand creeping over her hip, that sign. "No, wait," she'd pushed him onto the pillows and stripped the T-shirt over her head. Straddling him, she reached behind to find him and slip him inside. They moved quickly, urgently, secretly in the night, trying to keep quiet. The bed squeaked beneath them. It was all so lovely, and her cries were soft and like prayers. "God, God, God, Royce" she kept calling and was answered at last in the flesh, her flesh, her husband's returned to her. They were one. And she moved above him as long as she could, until she shuddered and covered herself over his chest. He came as well, those familiar spasms as if his joints were uncoupling from the stiff hauteur his body carried from habit.

They lay in the calm reassurance of long marriage, no pulling between them, no pushing. Lying naked together, unafraid, finally unashamed, they talked. Royce dropped that constant guard of his and Eva let go of her worry. Their flesh slaked at last of that urgent need, their spirits were free. They could face the future. "I missed you," she said.

"Um."

"Royce?"

"Yes?"

"Do you ever think about him?"

And they had been married long enough—almost twenty years next summer—that he knew exactly who she was speaking of, they were one flesh and of one mind at these times in their bed.

"Hunh," Royce's voice in the dark.

He'd told her at last about the little boy tied on the porch, that dark secret he'd carried so long, and about the man, Kyle McRae, whose hand he'd shaken. "We're kin, think of that." Cousins, maybe even half brothers, but what good did it do to think of that? Her husband was a stubborn man, like his father before him.

"Kin is who shows up at your funeral. Family is who you live your life with," Royce said, all he would say on the subject, but that was enough for Eva to hear. Their family was still nuclear, still intact.

The door to the sanctuary opened. Eva was stunned when the robed woman entered and bowed to the altar. Can you call a woman "Father"? She knew intellectually such creatures existed in the church now, had for more than a decade, but she had not experienced the presence of such a thing, a woman in priest's clothes, in surplice and cassock, the green sash around her neck. She was old enough to be Eva's mother, had she lived past her cancer.

Her name was Jane, no father, only the Rev. Jane Smithson, the first in the diocese, a woman from California, old enough to be her mother, Eva thought, her hair a dazzling silver. "You may have heard, but at his request to the bishop, Father Michael has taken a leave of absence. Until St. Dunstan's gets another priest, I'll be your temporary. We won't leave you stranded."

She gave a timid smile. "So where were we?"

The order of service. The stapled pamphlets they handed out each noon service taken from the dusty books in the pews.

At the invitation, Eva went up front for the laying on of hands, that gentle, feminine touch. No 'Bless me, Father, for I have sinned' mealymouthed contrition. Eva, for a change, chanced telling her truth in church. "I want to say a prayer of thanksgiving for the safe return of my son, and for my husband."

"Your name, dear?"

"Eva."

224

"What a lovely name. And your son and husband's?"

"Dean is my son, Royce, my husband."

"O God, lover of souls, hear the words of your daughter, Eva. Bless and thank you for the safe return of her son, Dean, and bless and keep her husband, Royce."

Jane's words were no different from the liturgy of the Book of Common Prayer heard all through Eva's childhood, but hearing them spoken in a woman's sibilant voice and not a cocky man's voice, in her mother tongue and not her father's weak command, it was as if Eva heard the word of the Lord for the first time. She prayed a different prayer today: Bless me, Mother, for I am happy.

And much later, looking back over her vocation, it seemed this was the first time she heard her calling, the start of a new career, as she would explain it to her husband, her friends. She could be those hands descending like doves on her burning forehead. There was no barrier beside her own fears that kept her from following in her father's footsteps. Why not the seminary?

47

Jake Wilder never really knew his own old man, Royce would realize much later in life. His grandfather was never spoken of, alluded to, nor much of Jake's youth or his life before he came to Beaverdam. Jacob Wellington Wilder was raised in lumber camps where the mountains' residents stripped the ridges where they lived of the giant trees, the last of the chestnuts, piling them on narrow gauge trains, snaking down the slopes to feed the buzzing saws or the pulp mills, lumber and paper for Northern magnates. Selling their birthright, the mountain men got to fill their gaunt bellies with a little grub, their empty pockets with a few coins to feed their rickety children and the hollow-eyed hags that raised their brood.

The older Wilder was not much of a worker but a hanger-on at these camps, and sired himself a son upon the plump loins of a Cherokee girl. He brewed a wicked popskull and sold it to the unsuspecting before they sobered up to his ways and he moved on down the ridge, melted into the coves, and came to the next lumber camp or work site, pulling the same stunt, anything to keep his shiftless body and shady soul together in the boom years of Calvin Coolidge's country club.

Jake grew up in such a camp, a toddler without a roof, only a canvas tent for most of his childhood. His mother wove together wigwams in winter, and once they lived in a cave, a hollow tree. As far back as he could remember, his father was always coughing, trying to force something lodged deep inside his thin chest, a hawking up of knotted phlegm, a catch in his soul.

Jake once took his own son on a pilgrimage to one of those forgotten places, a long day's drive over high ridges and deep into shaded coves, into an unknown country, maybe over into the next state. Royce reckoned it couldn't be Texas yet. They rode down a long road, beneath huge hemlocks and took a turn along a rail bed that petered out into a trace of young saplings and twisted rusted cable. Jake stopped the truck. "From here on, we have to walk it."

Royce didn't say a word but followed in the footsteps of his father as he shambled through the fallen leaves. The grade for the rail narrowed into a overgrown trail, the crossties rotted away where freshets of water sprang from the bank along the side of the mountain, then a series of switchbacks down the slope until Royce knew they were good and lost. And then they reached a clearing crowded with tall Queen Anne's lace and Joe Pye Weed. Jake walked the circumference, swinging furiously at the weeds with a broken branch, angry as if green had overgrown his memories, as if looking for some trace, some sign, hidden by the underbrush. Crickets flew up in the heat like sparks from a green fire.

Finally Jake Wilder stood still and turned himself in a circle. Looking for what, Royce couldn't be sure. The field was full of scraps of rusted iron cable that twisted from the ground, clawing toward the passing clouds. Royce sat quietly in the weeds, wondering when his father's fit would pass, waiting for when they could go home.

Dean was waiting at St. Dunstan's, lounged on the long stone steps, his elbows leaning on the stone, legs crossed in front of him, lankier looking than ever. Eva swore the boy had added an inch over Christmas, a sudden spurt that put him past all the clothes. They'd had to buy him a new blazer for the spring semester.

Dean gathered his ratty rucksack and loped over to the car, slumping in the seat and slamming the door shut.

"Hey."

"Hey."

"Good day?"

"Yeah."

"Yeah? Long day."

They could go on in monotones and monosyllables forever. Royce looked up through the windshield at the clouds through the trees, the first green buds still a ways from resurrection and Easter break.

"Dad?"

Royce was leaning on the wheel, his chin nearly touching the steering wheel. He wasn't sure how long he had been in this strange position, if he had fallen asleep, or if he had been dreaming.

"Shouldn't we go?" Dean asked.

He wanted to explain to his son today was different, that life would be different from here on out, or at least that they wouldn't feel the same about life. Or maybe not, it was hard to tell with a teenager. He remembered those years himself indistinctly, a hovering around the house, a hard yip always rising in the throat, something that had to be swallowed or shouted out. Royce looked at the trees, the green grass. "You want to take a ride?"

"Where to?"

Royce didn't answer. "You drive." He put the gearshift into park so they could switch seats, patting his son's shoulder in passing around the front of the idling car.

They rode in silence with only the squall of the tires in the hairpin curves, Dean deftly, unexpectedly, handling the wheel hand over hand while Royce bit his lip, kept quiet with any unwanted fatherly criticism. *Slow down, you're going too fast.* Royce stared out the passenger window at the tops of treetops and then at the rock face as they turned into the next switchback. Grooves in the rock showed where they had drilled the holes for the dynamite charges that had sheared away the granite face to allow enough purchase for the narrow blacktop. He swallowed hard. His ears popped with the pressure as the ancient orange Mercedes chugged up the mountain.

He had been in the driver's seat so long, it felt unfamiliar riding on this side of the car, no wheel to hang his hands on, bang his palms against impatiently. Riding shotgun with his own son, Royce found himself surprised that Dean's driving and his own lack of control would make him carsick.

"What the—" Dean stomped the brakes, which sent Royce bowing toward the dashboard, then bouncing into the springs of the seat, caught by the seatbelt cinched at his soft belly. He slapped the dash of the Mercedes with the flat of his hand. He clawed at the seatbelt and scrambled out the car door, swallowing the bile rising, burning in his throat. He felt like he was going to puke until he gulped mouthfuls of the wind whipping at the chained sign that blocked the road into Beaverdam.

A heavy iron chain stretched across the pavement, padlocked to yellow metal posts set in newly poured concrete at the shoulders. The sign was yellow, a traffic warning, reminiscent of the civil defense signs once seen in church basements and municipal auditoriums. A red DANGER oval over a magenta trefoil, three blades like a geometric angel of death. RADIUM.

"No," Royce said to himself. Then, "No," louder to the wind that blew out of Beaverdam.

"Dad? What does it mean?"

Royce rubbed his neck. The sign meant it was final what he had done, selling out his home to Landrum, that the radon was a reality, not just a ploy. He paced the length of the chain, stumbling in the makings of a pothole, nearly turning his ankle in his loafer, then caught his balance. Royce grabbed a chunk of the crumbling asphalt and hurled it over the chain and down the forbidden road. "No," he shouted. He rubbed his shoulder where he felt a twinge, something pulled, right after his angry throw.

They stood at the chain, looking down the road where it dipped and disappeared in the first of a dozen hairpin curves and switchbacks Royce knew by heart descending into the cove. They could easily step over the knee-high barrier, but it was three miles down the mountain to the creek and to the farm and even further to the church and the cemetery where they all lay now, his father and Wanda and Dallas, his dead baby brother, older than he, grandparents, all his people before him.

"What's with the sign?" Dean wanted to know.

"Radon. It means radioactive gas."

Landrum had said it was the highest level recorded in the gneiss of the Eastern shelf, whatever that meant. Royce couldn't shake the signs that Landrum had doodled on his sketchpad. How do you warn the Deans of the next millennia about the dangers? When skulls and crossbones have lost their meaning as pirate trinkets and T-shirt emblems, when waves radiating off a stick figure, or a bar through the mountain meant nothing to the dim-witted youth of the distant future?

"Is it really dangerous?" Dean kicked the dangling plate with his sneaker.

"No. Maybe. I don't know," Royce honestly admitted.

The boy kicked at the chain, then stood on top of it, balancing himself for a second like a tightrope walker before toppling off and onto the other side. Dean hopped the chain and walked down the road, disobeying the sign, "No Trespassing, Violators Will Be Prosecuted," that had been posted on the shoulder.

"Dean," Royce panicked, his son breaking the law.

"Just a sec." Dean kept walking. No respect for private property.

It wasn't theirs now. Royce had sold it all to Landrum and Matsui. The way that land worked in America. Once hunted by the Cherokee, then claimed and farmed by the first Scots-Irish settlers who came over the pass, then traded among the baptized at Beaverdam, all dead in their graves, their names transferred from the deeds of trust to the gravestones tilted on the hillside. Royce had signed over three thousand acres all told, the whole cove and a watershed, surrendered a hundred and fifty years of history with a series of stiff signatures and his initials RWW on a sheaf of papers.

Come back, don't go. Royce swallowed hard not to call out his fears to his son. Any second now he could bolt around the curve, disappear behind that rock face, and who knew what lay around the bend? But he didn't want to show his panic, the sheer terror. Coax him back gently now. Maybe he still has a little sense in his genes. "That's enough," Royce ordered.

Dean walked down to the curve and looked around the bend. He trotted up the road, then counted his steps, hurdling the low chain. "We won't ever get to visit?"

"No one lives there anymore. There's no one to visit."

"Then we'll have to remember it all, won't we?" Dean said.

Royce looked at his son, a double take, surprised he could utter something so wise. "You won't forget this now. Promise me, Dean. You hear? You won't forget?"

"All right, already." He shrugged away his father's sudden grip on his shoulder.

Royce let him go, but he saw the quick gap-toothed smile, a son's sense of being entrusted with a duty for the future. It would have to do, and it would. "Let's go on home, then. Your mother will be wondering where we've been."

"Should we tell her?"

"No need. It will be our secret."

The rusted chain still hung over the abandoned road. He kicked at the sign that said no trespassing and kept going down the broken curves.

It had taken days to get home when they finally turned him loose, ten years in a jail cell, sometimes in solitary confinement and in locked hospital wards, then all the sessions with the system's clinical psychologists until he had served his debt to society and posed no threat to himself or others, besides the mother he had had already taken care of.

The cove had changed slowly, inexorably in his time away. No one lived here anymore, only the wild came creeping in. No cows to graze the hilltop pastures, the woodlots gave way to new growth, kingdoms of briars and bramble. Kudzu swelled out of the creek bank and covered a barn, pulling it into a green disguise in summer. The second- and third-growth forests returned among the stumps of the great trees harvested in a prior century, the thrones of giant chestnut and dark hemlock, tulip poplars that a pair of men couldn't embrace between their outstretched arms.

Deer stepped out of the forests where the cattle had once grazed. Tracks of coyote, newly migrated from the west, ran down a few of the fawn. There were bobcat prints by the stream. Bear shambled from their dens. No hunters passed this way, and the animals lived out their short lives, generation after generation, undisturbed by the humans who always wore strange suits when they entered the empty cove.

He headed first to the cabin. The yellow ribbon of crime-scene tape still fluttered from the post of the front porch. The skins of the rattlesnakes had slithered free of the rusted nails and down the walls. He pocketed a scrap of the scaly diamonds. Dead leaves skittered over the threshold of the broken door, and inside a great shaft of daylight fell through the hole in the rafters. The rope still lay in the dust. He cut a great length of it, the sisal rough in his hand where they had pulled it free. He wrapped it tight about his pants, cinched it around his thin waist, bracing his gut against his backbone.

At first he kept to the weeds and woodlots, away from the road where he often heard heavy trucks lumbering over George's Gap. During the day he slept in ruined barns where the feeble sun broke through chinks in the falling roofs. When dark came, he wandered the road under the moonlight. He had forgotten a world without streetlights, only the moon and sharp stars stabbing at you from overhead.

He had the run of Beaverdam. He went from farmhouse to trailer, log cabin to brick rancher, all abandoned. The houses stood empty, the doors locked and the tumblers rusted inside the locks, but it was easy enough to break the glass in a window or a backdoor, force your way in.

On a back porch before the door, he found the remains of a bluejay, a crushed pile of feather and bone, a wing raised in the wind. The bird had likely died crashing into the glass of the storm door. Kyle squatted on his haunches and picked up a feather, running his thumb against the blue vane tipped with black and white. He stood and did what the bird could not and kicked the glass in, opening the door.

The houses were all empty and not that much different inside, the rooms bare of furniture, the run of raccoons and rats droppings by the floors. No juice in the light switches. He went from room to room, listening to the creaking of the floorboards underfoot, circling to find his own boot tracks in the dust. Some had left feedbags and trash, a mattress on the floor where an intruder might care to rest, to lie down and breathe the dust falling in the air, letting out a great sneeze that sent critters scurrying in the walls, mice and squirrels, but nothing else.

He found food left in the pantries, jars of old preserves or canned beans, not too dangerous to eat after he blew the dust off the lids and tested the lids to see if they had not popped. And so, like a man walking through a dream, he made his way from house to house along the road, down the cove, until he came to the church and the pond where it floated.

Only a few years after the last property owners cleared out, the beavers which had given the valley its name before the white settlers trapped them nearly to extinction, had found their way back to Beaverdam. They swam downstream and chewed at the softer trees on the banks of the creek, felled them into crude dams until the waters rose and spread over the bottomland. Hardwoods drowned in the spreading pond and the beaver's watery claim grew on the land. He saw the whitewashed church floating above the waters. He stripped off his clothes and waded, then swam in the still water through the deceptively deep pond. Long grasses waved in the murky water like the hair of drowned women. He hauled himself up on the rotted porch of the church.

The double doors had been left unlocked by some careless caretaker. The whitewash had peeled away with the seasons, but the door itself was still pocked with the old whispered wounds left long ago by a crazy woman chucking rocks, screaming curses at all the saints who had damned her.

He walked dripping down the aisle. The red carpet had turned to mud with the rising spring rains, and the beavers had gotten in and gnawed at the pews, great gouge marks in the varnished seats. The sanctuary was empty. He sat down on the pulpit for a while.

"Hey!" Enough echo was left in the empty church to sound hollow. Even the Almighty had had to evacuate this godforsaken place. There was nothing here but the four walls holding up empty air while the water flowed under the floorboards. In some places he stepped, a soggy plank would bow and water would gurgle through the crack.

He stayed a long time in the church, sitting in the pews, both front and back, and standing at the rotten pulpit, naked and slowly drying in the still air, looking out on all the empty seats, trying to imagine what had once transpired here. The hell they conjured for his mother. The hell they had put her through. Then he stood at the door and dove into the deep place and headed for the shore, newly baptized with the beavers splashing the pond.

❖

At daybreak, the work crew unlocked the chain and let the flatbed with the backhoe on through, then raised the chain again. Another day down in the poisoned place, but the job was different at least, none of the test shafts they usually poked here or the readings they took monitoring the radioactivity. A natural reactor, if they could find a way to plug it in.

"Take a deep breath. It won't kill you," they grinned darkly at each other. "Nah, just will fry your gonads for you." "Screw you, you're too dumb to breed."

It took a half hour to get the equipment down the treacherous curves to the church and unloaded and the tractor going up the hill. The crew stepped into the ungainly white suits, hoisted the heavy sleeves over their arms, then strapped on the head covers with the filtered breathing units as required by the federal manuals. Astronauts about to step onto an alien world. Limited exposure above ground was permissible, but digging into the earth carried certain risks. Lingering here too long ran the risk of joining these last inhabitants.

The cove was quiet. The leaves and birds, rocks and trees watched the alien intruders: slow, white marshmallow men moving across the forbidden hillside. Then all silence was lost as the diesel engines rumbled to life. Earth-moving machines ripped into rock and topsoil, reaching down into the graves. Winches yanked the rotten boxes into the air while workers steadied the sides with their white mittens. Names had to be entered against the records, the rotted remains of wood and bone and dirt poured into individual crates, stacked inside the tractor-trailer, husband upon wife, father on top of son, mothers and dead daughters, the short work of babies.

The stones were pulled up separately, carefully, and bagged with the proper tags. Jake Wilder, Dallas Rominger, Baby Wilder. Names unknown to the workers, breathing hard in their respirators, waiting to be done with this day, so they could go home out of this poisoned mountain to their homes, their own flesh and blood.

Other crews in white hazard suits would be here in the years to come, miners of a different sort, digging much deeper shafts for the coffins of uranium rods, the glass encased containers of spirits deadly, but dying slowly, for the half-life of a million years.

This was the last time the final residents of Beaverdam would be together, the democracy of the dead, raised not by the trumpet they had been led to believe would sound at the end of things, but by the backward beep of a backhoe. They had waited so long beneath the ground, but they were free now, rising up one by one, swinging their bones in clouds of dust in the swirling winches, then laid again to sterile rest in black bags, rezipped by their attendants in the white suits, awkward angels waiting for the end of another workday.

No name or headstone marked this last plot, the last of Beaverdam, Wanda McRae flying out of the earth, her cover laid bare. The driver couldn't see and the mechanical arm didn't care what marked the last grave. No headstone with Wanda's name, only a strange circle laid on the mound of clay—buckeye nuts, dried snakeskin, bird feathers, a plastic hospital bracelet—all within the loop of an old frayed rope. At the center, over the heart of the dead woman, rested the imprint of a man's hand, the splayed fingers of a son's touch. And the last of Beaverdam turned to a rain of dust, stone, vane, scales, and fiber. The wind gusted in this forgotten cove, scattering all in the air across a world that is forever ending.

Acknowledgments

A novel is written not by a single hand, but by many minds and warm hearts. I would like to thank my many faithful readers over the years: Lewis Buzbee, Ann Scott Knight, Kathryn Schwille, the remarkable roundtable duo of Nana Cuba and Faith Holsaert, as well as Virginia Weir and Hugh Himan. Over the twenty years that I've been at work on this novel, I would have quit long ago without the support and inspiration of the alumni of the Warren Wilson College MFA Program for Writers. This is a better book thanks to the sharp eye of my editor Lily Richards. Thanks too to the Virginia Center for the Creative Arts and Hambidge Center for offering space and solitude to revise this novel. Lastly, my gratitude to my wife and the woman who always makes me smile, Cynthia.

APACK

6579

CPSIA information can be obtained at www.ICGtesting.com
Printed in the USA
BVOW01s2000280514

354598BV00002B/58/P

9 781934 081419